HE WAS RUNNING FROM
THE TIME POLICE . . .

He heard the door open. A giant, distorted shadow fell across the stall as someone stepped in front of the small bulb hanging on the wall.

There was a quietness in the room when the door closed. He knew someone was in the bathroom with him. Just as he could sense that whoever it was didn't want him to know he wasn't alone.

Slipping the latch on the stall, Jackson opened the door and peered out, seeing the leather-clad man who had been at the pool table.

"Come out of the stall, Jackson," the man ordered. He lifted his right arm to show the pistol he was holding. With his other hand, he swept the dark sunglasses from his face, revealing the crystal eyes of a Time Policeman.

Volume 2

Trapped!

By
Warren Norwood

A Byron Preiss Book

LYNX OMEIGA BOOKS

New York

For Gigi and Karen

Special thanks to Richard Curtis, Michael Fine, Lou Wolfe, Judith Stern and Mary Higgins.

TIME POLICE
Volume 2: Trapped!
ISBN: 1-55802-007-1
First Printing/January 1989

Printed in the United States of America

0 9 8 7 6 5 4 3 2 1

Cover painting by Paul and Steve Youll
Cover design by Dean Motter
Edited by David M. Harris.

Acknowledgement

*The author would like to
acknowledge the special help
in the writing of this novel provided by
Gigi Norwood and Mel Odom.*

The Crain VERITAS Dagger used in this story was created for the TIME POLICE series by Jack W. Crain. It is an original design and the trademarks, VERITAS Dagger and Crain VERITAS Dagger, are his and are used here with his permission. My special thanks to Jack for his enthusiastic assistance, his willingness to give freely of his time and expertise, his generosity, and his superbly inspirational craftsmanship.

Warren Norwood

Chapter One

Dense walls of glowing dust swirled around the time machine in multicolored waves, moving with astonishing intensity only to burst and break with no recognizable force. The metallic smell of his chosen womb bit into Jackson Dubchek's nose as he waited to be reborn into a world he didn't know.

Discordant whines rose from the heart of the machine—some crying at a steady pitch, others wailing in alternating tremolo. Their overtones cut and crossed each other with hard edges of sound that shredded his ears and thoughts.

Stars flashed like strobes through the machine's crystel windows. Metal rattled like loose junk in a tin box. The center of darkness vibrated under the tremolo whines like a gyrobike out of balance, wobbling down the road, tearing itself apart, taking the universe with it.

Jackson clamped his hands over his helmet's earholes to cut off the sound and squeezed his eyes shut as he struggled to escape. The darkness grabbed him with tiny colored hooks and spun him in circles. His neck snapped. His head jerked. His eyes popped back open.

No, no. No, no. It's not how long you live, he thought as his time machine whined through eternity toward a past he had never lived, homing in on a heartbeat that had already been. "Not how long," he said aloud, "it's how well."

How well . . . how well . . .

His stomach growled, turned, and growled again, but he tried to ignore that unhappy beast gnawing at his gut with dulled fangs as he fought to remember why he was traveling back in time again—why, when he was sure he had sworn to himself never to do it again.

Jackson tried to remember. He tried to block out the sounds and the circumstances, tried to concentrate and remember, why, why, why was he traveling back in time? But he couldn't remember. Something blocked his thoughts. A dark, heavy forgetting oozed over his brain, smothered his mind like scorched gravy coating his tongue. It tasted of carbon and burned grease, of too much salt and garlic in a past he couldn't—

Needle sharp screams pierced his thoughts. Someone . . . or some*thing* suffered in the darkness. Animal or machine, he could not tell, nor where the scream came from, nor whether man or beast forced it out a too-tight throat.

The acid of panic bubbled and hissed as it ate away the edges of his sanity. *Why? Why? Why?* Satan asked in his ear.

Satan? The image formed in the dust outside the windows, complete with too-sharp eyes glinting cold obsidian over a yellow-fanged grin. Tysonyllyn? "Who? Why?"

Suddenly a million questions and a million new colored lights pulsed and flashed around him in a disorienting parody of all the laser concertos he had ever loved . . .

when he had loved . . . if he had ever loved . . . if he could remember . . .

Suzanne? A doorway. Chrys? A fire. Irene? Satan? No.

Who? Where was Martin? Who was Ana? Ana? Where was she?

A wave of darkness rolled over him, and his stomach rolled with it. The curling wave caught the lights, clutched them like little fishes, held them in its rising current, then crashed and twisted them down toward nothingness. One by one, with lifelong pauses between, the lights—the fishes, the lives of a billion souls—exploded in great phosphorescent showers of green agony, fauna dying in a galactic sea, until only black emptiness floated on the face of the universe.

Tears trickled down Jackson's face. The time machine moaned like a sometime lover in wretched ecstasy.

Bursting purple showers replaced the green death, but only for a moment before those, too, faded.

Jackson sobbed. His body shook from inside out. His heart throbbed with the closeness of death. The seat pounded against his back.

Blue suns burned through holes in the darkness where the purple showers had died. Only then did Jackson realize that if he did not soon escape, he too would die. But nothing—Nothing in all its dark emptiness—Nothing surrounded him with stiff cold arms. Nothingness kissed him with moldy lips. Nothingness swallowed him down a dry throat.

And Jackson fell . . . and . . . fell and . . . fell.

With a lurch of his stomach he lost everything he had ever eaten in all of his twenty-seven years. Then he lost everything his mother had ever eaten before him. Then everything his grandmother had eaten. Then everything every ancestor had eaten back past Lucy, past Eve, lost everything back to the embryonic stomachs of the universe. As his insides turned out, sobs clenched his lungs, madness filled his brain.

Time wobbled on an uncertain point between never-was and never-to-be. History made time spin. Eternity gave time its energy. Change blew against time like a wind shear at the edge of a storm that threatened to blow time down to the floor of Hell.

Jackson's time machine turned, tilted against the current of time, nosed up, lost its balance, and sluiced into the scent of orange juice, into the whiff of ammonia—fresh orange juice, hot ammonia—that burned sweetly through his nostrils. The deafening clang of a gong drowned out his screams.

Seconds later the universe exploded into time without moments, into fragments without pieces.

Ana. Oranges. Ammonia. Brother—big brother. Nausea. Time machines. Branson. Confusion. Ammonia. Gunfire. Jan and Pac. Insanity. What's-her-face? Pan. Dubchek. Oranges. Odar'a. Nausea. Gone. Music. Gone. All gone.

Jackson remembered the names, but somehow he had forgotten what they meant. Somehow he had forgotten every*thing* he ever knew and every*one* and every *place*. No, he couldn't forget. He wouldn't let himself. Not just like that. He couldn't. He had to remember. He had to force himself to remember.

As he gagged and retched, the first thing he remembered was Martin, his brother Martin, and because of Martin, their parents, dead two years in the Great Plaza

Fire. Because of Martin, he remembered his missing niece and nephew, and again, Ana, Martin's wife, gone, disappeared. Bits and pieces he remembered.

Like two hard cold hands, the orange juice and ammonia twisted Jackson's stomach and mind dry. A wave of memories flooded the emptiness inside him, memories and faces, names and places. Brelmer. Prague. Dr. Alvarez, dead. Lester Wu, dead. Slye, dead, by Jackson's own hand, the Time Policeman's head exploded so many times in the nightmares since. Ana, gone, without warning, without anyone even remembering she had lived—except Martin. Martin shattered, with tears running down to hang like dewdrops from his wiry beard. Martin, who, in the depths of his anguish, had made Jackson remember.

Dull lights flashed. The time machine slid roughly downhill. Metal grated against metal. New York. Gunfire. Time Police with mirrorshades and soulless crystal eyes. Dead people. Temporal Projects. *Irene, Irene, Irene* echoed in his head like a mantra as he stared blindly out the time machine window into a deluge of rain.

Irene? Who was . . . Irene, Irene, the Mnemosyne . . . Irene, the old acting teacher. She was Mnemosyne, and it was their time machine . . . their dirty dreams . . . their bizarre price for helping Martin . . . a piece of paper from 2091 . . . the constitution . . . a copy of the Second Republic's constitution. Jackson remembered, finally. What they wanted was simple, too simple. And he knew for himself that nothing about time travel was simple.

Moaning metal creaked and crunched as the time machine came to a shaky stop. The rain slackened. Dull gray light lit the cloud of steam that surrounded him, scorching from the friction-heated skin of the time machine. Jackson unclipped the nausea bag from his helmet and anxiously waited for the steam to clear. When he saw hundreds of time machines piled four and five high in long rows stretching away from him, he knew he had been there before, knew where he was and hated it. His stomach turned again.

Wheeling.

They weren't time machines. They were dead automobiles. He was back in Wheeling—in an automobile graveyard in Wheeling, West Virginia, in the rain—a long distance from the United Nations complex in San Francisco where he was supposed to have been. And *when* had he arrived in Wheeling? The calendar on his control board blinked unintelligibly almost in time with the light patter of rain on the roof of the time machine. Jackson wiped his face with a wettowel and rinsed the sourness from his mouth with a squirtbottle of water while waiting for the calendar to settle on a date.

9 JULY 1968. The Wheeling Loop, 1968.

Despite everything, Jackson laughed at himself and his predicament. There he was, traveling back in time in a machine that was the best technology 2250 could offer, and no matter where he tried to go, the machine could arbitrarily dump him in Wheeling, West Virginia in the years 1968 and 1969. Suzanne Brelmer had told him that no one at Temporal Projects knew why it happened or how to avoid it. Jackson didn't care why. All he cared about was getting out of there and on to San Francisco in 2091, where he'd been heading.

Where I was sent, he thought, 3 December 2091.

Sunlight flashed through the time machine, followed by a shadow, then more sunlight. Rain no longer tapped on the roof like a madcap metronome. Light gray clouds scudded across the mountains. Jackson rocked back and forth in the seat and, despite some protests of creaking metal from under him, decided that the time machine had settled enough to try moving. He dug several antacid tabs from his pocket and, as he chewed them, did a slow scan of the automobile graveyard, looking for signs of life and activity.

The last time he had been in Wheeling, two men had hunted him down, captured him, then chased him with a shotgun when he ran from their little house. He had barely escaped.

After a second scan of the area showed no signs of activity, he opened the time machine door, and stood on its sill to unroll the Portable Ovshinsky Energy System, which would convert enough energy from the sun to re-charge his batteries and let him try again to reach 2091.

The time machine had come to rest sideways atop two piles of rusting cars. Water still dripped from its roof. As Jackson unrolled the POES, the wind blew it back at him. Getting set up was going to be harder than he hoped . . . but everything was harder than he hoped it would be, and always harder than it looked. He crawled on top of the wet roof to hold the POES down as he secured it against the wind, and hoped that none of the locals would notice his shiny time machine or the POES. The crazy Mnemosyne had cleaned and polished the time machine after he had brought it back from Prague, and Jackson was sure anyone familiar with the junkyard would notice something that clean.

With the POES in place and activated, Jackson stood in the open door and decided his safest choice would be to wait in the machine itself. If he had to—

"And I'm a'tellin' you there's someone up chere."

"Well, don't you go shootin' 'em afore we git a chance to find out who hit is."

"If hit's them Jurdy boys, I'd uz soon shoot 'em uz near anything. They been tol' to stay out chere."

The words came to Jackson like a nightmare from the past. He had been in that very junkyard and heard those exact words in a past he would just as soon have forgotten. Twisting around to see if he could spot the man called Fratcher, who owned the junkyard, and his shot-gun-toting friend, Jackson's foot slipped on the wet sill. Stillborn seconds later he tumbled noisily down the stack of cars, clawing for any kind of purchase.

"Up chere! Up chere! I hear 'em!"

Jackson landed softer than he expected to and slid off a plastic-covered pile of something to the wet, stony ground. The strong mildew odor of the loamy ground snatched at his breath. How in the universe was he ever going to help Martin get his wife back if he got caught by those two old men again? He scrambled behind the pile, then slipped under the plastic as the voices got closer. The white plastic sheet covered bundles of newspapers, and he lay down on a shelf formed by a row of the bundles and waited, feeling the mud caked on his knees soak into his skin.

If they caught him again, they wouldn't be so care-less. Or had they caught him before? When had he been there before? 1969. He remembered that. But what day? What date?

"You take row nine. I'll take 'leben. We'll find 'em."

The voice sounded so close that Jackson stopped breathing. He had been there in summer. Some kind of music festival on the ancient vidscreen. Commie hippies,

Fratcher had called them. Maybe . . . Jackson shook his head. Woodstock, 1969. Maybe he hadn't been there yet. That was it. This was 1968, so he couldn't have been there yet.

"Keep lookin'. If they's chere afore then they's still chere."

Jackson let his breath out very slowly, and slowly took another. This was actually his first visit back to the junkyard—except it was his second—but Fratcher and his friend wouldn't remember the first because it hadn't happened yet, and they obviously hadn't found him in 1968, or they would have remembered him when he came in 1969, the first time he actually came, which would have been the second time for them . . . he thought.

The voices faded, but Jackson dared not move, dared not even look at his chronometer for a long time, tried not to think about the paradoxes involved in just this one incident. When he finally did look at his chronometer, he had to stifle a giggle. The chronometer couldn't tell him anything because, even though it wasn't concerned with what year he arrived, it didn't know what hour he had popped out of the time stream either.

He shifted slowly to his side, making as little noise as possible, and as he got comfortable, he found himself staring at the headlines of the ancient newspaper in the bundle in front of him.

VICE PRESIDENT FOSDICK DIES
President King to Appoint Governor Nixon VP

Something was wrong with those headlines, and Jackson knew it. His North American history wasn't the greatest in the world, but he knew there had never been a President named King . . . There had been one named Nixon.

Jackson squinted to read the fine print of the newspaper.

> *Presidential press secretary Sarah Shriver*
> *announced today that California Governor*
> *Richard M. Nixon will be appointed Vice*
> *President within the next two days.*
>
> *Vice President Harry Emerson Fosdick died*
> *yesterday at 11:00 p.m. and . . .*

Chapter Two

Vice President Harry Emerson Fosdick? Vice president of the old independent United States?

Jackson shook his head as he tried to comprehend that. The plastic sheet crackled with the movement of his head, and the sound froze him in place. He listened for a long time, but the only sounds that reached him were those of his own shallow breathing, the wind, and the drip of water through the rusting skeletons surrounding him. Fratcher and his friend were no where to be heard at the moment, and Jackson's body sagged in relief.

Harry Emerson "Fearless" Fosdick? Vice President. Jackson was almost positive that Fearless Fosdick had been some kind of religious cartoon character on the Sunday morning videos . . . Or had he been a famous Shane detective in the pulppocket books? One of those two, but certainly not vice president. How could a cartoon character have become vice president?

And *Governor* Richard M. Nixon? California governor? That didn't ring true, either. Nixon had been president of the old United States somewhere around the middle of the twentieth century, hadn't he? Didn't he lead the reconciliation with China and start NEATO, the New Extra-Asian Treaty Organization? Or had Richard Nixon been the cartoon character and Fearless Fosdick the president?

Jackson's head hurt, trying to remember the petty details of ancient history. Fearless Fosdick. Tricky Dicky. Which was which?

Even more confusing was the question of Leslie Lynch King. Who in the world was Leslie Lynch King? Jackson knew he had read the name somewhere, but not in a list of presidents. How did Leslie Lynch King get to be president of the United States in 1968? It made no historical sense—none of it.

Then in one brief, clear moment as Jackson Elgin Dubchek—citizen of the Second Republic in the year 2250—lay on a pile of newspapers under a plastic sheet in an automobile junkyard in Wheeling, West Virginia, 1968, he understood. The truth of what had happened flared in his brain like a pop-pill on his tongue.

Somehow, some way he had arrived in another past, a different past, one that had changed since he left the future—his future. The damned time machine had dumped him in an alternate 1968, one that didn't exist for him.

The 1968 where the machine had stopped was DIF-FERENT—totally different from the 1968 he had learned about in his studies. The 1968 he had learned about, the one his present, his 2250, depended on, was a 1968 that contained different facts.

In the 1968 of Jackson's life, Richard Nixon had never been governor of California. He had been somebody's vice president—Eisenhower's or Truman's. Years later, Nixon had been elected president twice before being driven from office by some kind of sexual scandal involving Defense Secretary Ames Watts, who had once been a tambourine player in a surfer's rock'n'roll band and who had also raised albino sheep—which had also figured into the scandal. That was the kind of bizarre information that lodged in Jackson's memory. He was a linguist, not a historian.

Names of presidents also lodged in his memory, and there had been no President King in U.S. history, and no Vice President Fosdick. Those few facts he knew were correct, but the very concept of alternate histories made him dizzy. How could anyone cope with getting plopped into the middle of a past that didn't exist?

As suddenly as understanding had struck him minutes before, something just as important grabbed his mind and held him still. At the very moment it didn't matter which past he was in. All Jackson had to do was get out of there and on to San Francisco in 2091. Period. Simple. End of problem.

If San Francisco turned out to be part of the *wrong* past, or if he didn't make it to San Francisco 2091, then he might have the luxury of time to worry about alternate versions of 1968. But for the moment, the most important thing he could do would be to get his tail back into the machine and get the machine back into the vortices of time and get both of them on their way to 2091. The very thought of having to travel again so soon made his sour stomach roll over.

For a long moment Jackson lay without breathing and listened again for the old men who were looking for him. Water dripped, plinked, splashed, trickled. The wind played eerie minor key aeolian melodies through the cars. Small creatures scuttled in and out of hearing range in brief bursts of scratchy sound. He heard nothing else.

Still he waited and listened and wondered until he finally screwed his courage to the sticking place and decided it was time to get back to the time machine. After taking a deep breath and letting it out slowly, he lifted the plastic sheet. It crackled with every movement as he crawled out from under it into the cool damp air.

"You just watch his machine, Corporal Henderson."

Half bent over, Jackson froze at the sound of the no-nonsense voice.

"He'll come back sooner or later, and that's when you hit your caller and bind him. Got that?"

"Yes, sir."

Time Police.

Jackson couldn't believe it. Every muscle in his body trembled. Who else could it be?

"Good. Corporal Noe, you take Adcock and Owen and zigzag down toward the gate until you find old man Fratcher and Mr. Heald. Then you put those two old tooters under house arrest and make sure they stay there like I told them to."

"Alabama, Captain."

No doubt about it, they were Time Police. Their accents weren't local. Their accents weren't even twentieth century.

"Markwardt, you, Evans, Cummins, and Milling go on back to the station and one of you bring the fogger back up here. We may have to use a little gas to smoke out our traffic."

"Yes, sir."

Afraid to crawl back under the noisy plastic, Jackson was just as afraid of staying where he was. They would find him any second. The muscles in his back and thighs burned with the strain of remaining still in his bent over position.

"Bessle, you take Gill, Litman, Jojobolendez, Proctor, and Frei, three on each side of a row, and work your way up the hill to the fence. See if you can't roust the traffic that brought this baby in."

Traffic. Traffic. Jackson had been called traffic back in 2183 when the Time Police had displaced him in the Federal District of New York because they thought he would be trouble to them later. Once again he had become traffic.

Now, he thought. Now. Get out of here. Still bent over, filled with frustration, he tiptoed step by cautious step away from the plastic-covered pile of newspapers.

A year before, he hadn't even known the Time Police or their Temporal Project in Kansas City existed. He had barely known Senator Voxner's name, and had never heard of Praetor Centurion Lieutenant Colonel Friz Brelmer. A year before he hadn't known Suzanne Brelmer, and she hadn't talked him into working for her father, for Temporal Projects . . . But he had known Lester Wu, who had died later in Brezhnevgrad, killed by the Time Police—by Captain Laszlo Slye, who Jackson shot in Prague, losing an innocence he had never thought anything of, never really noticed, till he had to step around its absence in his mind.

Jackson paused between two close stacks of cars, leaning against them to steady himself, searching for a place to hide, listening for the Time Police or Fratcher and the old man they called Heald. When he couldn't hear anyone, he sank slowly to sit on the damp door sill of the nearest wreck.

All the time travel business had threatened to drive Jackson insane once before. Now it was going to do it again. He thought he had gotten out of time travel for good. Jackson stifled a grim chuckle. Out, indeed.

As a pickup dulcimer player in Branson, he earned a decent hand-to-mouth existence, and had been relatively happy until Martin's call. Then everything had fallen apart. Martin's wife, Ana, and their kids were missing, gone, disappeared completely as though they had never existed—except that Martin remembered them all too clearly, and because of Martin's memory, somehow Jackson remembered niece, nephew, and sister-in-law, too, and when he did, knew what had happened to them.

A voice shouted something from up the hill, and Jackson pulled himself farther back into the wreck.

After calming Martin as best as he could on the phone, Jackson had contacted the Mnemosyne Historians to see if they could help. Irene had insisted on a face-to-face meeting at the Landers Auditorium and Vandivort Center for the Preservation of the Live Performance Arts up in Springfield. Jackson had gone with a mixture of reluctance and great hope that they could help Martin. Their proposition had been simple. If he would make a little trip for them back to 2091 to pick up a copy of the original Second Republic constitution, they would do what they could to find out what happened to Martin's family.

Again a voice called from up the hill, closer, more urgent. It was answered by a second before he heard booted feet running away from him. Jackson was sure they couldn't see him, but he didn't know what to do. The guard on the time machine would keep him from escaping unless . . .

With sudden determination, he pushed himself out

of the wreck and looked up the hill. No one was in sight. Good.

Walking as softly as he could, he crept around the wrecks until he could see his time machine. To his surprise, there was no one in sight there, either. His legs shook as he tiptoed between the stacks of cars. The stacks shook as he climbed up to the time machine.

Metal sandpapered on metal. Shouts echoed down the hill. Jackson pulled himself up into the time machine and tried to pull the door closed. It wouldn't budge.

Suddenly a hand slipped over his mouth.

He panicked and shook his head, feeling the fingers clutch and rip his breath away.

Jackson opened his mouth and bit the hand.

A man screamed, ripping into his ear.

Angry and scared, Jackson bit harder.

The hand jerked from Jackson's mouth. He tasted blood as he twisted in the seat to see a furious Time Policeman, crystal eyes pulsing at him from the back seat. Besides the characteristic eyes, there was no mistaking the elongated and flattened ears and broad nose.

On impulse, Jackson grabbed the helmet from the seat beside him and swung as hard as he could. The Time Policeman raised an arm. The polychromatic helmet glanced off the arm and hit the end of the man's nose.

To Jackson's surprise, the Time Policeman slumped forward with a moan, his body slack. Then Jackson smelled something like sewage and realized the Time Policeman had soiled himself. Jackson didn't care. He grabbed the unconscious man by the collar, pulled the heavy body past the end of the seat, and shoved the guy out the door.

The Time Policeman hit the wet ground with a high-

C splat and didn't move. Only then did it occur to Jackson that the Time Policeman might be dead instead of just unconscious.

No, he's not dead, Jackson promised himself as he stared down. Can't be. But the man lay perfectly still, crumpled in an awkward heap.

"Henderson?" a commanding voice bawled.

Jackson looked past the body to see another uniformed man wearing the silvered face shield of a Time Police officer. The officer was looking down at the body. With a frightening surge of energy, Jackson yanked the time machine door closed. After a few seconds fumbling, he activated the security system.

Then the machine started rocking.

Chapter Three

Praetor Centurion Lieutenant Colonel Friz Brelmer moved his weary legs with unthinking discipline as he and his twenty men marched through the forest back toward Natchitoches. We did a good job, he congratulated himself again, and soon the Republic of Texas will turn down the United States' offer to join the Union. History will shift in favor of the formation of the Second Republic, and the way to a safer future will—

A shot rang through the trees, signaling a fusillade. Brelmer yanked his pistol from his shoulder holster and threw his body flat on the hard-packed ground. Pine needles lanced through his clothing, drawing blood. But he pushed the pain away, made it serve him as he scrambled for cover. Still, he was more scientist than warrior, and within seconds the question of who had attacked the party seemed more important than survival.

Brelmer raised his head cautiously.

Muffled shouts filled the air, pierced through by screams of agony. Thunder cracked. A racket of shots, sounding like a handful of pebbles in a stainless steel pan, splintered trees nearby. Furrows of dust and needles exploded from the forest around him.

Brelmer cursed as he searched through the slanting shafts of light and shadow for a target. Nothing. He saw nothing.

Then the forest shivered with movement. Suddenly he had more targets than he could aim at. Screaming, yelling targets rose from the ground, swung from the trees, and appeared almost magically out of the shadows. Indians!

Brelmer fitted an attacker into his sights and fired. Once. Twice. Again and again without counting, he fired at the red-and- yellow-painted figures that swarmed through the Louisiana forest, feathers twined in their hair, madness shining in their eyes, clubs and stone axes swinging in their hands.

Body after body fell under the incessant firing, but still the figures came, rising from the ground, moving through the trees. The forest bulged past overflowing with shots, screams, and growls.

Brelmer fired at them until the fifty-round magazine in his Matthews/Bigen was empty. Only as he slammed home a fresh magazine from his backpack and tried to analyze the ringing din that surrounded him did he realize what was actually happening. Beams of light pierced some of the attackers.

"Holos!" he shouted above the chatter of fire. "They are using holos! Hold your fire!"

Ammunition popped with no slackening of its pace. The holos kept coming—with the real enemy between and behind them.

Brelmer did not know how the enemy could project so many holos in such a natural setting, but as he recognized what they were facing, he was startled by how physically convincing the holo projections looked. He shot one of the more solid attackers in front of him four times in the center of her chest, watching as she fell away with blank eyes staring at him.

Then came his second realization—the one that should have come to him first.

The attackers were time rebels.

2250 had no such sophisticated technology—not that Brelmer knew of, and, as head of Temporal Projects, he was on almost every need-to-know list. Nothing in 2250 could project that many holos at once in the middle of a forest. Again he fired at a solid target, and again a body crashed bleeding on the carpet of pine needles.

"Time rebels!" he shouted as he found another target and locked into target acquisition. "I want one alive!" His ears rang so loudly from all the discharges, he could barely hear his own voice, but he knew he needed one of the time rebels alive so he and his team back at TP could find out what time in the future these rebels were from.

"Time rebels!" he repeated at the top of his lungs. "Capture one!"

The firing rattled louder. Bark and splintered wood pulp showered down on Brelmer. With steady patience and a researcher's dispassion, Brelmer fired at the charging figures, trying to shoot only the most solid of them. Some fell, others did not. Around him voices shouted and figures grappled in the dim light. In leather breeches and tunics that suited this century's mode of dress, in the dim light presented through the thick canopy overhead, it was hard to separate his Time Police from the attackers, but surely their artificial physical enhancements would allow them to carry the battle. At least Brelmer hoped so. Never, not once, had he even dreamed that he might die with a stone axe smashed through his skull.

Suddenly the holos stopped, then blinked out of existence, leaving nothing behind but whirls of dust in the silver shafts of light. The firing slowed. Shadows slipped away into the darkness of the forest. Occasional shots followed them. Then came a silence warped by groans of physical distress.

Brelmer watched Sergeant Ghardtep push her large-boned frame to a standing position beside a tree, changing magazines in her Matthews/Bigen. Her crystal eyes glistened wetly as her gaze roved over the battlezone. "By the numbers," she ordered, "check off."

One by one, eleven uncertain voices sounded off by the ragged numbers—eleven voices where twenty voices should have answered.

"Meserole's hurt bad, Sarge."

"So's Carl. Head wound."

"Nicholson, help the wounded. The rest of you check your buddies. Then check the TR's. But be careful. If you find any TR's alive, Colonel Brelmer wants to kept them that way for questioning."

"Green is dead."

"Bastards."

"Where's Adams?"

"She's dead, too."

"I can't find Matthews. Where's Matthews?"

"I'm here, asshole. Where are you?"

"Behind this tree, you idiot. Where the hell—"

"At ease!" Brelmer's command knifed through the chatter.

"Shut up, all of you," Ghardtep roared. "They could

come back, and we won't hear them if you keep rattling. Matthews, check everybody and give me a damage report."

"Alabama, Sarge."

Sergeant Ghardtep crawled up beside Brelmer. Her face was composed, a study in wintery emotions, but he could hear her concern for him in her voice. "You all right, sir? You hit?"

"No, Sergeant, I am not hit, thank you. What do you make of all this? How did this happen?"

"They was obviously laying for us, sir. Knew where we would be and when . . . like someone who knew must of told them just where to set up and wait." As Ghardtep talked, her eyes never stopped roaming the shafted lights of the forest.

"It would seem that way, Sergeant, but we do not yet know how the time rebels acquire their information. They could get it from our files in the future."

Ghardtep shook her head and ran thick fingers through her short-cropped hair without looking at Brelmer. "I don't like to think about those things, Colonel. They twist around and get real confusing too damned quick, if you know what I mean."

"Of course. The paradoxes confuse us all."

"They're all dead, Sarge, Colonel," Matthews called. "The time rebs, I mean. We have five dead and three hurt bad."

"Sergeant." Brelmer caught the woman's eye. "I want them all taken with us—dead as well as the wounded."

"But, Colonel, we still have another six klicks to get back to our machines."

Brelmer made his voice hard, not wanting to have to

make her understand the responsibility he felt to the dead.
He was a scientist, not a soldier, but he was caught up
in a war in a land only he came close to understanding.
"We take our dead with us. I also want you to strip the
bodies of the time rebels for anything useful. In fact, bring
one of their bodies."

"But, sir, we can't—"

"Yes, you can."

"Yes, sir." Ghardtep moved away, her back rigid.

Forty minutes later the party returned to the trail,
six troopers each carrying a body, three walking wounded
shepherded by the medic, Nicholson, and Sergeant
Ghardtep leading the way. Brelmer took the rear guard,
letting his mind work the way he had spent years teaching
it.

He fully understood that taking the dead with them
made them more vulnerable to further attack, but he refused to leave the dead behind unless he had no choice.
The time rebel's body was a plus and would give Research
the chance to localize what time period the rebels were
coming from.

Temporal Projects needed that information for very
specific reasons. If they knew *when* the rebels were coming from, TP might be able to do something to stop them.
It would be even better, of course, to obtain a list of *who*
would return to the past. Knowing who formed part of a
plan Temporal Projects had been implementing for the
past several months—a plan known as Ancestor Adjustment. Disrupt the rebels' ancestral bloodlines, the theory
said, and the rebels would cease to exist.

At least, that was the plan.

In actuality, it hadn't seemed to work yet. New time
rebels kept showing up in the past as though nothing had

happened. That puzzle Brelmer hadn't figured out yet . . . and he was not sure he wanted to know the solution.

The group stopped and unceremoniously dumped the bodies on the ground as they drew their weapons and fell into battle positions. Sergeant Ghardtep signalled activity ahead with several quick hand signs. Brelmer moved up the line as quietly as he could to see what was happening. To his surprise, Ghardtep was grinning when he reached her side.

Following the direction scribed by her pointing finger down the hillside, Brelmer saw a group of almost-naked men squatting around a small, smokeless fire.

"Indians," Ghardtep whispered, "real ones this time, I think."

Brelmer nodded, then motioned back in the direction they had come from and made a circling motion.

Ghardtep saluted, and together they crept back to the group. With as much caution and as little noise as they could manage, the group reshouldered the stiffening corpses and set off back down the trail.

After retracing their path for a while, they left the trail and struck out into the woods. It slowed their progress even more, and made carrying the bodies that much more awkward and demanding, but if Ghardtep or the troops objected they didn't do so out loud. Brelmer heard nothing but their labored breathing and an occasional curse from them as they hacked and stumbled their way through the dense undergrowth.

Brelmer pressed ahead with grim determination, as anxious as the rest of them to get back to the camp and the time machines. He hated the woods. It was bad enough on what had passed for a trail, but this unbroken wilderness was almost more than he could stand.

He knew it was irrational, but the forest didn't seem natural to him somehow. There were just too many trees. He understood that in this remote and primitive time the oxygenerators hadn't been invented yet, and trees were still necessary, but he hated them anyway.

They were just too messy. Something tickled the back of his neck, and he swatted it, suddenly panicked at the idea of some ancient insect infecting him with diseases the doctors in his time had forgotten all about. TP groups had returned with smallpox or measles, and he'd had to keep them in quarantine until they died, then burn the bodies. Even though this group had received all the universal inoculations, he knew it could happen again.

Angrily, he hacked away a vine that trailed from the branch in front of him. Trees should be kept in green belts and ornamental gardens where they could be carefully trimmed to manageable sizes. Better yet, preserve them on holos in botanical museums.

He thought about the real Indians they had seen at the campfire, and wondered how anyone could stand to live like that, dressed in loincloths, dirty, having to hunt down and butcher everything they ate, and always surrounded by forest so dense any kind of predator or enemy could creep up on them from any direction without the slightest warning.

He felt a hand on his arm and jerked back in alarm. It was Ghardtep.

"We ought to be around them, sir," the sergeant said. "I think it's time we cut back to the path." She carefully avoided his eyes, not acknowledging that she had startled him.

"Very well, Sergeant."

She turned and motioned for the troops to move back

onto the trail. Brelmer watched them as they filed past him, taking note of their relieved looks, and trying to get his own racing heart back in control. He slowed his breathing to a more deliberate pace and cursed himself for letting the trees get to him. He felt like a fool. But control was everything in his life. Control had allowed him to discipline himself to the skill level he achieved in school, earning him the right of advanced learning. Control had to be exercised in every experiment set up. His life turned around control, of himself and of others. Yet, it was this attempt to control time that had broken the bars holding time in a constant framework. Now, time spun and spiraled at the bidding of others. Some of them people whose goals were at right angles with the Second Republic's. Even a tightly controlled system of progressive days and nights had been converted into seeming chaos.

Silently, he fell in behind the last soldier, and checked his chronometer. The detour had cost them almost an hour. As he stepped out from under the sheltering canopy of branches onto the path he realized the light was already fading. He hoped they'd be able to get back to the camp before dark. By night they would be too vulnerable.

The thought had barely entered his mind when he heard a shout from up ahead and smelled the hot breath of a laser. Instinctively, he hit the ground and rolled off the path, scanning the woods in front of him for a sign of their attackers.

He saw someone fall, dropping a body as she crumpled to the ground, and cursed the time rebels for getting the drop on them again, cursed the trees for hiding the enemy, and most of all cursed himself for deciding to go around the Indians rather than going through them. Right at this moment he would much rather be the side with the advanced technology.

Slowly he worked his way up the line to Ghardtep's position.

"The camp is just over that ridge," the sergeant said as she pointed to a slight rise a few meters ahead of them. "The best I can tell, the firing is coming from over there." She pointed again, this time off to their left.

Brelmer nodded, surveying the terrain. "How many?"

The sergeant shook her head. "Ten, maybe less. I think we might have gotten one or two. Only one of ours is down so far, that I can see. If we make a run for it we might just be able to make it."

"Any chance we could take one of them alive?"

"Christian Bible says all things are possible with Jesus."

"But you are not a Christian." Brelmer turned away to look back down the line. The troops were firing with a will, and as Ghardtep had said, only one was down. Despite her pessimisim, he still thought there might be a chance to capture one of the time rebels.

"You round up the troops and make a break for the camp. Let me have Matthews and Schweikhard, and we will see if we can circle around behind those rebels and capture one alive."

Ghardtep nodded. "You hold 'em off till we get over the ridge, sir, then we'll take over and give you a chance to get around 'em."

"Carry on, then." Brelmer worked his way back down the line, firing when he had the chance, passing the word to the troops, and calling Matthews and Schweikhard aside.

They set up a firing pattern that pinned the rebels down while the rest of their troop worked their way toward the ridge. Ghardtep signaled that they had made it by opening fire from their new position, and the rebels turned toward the larger group.

Brelmer signaled his group to cease fire, and they began to work toward an outcropping of rocks he had spotted as a rebel defense.

Matthews broke away to the right, and Schweikhard took the left, leaving the most direct middle approach to their colonel. As he moved nearer to the rocks he caught a glimpse of bright hair, and a flash of uniform each time the rebel rose to take aim.

With a quick hand signal he ordered his troops to move in, then sprang from his crouch to the top of the rocks and over onto the startled rebel. He saw a brief image of her startled face as she swung around to fire at him, and then he was on top of her, riding her shoulders down to the rocks and pinning her as Matthews and Schweikhard closed in to disarm her and bind her hands.

Matthews took a handful of the woman's golden hair and yanked her head back, and Schweikard whipped out a gag. The rebel twisted away, her green eyes focusing all her hate on Brelmer and her full lips working up a glob of spittle to fling in his face.

Matthews yanked again, and Schweikhard wrestled the gag into place as Brelmer wiped his cheek and studied his captive. Then he turned his attention back to the fight as the firing stopped, and the rebels fell back into the woods. Up the path he saw Ghardtep signal all clear, and he signaled back. Matthews and Schweikhard hauled their prisoner to her feet and fell in behind Brelmer as he headed up the hill toward their camp and the time machine.

Chapter Four

For the first time in all of her twenty-four years, Suzanne Brelmer felt uncomfortable in her parents' house. She sat across the small breakfast table in the kitchen where she had learned to cook, sharing a fruit drink with her mother, whom she had learned to trust with all the things a maturing girl discovers on her way to adulthood. Maybe it was even more than just discomfort, she admitted to herself. Would "threatened" cover the feeling she was experiencing?

"How far back in time have you traveled?" Mrs. Brelmer asked in an innocent voice.

Suzanne tried to remember how many questions and references her mother had made to Temporal Projects in the hours she had been there, finally giving up because she honestly didn't know. "Why, Mother?" she asked, fighting the resentment she felt about her mother's sudden curiosity.

"I'm just interested, dear," Mrs. Brelmer replied. An odd smile distorted the corners of her eyes and mouth as she avoided looking directly at Suzanne. "Can't a mother be concerned about what her daughter and husband do at their work?''

"Of course. You know that's not what I meant. But Daddy and I have both told you we're not allowed to talk about what we do at Temporal Projects.'' Suzanne pushed a smile onto her face, wanting to break the tension between them. ''It's all top secret, hush-hush, and all that.''

"I'm your mother, dear, and I resent being treated this way. Surely, you and your father can trust me. If I need it for my peace of mind, what harm is there in telling me what you two do over there?''

"We could be sent to prison, Mother.''

"Nonsense. Why would anyone want to send you to—''

"Because it's against the law.'' Suzanne shook her head, working out some of her nervous energy by drawing faces in the film of perspiration covering the glass in her hand. ''You really don't understand, do you?''

"No, I don't.''

"Then that makes two of us, because I don't understand why it is suddenly important for you to know what we do.''

"I'm tired of being pushed aside, Suzanne.''

"Mother! Neither of us has pushed you aside.'' Irritation flared inside Suzanne. She flicked a fingertip through a pair of faces, flawing the cartoon features.

"You most certainly have. Friz says I have no need to know, but I do. I need to know so I won't worry about you. Have you noticed the stories the *Republican Enquirer* prints? I do, every time I go to the supermarket. Horrid things about people in the time machines who have rematerialized inside the stone foundations of buildings, underwater, in fires. Others say time travelers are responsible for assassinating people in the past."

Suzanne winced, thinking of Laszlo Slye and how some of those stories apparently were closer to the truth than anyone at TP would care to admit. Especially her father. She made a mental note to pick up a couple of recent copies of the magazine, hoping no one she knew would see her actually purchasing it. At least the mystery of TP had caused a momentary cessation of the three-headed baby stories that were standard fare for the ENQUIRER. Obviously, articles about Elvis having an affair with an extra- terrestrial back in the late 1990s were losing headline space. She wished she understood her mother's sudden interest and had an answer for it. "Just don't worry, Mother. There's nothing to worry about." The lie slipped glibly from her lips, hurting just the same. But she had been pushed into it, hadn't she?

"Then why can't either of you tell me—I mean, if there's nothing to worry about, surely there's no reason why one of you can't tell me what you do at Temporal Projects. I'm not asking for details, just—"

"Mother, we can't. We're not allowed. Forbidden, *verboten*, all that. The government made the rules, not me. Daddy's right. You have no official need to know."

"You always were your father's daughter." The harsh bitterness in her voice could have cut glass. Mrs. Brelmer stood up in an agitated rush. Her clenched hands trembled at her sides. Her lips quivered.

"What is it, Mother?" Suzanne asked as she, too, stood. She didn't know what to do next, and her indecision was like a knot in the top of her stomach. "What is the matter with you? Is it your back again? Is that what's upsetting you?''

''No!''

''Then what is it?''

''Nothing.'' Mrs. Brelmer turned away with shaking shoulders. ''Just leave me alone.''

''It *is* your back.'' Suzanne stepped closer, but knew better than to touch her mother when she was upset. Mrs. Brelmer hated anyone touching her when she did not have her emotions under control.

''Please, Suzanne, go away. Go to your apartment. Or go to your precious Temporal Projects. If you don't trust me enough to tell me what you do with your life, then how can I trust you with my problems? Just leave me alone.''

''Not until you tell me what's wrong, Mother. You've put me in an impossible position, and that isn't like you. What is the doctor saying about your back?'' How long ago had it been, Suzanne asked herself, since the bullet wreck that had claimed her mother's comfort? She had been eight then.

''Nothing. He says nothing.'' Mrs. Brelmer spun around, her red face contorted by frustration. ''*They* say nothing. I have four, now, you know, four doctors, and none of them can do any more than prescribe physical therapy and placebos.''

''I thought those new analgesics had helped you.''

''Only for a few weeks.''

''Then what?''

''Then they ran blood tests and decided I couldn't keep taking them because they were ruining my liver, so they gave me something else, and that made me sick to my stomach, and then they tried three or four other things that didn't work, until finally they got back to CASA, and that makes me itch, because the other drugs sensitized me to it, so I—"

"What is CASA?"

"Fancy aspirin."

"That's it? Fancy aspirin is all they're giving you?"

"Yes." She met Suzanne's gaze for a second, then looked away and sat on the window seat. "That's the problem . . . or part of the problem."

Suzanne waited, expecting more, but when her mother didn't continue, she said, "Then we'll just have to find you a new doctor."

Her mother's head whipped around and her eyes glistened under dark brows. "What good will that do? I've lost count of the new doctors I've seen. You find me another one, and I'll take an hour explaining what my problem is and the whole history of my treatment, then the new doctor will want to try something that we've already tried, something that I know from experience won't work, but I'll agree to try, because I won't see where I have any choice, but the new therapy won't work, and I'll just be two weeks worth of pain older. Damn doctors get angry with their patients if the cures they prescribe don't work, and they won't trust the patient's judgment, so in the end all they do is run a lot of tests, take our money, and frustrate us."

"Money? Why are you paying doctors? Or should I ask who you have been paying, Mother? Black market doctors? That's it. You have been, haven't you? You've been getting black-market medical treatment."

A long pause tightened the knot in Suzanne's stomach before her mother answered.

"Yes." She stared defiantly at her daughter. "But

it is worse than that." Tears ran freely down her face, smudging the otherwise immaculate make-up. "Much worse."

"Like what, Mother?"

"Capricodone."

"You're taking Capricodone? You mean Capricorn? The street drug? That's illegal. I don't understand. Why would—"

"It is Capricodone, and it is only illegal in parts of the Republic. It's not illegal in South America or Japan. Besides, it controls the pain, and that's all—"

"But, Mother, why would you take—"

"—I care about. My doctor gets it for me . . . at a considerable price."

"Information," Suzanne said. The pieces suddenly fell together and she realized she was facing something much bigger, much more evil than she could have imagined.

Mrs. Brelmer nodded almost imperceptibly. "Yes. They want to know things. If I can't find out what they want to know, they won't sell me the Capricodone."

"It's drugmail."

"It's relief."

Suzanne shook her head. "Mother, I'm sorry, but that's not right. If there's nothing legal you can take, you may just have to learn to live with the pain. Lots of people have to do—"

"I'd sooner die."

"Mother! Don't talk that way. That's stupid."

"Oh? Am I stupid as well as untrustworthy? Well, then, let me live a few less years with the pain under control than suffer with it every day."

"That's not what I meant."

"What the hell do you know, daughter of mine? Does the pain wake you up at night? Does it hurt you all the time?"

Suzanne stood mute before her mother's withering anger, wanting to sympathize, knowing that she didn't really understand how her mother suffered, searching her mind for some way to lead her mother out of the trap she had fallen into.

"Suzanne, do you know what happens if I sleep fairly well? I wake up in the morning with a back so stiff and painful I can barely move. But if I toss and turn because of the pain, I wake up with less pain, but I feel miserable because I didn't get enough sleep. You people lucky enough not to have constant pain will never understand how miserable pain can be. It distorts—"

"Mother, please, I try to understand. So does Daddy, I'm sure."

"Yes, well, that's very nice, dear." Her eyes had dried and her face had taken on a cold, pale calmness. "Now, why don't you run back to play secret games with your father while I find something sharp to fall on."

Suzanne winced at the image that formed in her mind.

Her mother turned away from her. "Oh, please, spare me the dramatics."

"No, you're the one being dramatic. Threatening suicide won't solve anything."

"Suicide will. It will stop the pain."

"That's a selfish way to look at it."

"Whose pain is it? Yours or mine? When it's yours, you will be selfish, too."

"What kind of information do they want?" Suzanne asked. "And just who are they?"

Mrs. Brelmer laughed bitterly. "They want to know

everything about what happens at Temporal Projects. And they don't tell me who they are, but I've been led to believe that they are Licinians, or at least in league with the Licinians.''

Suzanne took a deep breath, then blew it out slowly and loudly. The Licinians represented more powerful interests than she wanted to face on her own. Even Senator Voxner did not tangle with the Licinians if he could avoid it. They had too many friends in positions of power. ''What's your doctor's name?''

''I can't tell you that. You'll do something stupid, like have him arrested, when all he's trying to do is bring a little relief back into the practice—''

''He's giving you illegal drugs in exchange for illegal information, making you at least an accessory to two felonies—the information-selling being punishable by death, and—''

''He doesn't give me anything, dear,'' she said. ''He sells me Capricodone.''

''That's even worse. He's making a profit from your—''

''Why? Why is that worse? He has to pay for it. He takes his risks too.''

''I know, but Mother, that's a terrible thing to do to someone like you who suffers from chronic pain.''

''No worse than what you and your father do.''

''What do you mean?'' Suzanne realized her mother was full of self-pity, and used that to manipulate her, but at the moment Suzanne felt powerless to escape it.

''The two of you basically ignore it, as though it will go away if you don't talk about it or face up to it.''

''That's not fair. We don't—''

"That's as fair as it gets." She stood. "I believe you were about to leave?"

"Not unless you promise not to do anything foolish."

A bitter laugh was the only reply she received.

"I mean it, Mother. I will not leave this house until you promise me you're not going to . . ." She couldn't bring herself to say it.

"Not going to what? Not going to kill myself? No, Suzanne, I won't promise you that. I won't promise any-one that. If your father gave a tinker's dam about my problem, I might—just might, mind you—just might promise him, but he doesn't care, so I refuse to promise anything. Goodbye, dear."

"No goodbyes, Mother. I'm staying. I'm going to stick closer to you than your shadow—twenty-four hours a day, every day until you promise not to kill yourself, and also promise to get help."

"Psycounseling? Shrink testing? Never. I've talked to those people—or rather, I've listened to them talk. That's what they do, you know, those headachers. They try to fit you into their pet theories so they can sell the story of your disease and recovery to some damn journal or another."

Suzanne met her mother's angry gaze with as much calmness as she could. "Fine. Have it your way. I'm staying." She realized they were at a standoff, but she didn't know what else she could do. "I will not leave as long as you're thinking about . . . that."

Mrs. Brelmer shook her head. "It's a nice gesture, dear, but we both know it's meaningless. You'll stay for a while, maybe for dinner so you can tell your father all about my terrible sins, and then sooner or later I'll make nice and pretend I've come to my senses, and you'll leap at the chance to believe me so you can get on with your own well-ordered little life. And that will be that. If you think that's enough to prevent me from killing myself, or even to stop me from going back to my doctor, you're more naive than I think you are.''

Suzanne looked away from the smug little smile on her mother's face, knowing perfectly well she was right. But there had to be something she could do.

"If you really cared," her mother said, "you'd use some of your fancy government contacts to get me the Capricodone without the doctors. I may not know much about Temporal Projects, but I do know it's some sort of research facility. Surely someone Suzanne's.

"You want me to get you the drugs?" Suzanne's mind raced. Could she? She knew they weren't doing that kind of research, but maybe there was a way, maybe in another time . . . "Won't your doctor get suspicious?"

"I can take care of him."

But can you take care of the Licinians? Suzanne wondered. And if you can't, can I?

"If you try, I promise I won't kill myself," her mother said.

Suzanne looked back at the woman who had given her life, and wished for the thousandth time she weren't so susceptible to her mother's manipulations. She knew now that this was what her mother had wanted all along. And she knew, without a single doubt, that whatever she could do for her mother, she would do.

Chapter Five

Eternity blinked off and on like a malfunctioning strobe light in a million colors of confusion. It burped and gurgled, sang and cried, screamed and whimpered—ignorant and unsure of where it traveled or why.

In the midst of that vacillating eternity, Jackson clung to the threads of himself, demanding life from a body torn and dying, demanding clarity from a brain awash in chemical tides from overloaded sensors. Something had to make sense, something soon, something said, something silver, something sand . . .

AND IN THE WORLDS WROUGHT BY WORDS *á jamais*, FOREVER IS THE *nicht, nacht, nyet,* CRYING FOR HELP. PLEASE HELP. *Auito!* HELP ME, SOMEBODY. HELP ME! *Apopo,* TOMORROW, THE BROWN-AND-BLACK-STRIPED MAN ANSWERED FROM THE CENTER OF HIS DANCING BOAT. I AM THE DICTION FERRY OF YOUR MIND. I AM THE—

The world lurched. Jackson threw up, and the sour citric stench of it pierced his darkness with the smell of reality. Hot hands wrung his empty stomach dry.

B MINOR NINTH DIMINISHED WITH AN AUG-
MENTED SIXTH IS NOT THE JAZZIEST CHORD
WHEN A PLAYER HAS SIX STRINGS, BUT EVEN
WITH ODAR'A STRUNG FOUR APART, THE NOTES
WERE MISSING AND PRESUMED LOST UNTIL
FOUND GUILTY IN THE *alflandege,* WHERE THEY
COLLECT THE CUSTOMS OF HEMIDEMISEMI-
QUAVERS WEIGHED ON THE MUSICAL SCALES
IN TORONTO OF—

The time machine rocked and groaned. It rolled and
moaned, hissed and whistled, bumping through the ether
like a wired but weary sex dancer at the end of a long
exhibition night laden with endorphins and phets, weighted with words. Then it peaked and collapsed through the
shuddering spasms into the heel of a shadow where bodies
rocked to the rhythm of their own musical deliverance.

9 January 2091

Jackson fought the sticky nets in his brain and tried
to understand what he saw. Lights flashed lazily—lights
from nowhere. Music dribbled from the ar. It coated his
ears like artificial butter. Ammonia and bile mixed with
the acidic odor of oranges. He coughed and cursed.

"Bill Truman's voices make us run around."

The sound of his own voice woke him. Jackson
wrapped his arms around his aching body, opened his eyes
again. Without sympathy or understanding, he stared at
the flickering calendar on the instrument panel as the time
machine whined down the winding road of eternity toward
a chablis of slow silence.

22 May 2092

At that moment he would have given almost anything
he owned to be back in Branson playing his dulcimers in

one of the revival clubs for just enough money to eat the next day.

8 April 2091

He would have given almost anything to be home in his little rented room for one of Chrys's marathon sex visits . . . or curled up on his sleeping mat for one of Suzanne's rare calls to see how he was faring. Ah, Suzanne . . .

17 November 2091

He would have given anything he could for Martin to have Ana and the kids back again.

9 January 2092

He would have given absolutely anything to be out of the time travel business once and for all and forever. He would have even given his dulcimers, Odar'a and Jenny.

3 December 2091

Anything, everything . . . except he had nothing to give.

3 DECEMBER 2091

Nothing except his life.

3 December 2091

The calendar held, repeatedly blinking the same date—bright, dim, bright, dim. He changed his mind about the dulcimers. Some things were just too precious to give up.

3 DECEMBER 2091. Incredible. If the calendar was correct, the machine had stopped in the right time. If it had reached San Francisco as well, that would be a major step toward overcoming Jackson's time travel blues—not to mention the time travel nausea and disorientation. And he could do with some fresh air.

Jackson took off his timesickness bag, blinked, and stared uncomprehendingly out the window of the time machine. He couldn't see anything. Nothing. He switched off the lights on the instrument panel. Total nothing. Complete darkness. He couldn't even see his hand in front of his face. The air weighted his lungs. Death tapped on his windows.

Panic clutched his throat and he gasped for breath. An idea that had never occurred to him before suddenly loomed around him. Suppose he was underground? But what would be tapping? Suppose the time machine had stopped buried in a rock? He'd seen an old holo about time travel, and the man in that had been trapped in a rock. Suppose . . .

If it was underground, Jackson knew he couldn't use the POES to recharge the batteries, and if he couldn't recharge the batteries, then he couldn't leave, and if he couldn't leave then he'd die in 2091—stuck in a rock in a time machine made one hundred fifty-odd years later. Again death tapped on the windows, and on the roof, and on the sides.

No. No. He couldn't be in a rock. Wait. Something . . . something they had told him when they first trained him at Temporal Projects . . . something about the time machines seeking empty spaces. TAP, TAP, TAP.

Damn! Why couldn't he remember? After a few seconds of fumbling over the instrument panel he found the switch that turned its lights back on. TAP, TAP, TAP, TAP. Then he started reading all the labels on the panel until he found one marked EXT ILM. Exterior Illumination . . . he hoped. It had no safety cover, so he took a shallow breath and hit the switch.

Blue light filled the space around him, bluelight filled with moving objects . . . bugs.

He laughed.

Bugs! And grass, using the vernacular of the times! Marijuana! The damn machine had parked itself in a marijuana field. Jackson hadn't realized that marijuana was legal in 2091 . . . or maybe it wasn't. Maybe he was in the middle of an illegal marijuana field. Quickly, he shut off the lights, but even as he did so, he laughed again.

Time to get out and see if he could figure out where he was. As soon as he climbed out of the time machine he understood part of the problem. He had indeed arrived in a field of marijuana. The time machine had come to rest on a low platform in the middle of a greenhouse.

That was bad, very bad, because whoever owned the greenhouse full of marijuana probably wouldn't take kindly to a machine that looked like an antique automobile—a nineteen fifty-four Buick, according to one woman he had met—parked in the middle of his crop. If the marijuana was still illegal in 2091, the owner would certainly be even less pleased.

Jackson got a flashlight from the toolkit inside the machine and did the only thing he knew to do under the circumstances. From the back of the time machine he pulled a long extension cord and dragged it between the rows of plants until he reached a wall. After some searching he found a socket. A red light came on at the head of the cable when he plugged it in, to tell him it was working. He then pressed both his hands and his nose on the security panel beside the door, activated the security system, and shut the door. Now no one else could get into the machine or unplug it, and with direct power it would be charged in less than two hours.

He wasted almost an hour of that time finding his way out of the greenhouse. Row after row of two- to three-meter tall marijuana plants blocked his view of the walls and doors, and forced him to wander for what seemed like an eternity. Just when he was ready to welcome even a surly guard who could show him the way out, he found a cross-row that led at last to a narrow stairway.

The echoing metal stairs took him down into musty darkness and the smell of baled grass. He shook his head and tried not to breathe in the dusty air. "This has to be legal," he muttered. "No one could run an operation like this if it wasn't." But he had to admit there was probably enough marijuana here to pay off an entire police force with plenty left over for profit.

He recognized the building as some sort of warehouse long before he reached the bottom of the stairs. When he finally did reach the floor he realized that he was faced with a variation on the same problem that he'd faced in the greenhouse. Huge piles of the marijuana bales were stacked up to the ceiling, and he had only the vaguest of ideas where he was, or how he could get to a door.

He ended up following the wall at the foot of the stairs until he reached a row of windows. These he tested until he found one that was unlocked. Climbing up and out wasn't as hard as it looked, but he had a long teetering moment of indecision before he could force himself to drop the six feet to the sidewalk.

"I need an accomplice," he muttered as he dusted himself off. It didn't seem right to be bumbling through time all alone like he was. Or maybe, he thought, he was just remembering how much easier it had all seemed when Suzanne was along with him in Prague.

Looking up, he saw the lights of the city and knew from photographs Irene had shown him that he had arrived in San Francisco. The relief allowed his body to relax in places he hadn't realized he was tense. As he drank in the reassuring sight of the old Transamerica tower he felt his mouth curving up into a smile. Now all he had to do was figure out where to find a copy of the constitution of the Second Republic, find his way back to this building, jump in his time machine, and head back to 2250.

Nothing to it.

As he stood on the sidewalk wondering which way to go, a black bullet limousine swept around the corner, filling the street with light and shadow.

Jackson took an automatic step backward. The limousine halted at the curb. He looked left and right, wondering which way to run. The limo was too big and sleek to belong to anyone but a high-ranking official, or maybe the owner of the greenhouse, and just at that moment Jackson didn't want to attract the attention of either.

He turned away from the curb and started walking down the street, hoping he would look like he belonged there.

Behind him he heard the soft whoosh of the limousine's door peeling open. "Jackson Dubchek?" a female voice called.

He could not have been more surprised if a tiger had leapt out of the car. His astonishment halted him in his tracks.

"Huzzah, hurry," the woman called.

A siren wailed close by.

"That guardians comin' for you. They buzz wit you any sec. Come, come! Get in! I be Tysonyllyn. Huzzah."

The approaching siren and a crazy kind of curiosity made him turn toward the car, then, with a what-the-hell mental shrug, dash to the door and climb in. Nothing ever made any sense to him when he was traveling like this anyway, so why not go with it?

The door swished shut behind him, and the bullet limo jumped from the curb before he had the chance to change his mind. He turned toward his companion in the dimly lit seat, and realized immediately that the dark-skinned woman in a see-through white lace dress did not even come close to resembling the Tysonyllyn he had met.

"Who are you?" he asked.

"I be Tysonyllyn," she said, holding out a hand as graceful as the rest of her body.

Her accent was unlike any he had ever heard before in any of his linguistic classes—impossible to place in time or region. He took her hand and shook it, unable to take his eyes off hers. They seemed to glow like pearls. "I met a Tysonyllyn once," Jackson sad as his fingers tingled in hers. "He was a man who looked like the devil."

She laughed, and for the first time in his life Jackson understood what tinkling laughter was. A wall separated them from the driver's compartment, and Jackson realized that the limo could be the world's plushest trap. With her there, he didn't mind nearly as much as he thought he should have.

"Tysonyllyn is name used by many," she purred. "Should have told you that, they should have." She squeezed his hand and leaned forward. Her breasts pressed out against the white lace, darkly purpled nipples visible through the gauzy material. Were they erect, peeking at him? "I have what you want . . . everything you want."

Suddenly he wanted her and swallowed hard to break the tension inside himself. "How do you know who I am and what I want?"

Again her laughter tinkled through the limo. "A message zip down the line, say where and when and what—Toke's warehouse, tonight, copy of new constitution, TLC. And here I be, all of me, just for you. You be famous."

"I don't understand any of this."

She reached into a large leather case and pulled out a portfolio, which she handed to him. "This be new constitution, one of three hundred seventeen copies sign by all parties. You like sex?"

He stared from the portfolio to where her hand kneaded his thigh. The scent of her made him dizzy. Her touch made him crazy. As he pulled her closer, she responded by climbing on top of him, pushing him down in the soft seat, smothering his mouth with hers, tasting of mint-sweetened breath, grinding her lower body against his, whimpering in unrestrained anticipation.

As they struggled to get enough of their clothes off to join their bodies, Jackson caught crazy glimpses of the city whirling by outside. Bits of architecture from three centuries and at least five cultures swooped and dipped past the limo's window as he and the woman came together in a mad coupling that left him panting and exhilarated.

The sharp nip of her teeth on his neck blended into the flashing nipples of a neon sign in what must have been the historic North Beach restoration area. The strangely peaked and tiled roofs of Chinatown fluttered over his senses with her tongue, flashing over her smooth shoulders and upturned face as she pounded against him like a perpetual motion machine. He caught just the briefest image of a tall gray tower shaped like an antique fire hose nozzle before he closed his eyes and let her insistent inward pull carry him away from all consciousness of anything but her and himself and the two of them struggling for a common goal.

It was all so bizarre and so joyous that he laughed from the sheer pleasure of it.

She responded by working the rest of their clothes off and taking him again after a little oral encouragement, riding him to a slow peak with little bursts of energy and grunting, high- pitched moans of pleasure. When he fell off the edge the second time, he thought he'd died and become a Buddha.

He rolled back into the soft, padded seat of the limo and let his mind drift away on a tide of endorphins. Never in his whole life had he felt so relaxed, so complete . . . so loved.

He felt her fingers smoothing back his hair and gently massaging his scalp. "You be feeling better now?" she murmured in his ear.

"Mmmmmm." He wasn't sure if it came out as a purr or a moan, but she seemed to interpret it positively.

"You fall asleep, we can't do it again, Jackson Dubchek."

"Doesn't matter, I couldn't do it again anyway," he mumbled, on the edge of oblivion.

"In all my dreamy days I never thought it like this. You better than famous, Jackson Dubchek. Now maybe be famous for more, when I tell how good." Her laugh dropped from tinkling bells to throaty woodwinds. "But maybe you forget soon, hey?"

"Never. Impossible. I couldn't possibly," Jackson said, wondering how she could think such a thing.

She shrugged. "Not so special for you, maybe, with women of all times who love you like me. I know. I have memorized the lessons. But I have something no one else have for you. See."

Jackson felt her move underneath him, and forced one eye open to look. The dim light from the streets filtered in through the windows and danced along a streak of silver metal in her hand.

Knife.

She has a knife.

The thought splintered through Jackson's sex-addled brain and charged him with adrenalin, bringing him upright in the seat, suddenly wide awake.

The woman's laughter mocked his fears. "Never hurt you, never. Is your friend, this blade. To help you when I can never ever." She held it toward him, and hesitantly he slid his fingers around the cool haft.

It settled into his hand as if it had been made just for him. The balance was perfect. Holding it up to the light, Jackson saw that it was a dagger of a nearly timeless design that would look equally right as far back as the First Republic of Rome. The handle was smooth, black wood, and the blade was polished steel. One side held Roman characters that read "VERITAS" Just below the hilt guard he made out the maker's mark in the shape of a tiny crane.

"One of a kind, that." The woman's lips slid over his ear and her tongue darted out to tickle him. "Like you."

He turned to her once more, ready to try to recapture the wild passion he'd sworn he was incapable of a moment before, but she pushed him gently away.

"We be back," she said, and handed him a simple leather sheath for the knife. "Cannot wait now. But here." She pointed to the wooden inlays on the limo door. "Carve for me. J plus T, with the knife, so I can prove I don't make it all up."

"You want me to carve our initials?" Jackson was confused, but willing to do whatever she wanted.

"Famous man. I want something to take back with me." She giggled. "Or forward. So confusing to you too?"

"Always," he said, taking the knife out of the sheath and slicing into the wood where she was pointing. Did she mean to say she was from the future too? he wondered. She kept saying he was famous, but he couldn't be known at all in 2091. Or could he?

"There," he said, finishing the cross stroke on the T. "J plus T. Are you happy?"

"Happy, yes." She smiled. "But sad you have to go so soon. Here is Toke's." She turned and rapped sharply on the privacy panel between them and the driver, and the limo swept to a stop at the curb.

"Have constitution? Have knife?" She checked to make sure his hands were securely in possession of the sheath and the leather folder, while Jackson struggled to button his shirt again and tried to remember if he had put his underwear back on. "Go then now before I cry for you." She touched a button and the limo door sprang open, tipping Jackson back out onto the same sidewalk where she'd first picked him up.

"But wait," he said, confused all over again.

She shook her head and blew him a kiss. "Be most of care, Jackson Dubchek. We will all remember you." The door slid shut on her shadowy face, and the bullet pulled away, leaving only a heated curl of dusty air in its wake.

Jackson blinked and looked around him. The skyline with the Transamerica tower was the same as before. So was the anonymous facade of the warehouse. Only the folder in his hand and the knife that she'd slipped into his belt told him the whole experience hadn't been some wild erotic fantasy out of the blue of time travel confusion.

"Well, I guess I'd better go back," he said, feeling more than a little bewildered by it all. He turned toward the warehouse and realized with a nasty little jolt that it was going to be a lot harder to climb back in the two-meter-high window than it had been to jump out. Especially in his condition.

He remembered holos where the dashing heroes made love to beautiful ladies to gain secret information, then performed all kinds of athletic feats to escape from the bad guys, all without ever seeming winded, and he knew he would never be in their class. But at the moment he didn't seem to have any choice. Wearily, he walked to the window, looked for a foothold, then hitched himself up high enough to work a foot over the top. He teetered painfully on the edge for a moment before dropping down into the warehouse, stumbling toward the foot of the stairs.

It was all catching up to him at once. The fatigue of time travel, the confusion of the woman's appearance, and the exhaustion of their passion were all working against him, making it all but impossible for him to put one foot in front of the other, much less think about threading the maze of marijuana plants back to his time machine.

Images moved past him as in a dream, and he couldn't be certain whether or not he was actually fighting his way through a forest of pot plants, or just dreaming about it. At last he found himself standing beside the time machine, not knowing exactly how long he'd been there, or what he ought to do next.

"The plug," he muttered. "Pull the plug," and he followed the machine's long slick tail back to the wall outlet, where he disconnected it. Then he had to follow the same tail back to the machine.

"Deactivate the security."

It pleased him in a remote sort of way that at least some part of his brain seemed to know what needed doing. He pressed his face and hands against the security panel, and thought it might be a nice place to take a nap.

The door hissed open underneath him, lifting him off the security panel and nearly dumping him onto the greenhouse floor.

"Time to get in and go home, Jackson, old boy," he told himself finally, then giggled. Crawling into the seat and strapping himself in seemed to take an eternity. "But you've got an eternity, son," he said. "And if you fuck up the first time you can always go back and try to do it again." He thought about going back and trying to do the woman again, but it was more than he could imagine. Wearily, his fingers moved over the control panel as he set the buttons for his return trip.

"All done. Aaaalll done." He punched the transmit button. "All done and ready to go back to good old 2205." That was right, wasn't it? Or was it 2250 instead?

Sudden panic gripped him in a fistful of edged talons and he stared at the control panel. He could hear the time machine's whine building into a howl, but the flickering numbers on the control panel refused to hold still long enough for him to make any sense of them. Had he set them right or not? He couldn't tell, and as the howl grew into a scream he began to scream too, until everything was lost in a tidal wave of orange juice and ammonia.

Chapter Six

The wave washed him onto a shore of light. Bright, blinding light flooded his senses from all directions, and poured into him through his eyes, through his mouth, through his skin itself. Warm, white light cascaded into the time machine and pulled him out of the tunnel of his abstract fears into a reality that burned his unprotected corneas.

"Look! Over there!" he heard someone shout.

Jackson squinted through the milk-white light at the dimly blinking readouts.

9 January 2205

Shadows danced over the translucent dome of the time machine.

"It's one of them all right," someone said.

"Move around to the other side. Don't give him the chance to pop that hatch. Simmons, Halstead, cover the back."

People out there, Jackson realized. Maybe not friendly people. He cracked his eyes against the flood of white light and tried to make them out.

Seven or eight of them surrounded the machine—all

armed, all pointing their guns at him. Panic jolted Jackson's eyes wide open in the painful light. He knew the security field would hold them at bay, but he didn't have any idea how long it would function. Would it last long enough for him to recharge for the trip back home?

Hastily he fumbled at the reset panel and corrected the target date. The power meter showed he still had some juice left, but he had no idea if it was enough to make the short 45-year hop back home. And there was something else, digging at the back of his conscious mind like an insistent mouse . . .

"Youse are surrounded, qwerk. Get your effing ass out of that damn thing wit' your hands high in the air."

"I may be dumb, but I'm not stupid," Jackson muttered. Who were these people anyway, with their rough voices and their damned lights. He squinted up at them through the protective dome and caught a glimpse of striped overalls and a matching visored beanie.

Republican guards? Impossible. Their only duty was to guard the government's supersecret research facilities. And if he had accidently landed at one of those there was no way he was going to open the hatch.

He hit the displacement Initiation switch, and the time machine started its familiar whine. Suddenly the whine trailed off and OVERLOAD, OVERLOAD, blinked at him from the instrument panel.

"He's firing up! Don't let him move it," warned a voice from the left.

With great deliberation Jackson forced himself to breathe slowly and deeply, trying to ignore his improbable surroundings. As calmly as he could, he examined each complicated cluster of instruments on the panel in front of him, not understanding what was wrong, knowing he had to find the answer. In the rear galleries of his mind a hard piece of essential information rattled around just beyond his reach.

"Youse got five seconds to get your ass out of that car."

Jackson blinked, but would not let himself look up. He had to act as though he were unafraid. Besides, somewhere on that instrument panel lay the tools for escape—escape by some method he almost remembered from the training Temporal Projects had given him, some sequence that . . .

MAN O-RIDE! . . . No, not Manual Override.

"All right, damnit, shoot the qwerk."

EQ BAL? No, not the Equalizer Balance. What in the name of blessed Gautama was Equalizer Balance?

Bullets rattled off the windows under the muffled chatter of gunfire. A chill ran up his spine, but Jackson knew from his experience in Brezhnevgrad that even without the security system on, the bullets couldn't hurt him. If Slye hadn't pushed Lester Wu from the machine, Lester would still be alive.

With a shake of his head, Jackson shifted his gaze to the next cluster of switches, guages, and readouts—each device labeled in black.

SYNCH PHASE <98,325.6>. SYNCH PAUSE—ON. COULTER PT. <10,000.0>. PREP-DEF <01,674.4>

No. Not that one. Next group.

More bullets pelted the time machine. He started and looked up. A round-headed man puffed his angry red face at Jackson.

"Youse got one more chance, qwerk. Get out."

Jackson shook his head and shivered. Instruments,

dummy, he thought, forcing his attention away from the people surrounding him. Concentrate. Where were you?

Green-labeled row. LIFE-SYS-MON. No, not those. Not the blue ones, either.

"Get him out of there!"

Red labels. Yes. Shouting outside. Don't look. Stop panting. Breathe easy. Concentrate.

Read the red labels. There. Small cluster with safety covers. TECH E—1/3—1/2—3/4—FULL. E-PWR FULL.

"Gunter, Kobler, Heezon, I want that bastard out of there right now."

Emergency Power Full. That was it!

But what was the sequence? How was he supposed to start it?

"Lavendar, get the cutting acid."

INIT E-TRANS.

The time machine shook. A man roared in pain. Jackson looked up to see a man falling backward with a sledge hammer flying over his head. Blue lights on. Security system still functioning. He racked his brain to remember the sequence they had told him to use for initiating emergency transition. Power switch first? Or INIT E-TRANS switch first?

Lights dimmed. Instruments flickered. The rear of the time machine bounced up and down on its fat shock absorbers. The faint scent of acid burned Jackson's nose. Panic held him captive for a second, then kicked him in the heart.

One hand flipped the safety cover off the INIT E-TRANS switch. The other hand grabbed his mask. Watering eyes threatened to blind him. He sneezed and coughed but managed to switch on INIT E-TRANS. Then he uncovered and switched on full emergency power, then dragged the mask on over his face. His tears formed a wet seal against the acid fumes.

"Drag him out!"

The machine whined. Threads of white mist wove through the cabin. A second whine crossed the first, higher, hotter, as the time machine vibrated over a low hum.

"Shoot him!"

Butter melted over his eyes. Castenets chattered. His skin itched and burned. Sirens wailed. He heard the door open.

Hands grabbed his arm. He twisted away and somehow found the door handle. Hum, whine, and vibration rose like a wave around him. Blood dripped on his tongue. Fire roared. Pain jerked him out of the seat.

Jackson screamed.

The universe collapsed into a darkness of crying mothers, a darkness of wailing children. Jackson cried and wailed with them. He cried for the stars that exploded, wailed for the world that was no more, wept for the life he'd never live. Then he lost everything in the void.

Hunger. Pointed hunger that held on as surely as nursing vampire bats.

Pain. Sharp pain that nibbled on his skin with needle-fine teeth. Aches throbbed in his ears with the sound of a double bass. Cold liquid edged down his throat. Glue held his eyes shut.

"Must've been a real rat tail for him back there," said a voice from the distance.

Confusion kept Jackson's tongue still. He couldn't remember. Back where? Where had he been? He couldn't remember much of anything.

"Did you see the time machine?" another voice asked.

Jackson listened with great interest, wondering who and what they were talking about, recognizing one of the voices, but not knowing who she was.

"No."

"Looks like it came through a fire—paint burned off, windows cracked, plastic panels warped. But that's only half of it. They found a woman's hand in the machine with him."

"A hand? You mean . . ."

"Just a hand—cauterized. Charred, actually, at the wrist."

"That's disgusting. What happened?"

"We don't know. Irene said that if we had thought of it, we could have put a recorder in with him—should have."

A gust of memory hit Jackson like a fierce wind. The woman, Tysonyllyn, the limousine, the escape. Was it her hand? A coarse moan rasped from his throat.

"Ah, Mr. Dubchek, are you awake under there?"

"Uh-huh."

"Here, drink some more of this."

Something wiggled in the corner of his mouth. He sucked greedily on a tube he realized had been there all the time. Cold sweetness flooded his throat.

"Margaret, go tell Irene he's come around."

Irene . . . Jackson knew that name. He poked at it with mental fingers, waiting to see what what kind of reaction he got. Almost, but still it evaded his grasp. "Where?" he asked hoarsely, lisping around the tube. "Can't see."

"Your eyes are bandaged, Mr. Dubchek, and you're back in Springfield . . . at the Landers."

At the Landers . . . with the Mnemosyne . . . back from . . . where had he gone? . . . San Francisco. Back from San Francisco. And that other place. A woman's hand had covered the years with him.

"What happened?"

"That's what Irene and the council will surely want to ask you, Mr. Dubchek."

He thought he recognized the voice, but then couldn't place it. "Who are you?"

A hand patted his. "I'm Cheryl. I treated your arm when you were here with Bryan last year."

Another gust of memory shook him. Last year. Last year he had never heard of time travel. Last year Martin had a wife and two children. What did last year mean to anyone when time travel could make any year last year and any day already lived a tomorrow yet to come?

"Do you remember that?"

"Baby," he responded. "You were pregnant."

"Twins." Pride filled Cheryl's voice. "Erica and Elgin."

"Elgin? You gave my name? My middle name?"

"That's interesting, but I named my son after Secretary of Culture Elgin. Is she a relative of yours?"

"Cousin, second cousin. Why?"

"Oh, nothing. She's just a friend."

There was something secretive in Cheryl's voice, and Jackson wished he could see her face. Studying languages at the universities had built his vocabulary considerably in body language. "Never met her."

"You should. It would be—ah, Irene's here."

"How do you feel, Jackson?"

A dryer, cooler hand took his and squeezed it gently, then held it.

"Sore. Cold. Tired. Confused. What happened?"

"We want to ask you that very question."

"Don't remember much. . . . Shooting . . . machine wouldn't start . . . maybe my fault." He sighed. "Met a woman . . . no, she met me—was waiting, she said—was expecting me. Gave me the constitution."

"Yes. We read it. It is a very disturbing document, Jackson, much different from the constitution the Republic touts so proudly now. Did you say her name was Tysonyllyn?"

Jackson remained silent, wondering how Irene knew that. He couldn't remember talking to her before. But the woman always knew more than she let on.

"You talked in your sleep, Jackson," Irene said.

Jackson felt his face go red and hoped Irene wouldn't notice. How much had he said about the dark-skinned woman? Had he fantasized about their sexual encounter? "That's what she said, but . . ."

"I know. You can't trust anyone you meet back there. Who knows for sure how many sides are involved in past events spiralling into our present?"

"She implied that she was from the future."

"Hopefully, she was from Bryan's future," Irene said. "His seemed to dovetail nicely with what we are living now. And he did mention a movement in his present to preserve what we are doing now."

A long silence filled the room as Jackson remembered how the old Time Policeman had fallen in battle to allow him and Suzanne a chance to return to Prague for Dr. Alvarez.

"You are not badly injured, you know," Irene went on.

"What do you mean?"

"We'll take the bandages off your eyes tomorrow. You experienced something akin to an arc welding burn, I am told. Nothing serious, but extremely painful. You should be up and around in two or three days."

Jackson waited, knowing there was more, dreading it. "So? What are you going to do for my brother? Can you help him find his family?"

"Yes. Something happened in 2074n75, we think. We're trying to narrow it down."

"And?"

"The copy of the constitution you brought back differs from current copies in three major ways. The one you returned with is greatly concerned with human rights, and details violations that it will never allow to happen again. Second, it guarantees individual political rights which are not guaranteed now. And thirdly, it pays particular attention to a historical period called the Holocaust, claiming that twelve million people—mostly Jews, but also dissidents, Gypsies, and homosexuals—were slaughtered in huge death camps in Europe."

"I've never heard of that."

Irene exhaled loudy. "We've had hints, suggestions, traces of memory—suspicions we couldn't confirm. Now we have this. Now we know when and where. We want to verify it."

"So what's stopping you?"

"We . . . uh, we want you . . . uh, that is we would like—"

He jerked his hand from hers and crossed his arms over his chest. His solar plexus felt like a stone knot.

"No. Absolutely not. No more time travel for me. Send someone else."

"There is no one with your qualifications. We have a sense of history, of events, but not of the languages we would encounter hundreds of years ago. It was something we did not consider." Irene seemed embarrassed. "But who the hell could have expected our present to be sucked down a whirlpool in time? We didn't know."

"There has to be someone else. I'm not going."

"We have to know, Jackson. It's imperative. Is this document you brought back the real thing, or is it another of the Temporal Projects lies, buried in an altered past?"

Something skimmed along the surface of Jackson's thoughts, finally coming to a rest so he could examine. "What about President King? Is he a lie or a plant?"

"Who?"

"President Leslie Lynch King. The machine dropped me into Wheeling again, in 1968 this time, and according to the newspapers he was president of the United States."

"We'll check on that, too. But who was president in 1968 doesn't affect what happened in Europe in the so-called Second World War."

"Doesn't affect me either." He tried to sound defiant, but all he heard was hoarse weariness.

"It could. That could be where your sister-in-law's family was lost."

"Damn you. You said 2075, something happened in 2075."

"I said we thought that might be the date. Given this," a paper rattled, "how can we be sure of anything?"

"How can you be sure even if you send me back? What guarantees do you have that anything in the past is real?"

"None. We remember as best we can, and that is all we can do. Sometimes it helps. Sometimes we save the original past. Sometimes it fails. Then we lose the past . . . and we lose part of ourselves as well . . . or part of our family."

"Why me?" Jackson ased, wishing the bandages were off so he could see her face in the long pause that followed.

"Two reasons," she said finally. "The first is that your whole life was disrupted by Temporal Projects, especially through your brother's, and this is your way to strike back at them—and help your brother at the same time."

Jackson was silent.

Irene sighed loudly. "The second reason is that we—the Mnemosyne, that's all of us around the Republic—have sent nine people into the past. You're the only one who returned. Praetor Centurion-Lieutenant Colonel Brelmer's staff has become infallible in weeding our people out of their lists of applicants. And we think that is the key to time travel in the machines. The Time Police are subjected to successive operations and genetic tampering that are lasting in their results and enhance their physical skills to make them more able to cope with the rigors experienced in whatever year they pop into. At the present, they are the only people who are being cleared for Temporal Projects. There is a theory among us, and I share it, that there is something done to everyone who uses the machine. Some small adjustment in the body's make-up that allows a person to move through the ages without going mad. The only avenue we have open to us is if we can get someone into the ranks of the Time Police. But our chances of that are dismal. Brelmer culls his recruits from prisons, from the ground military, from people whose learning is far below even our beginning students. Our people stand out every time. There is no one else, Jackson.''

Jackson opened his mouth, but words refused to form on his tongue. Eight Mnemosyne lost in the past? Plus Dr. Rosita Alvarez and Lester Wu and who knew how many other innocent people? Anger in his blood burned away his confusion and fed the spark of revenge in his heart as it spread to a conflagration. Someone had to help Ana.

Chapter Seven

As he sat in the anteroom of Senator Voxner's Moscow office, Praetor Centurion Lieutenant Colonel Friz Brelmer wished his flight had been smoother and briefer—or at the very least that he could have gotten some sleep. Transworld shuttle travel was almost as hard on his body as time travel. Acid gurgled in his stomach. Timpani mallets pounded behind his ears. Thick hide glue filled his sinuses, and rosin scratched at his eyes with tiny talons. Brelmer wished he had never made the trip at all.

Shifting his stiff body in the uncomfortable slouch-back chair, he breathed deeply and looked around the all too familiar room. In the course of many visits to Moscow, he had tried every chair in the anteroom at least once. None of them had been built for comfort. Their backs tilted too far away from the vertical not to have headrests, but of course none of them had headrests. Their seats stretched too far forward even for a man of Brelmer's height, so that his feet did not rest naturally on the floor, but they did not have footrests, either. The chair arms were either too high or too low to rest one's elbows. All of which assured Brelmer that no normal person could have found any of the chairs comfortable.

After working for the senator for the past few years, falling more and more under the other man's sphere of control as Brelmer's career advanced, Brelmer understood that Voxner had selected the chairs for the very reason that they were uncomfortable. Making the people who had to see him spend their time in discomfort effected a simple psychological edge for the senator. It eroded his visitors' confidence and self-control, took the edge off their concentration, and made them vulnerable without realizing it. Like much he had come to understand about the senator, Brelmer understood that almost by instinct. It worried him sometimes that the senator's ambitions and convoluted political tampering were so transparent to him. Did Voxner let him understand just enough to keep him satisfied with the events he could view for himself, to let him think nothing else was going on, or did his planning and procedure really match the man's? Either solution left Brelmer uncomfortable, slightly out of touch with the control that had been the unwavering guide in his life.

But one of the things that Brelmer did not understand was why Voxner always demanded to see him in person whenever they were working ten thousand kilometers apart.

The time and energy Brelmer spent traveling halfway around the world were a waste. He and the senator rarely met for more than one or two one-hour conferences on those trips. Two days wasted for two hours worth of meetings annoyed Brelmer no end. Surely the senator knew he needed no psychological edge with Brelmer. Or did the man not know that?

Brelmer shook his head. There was no way to ask

the senator that question, and there was no one else to ask. With his usual prudence, Brelmer had learned to keep most of his opinions and questions to himself and to humor his superior. If the senator thought it necessary for them to meet face to face in order to discuss Temporal Projects—if the senator thought he needed to make Brelmer physically uncomfortable in order to gain some edge, Brelmer would take the time, make the time for the meeting, and he would protest his discomfort in some quiet way he hoped would please Voxner. Brelmer would pander to Voxner's power, but for reasons totally different than Voxner might infer.

Duty demanded no less. Ever since the aftermath of Brelmer's trip to Prague, 1968, when he had almost been killed by Rosita Alvarez, Brelmer had learned to distrust the senator. After that trip—after having his life saved by that disloyal librarian, Dubchek—Brelmer had discovered more than a little evidence that Voxner had connections to Rosita Alvarez; connections that Brelmer did not know how to interpret. Most importantly, he could not determine if Dr. Alvarez had been a willing tool for change or a pawn in another of Voxner's larger history-altering gambits. All that had led Brelmer to believe that someone had to act as a buffer between Voxner and Temporal Projects—someone willing to resist the senator's occasional intemperate ideas, and willing to stand for what he believed was right—a control to match Voxner's chosen role as a variable.

"Well, Friz, are you going to sit there all day? Or are you going to come into the office?"

"Sorry, Senator," Brelmer said as he stood and met Voxner's scowling gaze. "I was lost in finding a solution to a current problem."

"You certainly have enough problems to work on. TP seems to generate them as fast as I can solve them." Voxner turned his back as he spoke, and walked casually back into his plushly appointed office.

Brelmer followed with a silent sigh and a roll of his stiff shoulders. "Yes, sir, I do. Temporal Projects does— by its very nature—seem to generate a multitude of complex problems."

Voxner waved to the chair in front of his desk—not the usual visitor's chair, but this time a duplicate of the uncomfortable chair in the anteroom. His scowl had softened.

Brelmer sat formally in the chair, back straight, shoulders back, chin slightly tucked in, eyes forward— the military posture of subordination. Tightly controlled.

"Tell me about the Texas problem, Friz."

The way Voxner said "problem" almost made Brelmer flinch, but he knew that, like everything else the senator did, the sarcasm was part of his defense mechanism. An unexpected yawn kept Brelmer from speaking for a moment.

"Does this bore you, Friz?"

"Oh, no, sir. Absolutely not. I am merely suffering from travel fatigue."

"Didn't you take your pills?"

"Yes, sir."

"Then I don't understand your problem."

"Fatigue. Partly a result of the Texas trip. We had a bit more trouble than we hoped."

"Nothing you couldn't handle?"

"Oh, absolutely not, sir, but you should know that we were ambushed by time rebels on our return to our machines."

"So your report indicated."

"Yes, of course." But Brelmer wasn't always sure the senator read the reports. Voxner had a handful of other sidebar schemes going on constantly.

"When were they from?"

"We do not know yet, sir. But we captured one of them, and we're in the process of analyzing her now."

"That's not enough to satisfy you? Or do I sense an additional problem?"

"Perhaps I need to back up a bit. If you remember my plan, in order to encourage the independence of Texas from the United States, we had to eliminate a few people and prepare the way for Bernardo O'Higgins as you requested."

"What does that have to do with the time rebels?"

"They knew we were coming, sir."

"So?" Voxner's brows formed tight waves of displeasure.

"Sir," Brelmer said, wondering why Voxner had such a difficult time understanding, fighting his own frown in response, "if the future time rebels know what we change in the past, and when—and they seem to be getting better and better about determining those things—then they can return to the past and attempt to change it themselves. Every time we make an alteration, we set up a paradox that informs them of—"

"Enough. I told you I didn't want to discuss paradoxes any more. They are your problem, not mine."

Brelmer forced himself to breathe easily before responding. "Of course, Senator, but if you will not let me discuss the paradoxes, I cannot explain the problems Temporal Projects faces because of those very paradoxes. You place me in an—"

"Don't push me, Colonel."

Brelmer's already straight back stiffened. "Sir, if you wish to relieve me of my duties, you have every right to do so. However, the person you put in my place will be faced with the same problems, but they will know less about—"

"I might just do that, Friz—relieve you."

"Do you want my resignation, sir?" Brelmer was surprised by the eagerness in his tone, but realized that at that moment, he would gladly have given his resignation to Voxner, to wash his hands of the problems.

"Perhaps you should prepare it . . . undated, of course."

"No."

Voxner started and leaned forward over his desk. "I beg your pardon? You mean you won't give it to me undated?"

"No. Absolutely not. I will not give you an undated resignation to hold over my head, Senator. If you want my resignation, you shall have it as quickly as I can prepare it, and I shall leave Temporal Projects immediately. I will not work under the sword of an undated resignation."

Voxner steepled his fingers under his chin and gazed thoughtfully at Brelmer. His frown softened before he spoke. "I have fired people for less insubordination, Friz. But I believe you are doing the best possible job at the moment, so I don't want your resignation . . . not yet. And if I must listen to them, I will endure your lectures about paradoxes . . . for the moment. But I warn you, Friz, I am concerned about you and your department. You have serious problems across the water—not the least of which are leaks, too much information getting into the hands of the media.''

"We have been working on that, sir."

"Not hard enough, apparently."

"As hard as we know how."

"Then the leaks must be coming from somewhere else. What about you?"

"Pardon?"

"What about you, Friz? Could you be the source of the leaks? How would I know? How would—"

Brelmer stood abruptly at attention. "You will have my formal resignation within the hour, sir."

"Sit down, Friz."

"If you do not trust me, Senator, I see no—"

"Sit down, Colonel. That's an order."

Brelmer sat, fury bunching along his spine.

"If I didn't trust you, Friz, you would no longer be managing Temporal Projects."

His anger still too hot, Brelmer kept his mouth shut.

"However, trusting you and suspecting that leaks are coming out of the highest level of Temporal Projects are two things not necessarily connected. Do you understand that?"

"No, sir, I do not."

"I have reason to believe that someone in your confidence—someone very close to you—is the current source of information for the Licinians. And they are the media's source of classified information."

Brelmer was stunned. "Someone in my confidence revealing classified information, sir? But who? There is no one in my confidence at TP who has not earned my trust."

"Be that as it may, I'm convinced that the leak originates near the top. There is too much—"

"Damn."

"I understand your displeasure, Colonel."

"No, you do not, Senator. You are accustomed to suspecting people. It is part of your nature. It is not part of mine; at least not suspecting those—those who have earned my trust." The words rushed out before Brelmer knew what they were. "I hate suspecting people close to me. I hate it. As soon as I suspect one, I have to suspect all of them. And where does that leave me? Isolated and lonely. Just like you. And that is not what I want for my life, sir. Not one Buddha-bedamned bit."

Voxner laughed. "Too bad, Friz, too bad. The more you get like me, the happier I'll be."

Brelmer worked at keeping his fingers from digging into the fabric of the chair. In a way, the senator's words and logic made sense. To monitor an experiment, you had to detach the control from everything else involved. Keep it from becoming tainted with what you searched for. And that would work in an exercise involving human dynamics as well. The control would become isolated and alone as a result, but it would be a true control. Damn! It made perfect sense, though. He looked into the senator's eyes with his crystal ones, seeing the trap he was stepping into with Voxner's help. The only problem was, Brelmer told himself as he kept his facial expressions in check, could the control handle the strain as well as the senator did?

Chapter Eight

Ammonia and oranges. The universe spiraled down through a series of nights and lights, through burning citrus and cat urine, through oranges and ammonia into the stink of shadows, into the pulses of blurry data flashing like a slow metronome on the instrument panel.

77 BQVVT 1888. 88.88 M 77.78 B.
BELLSLELL.

11 Bqvil 1885. 57.88 N 77.79 B Hellstell.
71 AQUIL 1554. 81.38 M 11.79 E. HETTELSEL.

17 April 1495. 81.88 N. 17.79 E. Hettstell, Berman.

11 April 1495. 57.38 N 11.29 E.
HETTSTEDD.
11 Bqvil 1885. 57.88 M 77.79 B. Hellstell, Bermnnmy.

77 BQVVT 1888. 88.88 W 77.78 E.
BELLSLELL.

11 April 1945. 51.38 N. 11.29 E. Bellstedt, Germany.

11 APRIL 1945. 51.38 N. 11.29 E.

HETTSTEDT, GERMANY.
11 April 1945. 51.38 N. 11.29 E. Hettstedt,
Germany.
11 APRIL 1945. 51.38 N. 11.29 E.
HETTSTEDT, GERMANY.

Dates and locations twisted through oranges, threaded through the instrument panel, curved around the ammonia and around the time machine, and the stinking time machine twisted heavy ropes around Jackson's stomach, wringing only bile from the emptiness.

11 APRIL 1945. 51.38 N. 11.29 E. HETTSTEDT, GERMANY.

Blink by belch by blip by burp, the twisting slowed, the retching stopped, and the nausea retreated. After wiping his face, Jackson summoned the strength to open the door to the time machine. The new odor that assaulted his nose told him in one primitive instant that the instruments were correct—Hettstedt, Germany, the village closest to Buchenwald. He had arrived exactly when and where the Mnemosyne had wanted him to.

The smell that attacked his nostrils made him wish he hadn't.

Death stench thickened the gray air. Nausea bubbled once more in his throat. Dismay watered his eyes with acid tears.

BUCHENWALD. *Einfahrtarbeiterin*, the sign on the brick gate building read. *ARBEIT MACHT FREI*. Women worker's entrance. Labor makes you free.

Irene and her team had warned him what he might expect to find if the constitution was correct—warned him based on what the Mnemosyne researchers had discovered about the death camps in South Africa, but Buchenwald . . . He belched up a sour bubble that burned his esophagus from the pit of his stomach to the back of his mouth.

BUCHENWALD. Buchenwald was already worse than the Mnemosyne warnings, worse than descriptions from the cold computers and research tapes. Buchenwald polluted the air with things worse than any information, any warning anyone could have given him. Because of the light wire fence between him and the forest to his right, Jackson felt sure he had not even entered the main part of the *konzentrationslager*—the concentration camp—but already Buchenwald clogged his nose and burned his throat. It wrenched tissue from his stomach. It squeezed tears from his eyes.

Sobibor, Woebbelin, Ludwigslust, Gardelegan, Belzec, Thekla, Penig, Ohrdruf, Auschwitz-Birkenau-Oswiecim, Bergen-Belsen, Fallersleben, Dachau, Wolfsburg, Bruanschweig, Flossenburg, Sosnowiec, Treblinka, Gusen, Natzwiller, Landsberg, Passau, Mauthausen, Ebensee, Monowitz, Oranienburg, Chelmno . . . The list seemed endless, but with the help of the Mnemosyne, Jackson had memorized the names of every concentration camp cited in the copy of the constitution he had brought back from San Francisco.

Now he sat and stared and understood that the original constitution had been correct. At least about Buchenwald. No one would need to get any closer or see any more than he saw to know what existed on the other side of the fence and barbed wire.

Death.

He could name death and taste it only because of some instinctive memory of his senses. What he saw, the vision of death itself, he could not name . . . not yet.

Less than thirty meters from where the time machine

had come to rest in the shadow of a low, barnlike building—on tracks that ran in front of the gate building, less than thirty meters from where he sat and stared, stood a topless railroad car, its wide doors hanging open like the gates of Hell. Darkness shone down from the gray sky upon the contents of that filthy railroad car.

Inside the car, stacked haphazardly like cordwood, was something . . . something so unbelievable that Jackson was out of the time machine and halfway to the railroad car before his brain would let him identify what his eyes saw . . . identify what his eyes saw but what he dared not let himself see . . . identify the stacks in the car under the dark light of Hell as naked corpses.

"How?" he whispered. "How in Buddha's name . . ."

Jackson saw the corpses, recognized what he saw, but did not, could not comprehend. For the sake of his sanity, he dared not comprehend the immensity of the sight. The grim eye of the universe focused on that railroad car, turned around it like winds around the eye of a monsoon, centered on that dark place and that cold moment, and narrowed down to one point inside the spinning of time and space. The eye of the universe—the cold, uncaring eye of the universe—focused, turned, and held Jackson at a center from which he could not move.

He knew the pale lumps and sticks on the flatcar were human corpses even though they no longer looked like real human beings. He knew the bodies of human beings stared blankly at him and he stared blankly back. He knew, not because his brain told him but because something deep in his gut recognized the indelible mark of humanity left on those stacks of skin-covered bones.

Still he could not comprehend the sight.

With great difficulty, Jackson swallowed the hard lump of disbelief in his throat, unable to stop staring at the corpses, unable to endure their persistence in his eyes. In those empty moments where the universe held him, his mind shrank from the acceptance of consciousness. His eyes watered. His head floated. His knees buckled. He wept.

As slowly as the movement of a nightmare, he sank to the ground before the railroad car. Deep sobs shook his body while he knelt in the mud and prayed without words. Life contained no words for the atrocity that confronted him. Religion contained no prayers. The primitive supplication that rose through him echoed only as the crying of his heart.

That cry went out to the unnamed gods—to the One, the All, the Infinite, the Finite, the Be-All-and-End-All—went wordlessly to all the gods of the Baha'i pantheon and beyond. He cried to every god and to no god in particular, cried for release, cried for relief, cried for himself and those who had perished in the death camp.

From some outside place, from some outside time, a faint voice asked in German who he was.

Jackson barely understood the words and did not understand where the question had come from. The voice asked again. A light hand brushed his shoulder.

Jackson looked up through his tears.

Atop a skeleton body dressed in striped pants and a shabby brown coat, a death mask with moving mouth and blinking hollows babbled to him in soft whispers.

When Jackson wiped the tears from his eyes, Skeleton looked worse than walking death. The words, what were the words? "Uh, ah . . . I, uh, *ich kein verstehen* . . . uh . . ."

"Amerikaner?" Skeleton asked.

"Ja. ich bin ein amerikaner," Jackson answered, unsure his phrase was correct.

Skeleton's lipless mouth moved in a grim parody of a smile that showed no more than three or four teeth remaining in his colorless gums. Then he pointed with a bony finger and again babbled something. The strangely accented German that Skeleton spoke tumbled so rapidly and quietly from his mouth that Jackson could understand only the repeated *Amerikaner*.

"Ich kein versthen sie, mein herr," Jackson said, shaking his head to reinforce his words. *"Oft langsam, bitte.* Slow down, please."

Skeleton made a croaking, cracking sound that might have been laughter, and Jackson guessed that his fractured German had amused the man, then felt amazement that the man could be amused by anything in the midst of this hell.

"Amerikaner. Soldaten." Skeleton pointed repeatedly toward the center of the camp with one grotesque hand. With the other hand he tugged at the worn woolen coat the Mnemosyne had insisted that Jackson wear. Only then did Jackson finally understand. There were Americans in the camp, American soldiers. What does that mean? he wondered as he climbed to his feet.

Skeleton pulled him along with remarkable strength and determination—through the *einfahrtarbeiterin,* past groups of seven or eight skeletons huddled around small fires—past open windows in unpainted buildings where skeletons stared out at him, the dark hollows in their faces following him along the muddy street—past one, two, three piles of corpses stacked beside the buildings with an unbelievable impersonal touch—to a wire mesh gate, three meters high, secured by a heavy chain.

Skeleton smiled and pointed through the gate. *"Amerikaner."*

Except that the living dead he saw on the other side of the gate looked even worse than Skeleton, Jackson saw nothing different from what they had just passed through.

"NAZI! NAZI! NAZI!" a voice behind them screamed.

Jackson turned in time to see a man running toward them waving a heavy stick, eyes gleaming with madness.

"Schweinefleisch! Kotkopf! Nazi scheissersack!" Behind the madman shuffled a ragged mob in an odd assortment of striped and tattered clothes. "Liar! Pig! *Nazi! Warmebruder!"* they croaked. In the hollows of their eyes gleamed small fires of the same madness.

Fear pushed Jackson's back against the gate, but he sensed something wrong. Even as he looked desperately around for a way to escape the cadaverous wave of humanity that closed on him, Skeleton stepped between him and the madman.

The madman slowed and lowered his arm. His eyes shifted toward uncertainty and, as they did, Jackson noticed the dulled crystal gleam in them for the first time.

A Time Policeman! But what was the man doing here? Had he been accidently left behind? Or had he been displaced? A chill shook Jackson under the woolen coat. So far he had been more skilled, or more lucky, than the man whose eyes he could not avoid. But how close had he come? How often?

"That man is a Nazi," the displaced Time Policeman

shouted, pointing his stick at Jackson. "He spies on all of you." The shuffling mob caught up with him.

"*Grosse fonfer!*"

"Yes, he is the liar," Skeleton said in his loudest whisper. "This man just arrived."

"*Schmuck!*" Another cadaver spat on the man with the stick.

"*Yentzer!*"

The ragged mob tightened its circle, forming a half-moon audience around the violence that Jackson could feel coming.

With an inarticulate cry of rage and resentment, the Time Policeman swung his stick at Skeleton. It connected solidly with the man's head, sounding deathly hollow, and spilled Skeleton to the ground. The Time Policeman grabbed the stick in both hands as he shifted to face Jackson. His voice was shrill, uncertain, as he screamed in a language Jackson knew only he and the other man understood.

"What time are you from?" the Time Policeman asked as he stepped forward.

Two men separated themselves from the ragged mob and seized Skeleton by the arms, dragging him to safety. His lipless mouth hung slack as bloody spittle made glistening threads down his cheek.

Was he alive? Jackson wondered, then changed his concern to his own survival as his attacker whipped the heavy stick at him. His fingers gripped the wire mesh as he flung himself to one side.

The stick rattled and popped as it skidded across the mesh.

For a moment an animal part of Jackson's mind tried to compel him to reach for the club before the man could drag it back. Once his fingers closed on it, he was sure his heavier weight would be a deciding factor in who kept control of it. Or would it? How strong were members of the Time Police? Jackson didn't know, but the rumors about their abilities were considerable. Increased strength had been one of the leading augumentations any member of the Time Police underwent. And how strong would one of them be when the genetic and physical alterations were coupled with the madness of being lost in time for Buddha only knew how many years?

"What time, damnit?" the madman demanded. The stick remained steady in the bone-thin hands, then flashed forward.

Jackson managed to escape the full force of the blow as it smashed into his ribcage, but enough remained to spin him around. He clawed helplessly at the mesh, knowing if he ever toppled from his feet he would lose any chance at all of escaping the man's blows. Tears ran down his face as the pain in his side took him like a sex-starved lover. Reach for the stick, the animal voice inside him said again.

But Jackson denied the impulse, capped it away in a small corner of his mind. He would evade the man when the chance presented itself. He would not try to capture the stick. That path led to agression, and it was that agression that had caused him to kill Laszlo Slye in Prague, chaining himself to the nightmares that still had not faded.

The Time Policeman drew the stick back with both hands.

Under the woolen coat, pressed into his back by the fence, Jackson could feel the knife he had been given in San Francisco. For a single, horrid moment, images of what the sharp dagger would do to the man in front of him played across the screen of his mind. No, Jackson told himself, there is enough death here already. Buddha forbid there should have to be any more.

"2250," Jackson said, feeling his body shiver in anticipation of the coming blow.

The information checked the Time Policeman's move. "2250?" The crystal eyes glowed with inwardly directed fires. The stick settled on one broad, unfleshed shoulder.

"Yes." Jackson straightened himself against the fence. He looked past the man for just a moment to see how Skeleton was doing. The two men who had pulled him to safety were administering first aid. Thank Buddha the man wasn't dead.

"Ten years before I was born," the Time Policeman cackled. He roared with laughter at the thought.

A stinging sensation burned along Jackson's hands. For the first time he noticed that the wire mesh had torn skin from his fingers and palms.

"But you didn't know that, did you?" the Time Policeman asked. An insane smile spread across his face. "Time Policeman Corporal Lance Paulson at your service, sir." He gave Jackson a mock bow but the gleaming madness housed in the crystal eyes never looked away. "And who is in charge of Temporal Projects in your time?"

"Friz Brelmer," Jackson replied. Maybe, just maybe, he could talk his way clear of this situation. Would Irene still have insisted he make this trip if she had known he would face an encounter like this? Then he thought of the iron will that powered the woman despite her being old enough to be his grandmother. Yes. She would have insisted. Even if she had had to shut him up in the time machine herself.

As long as he came back alive with the needed information.

And that was a sobering thought, Jackson whispered to himself.

"Brelmer!" The Time Policeman, Paulson, hacked and spit into the mud. "Now there's as fine a traitor as you would ever want to see in your life."

Brelmer? A traitor? The questions spun crazily in Jackson's head, threatening to overpower him and cloud his mind. Everything he had seen of Friz Brelmer, despite his being Suzanne's father, told him the man was the epitome of loyalty to TP. Had something happened to change that? Or was it going to happen? Or was Paulson from an alternate time line just as he thought Vice President Fosdick was?

A sly smile captured Paulson's hollow face, twisting the elongated ears further back on the hairless skull. "You have something I want," the madman said, "and I mean to have it." The stick lifted from the Time Patrolman's shoulder.

Jackson felt his body flinch involuntarily. Surely the man wasn't going to continue to try to kill him. He had answered the questions, had resisted fighting back. What more did the man want?

"I saw you get out of your time machine," Paulson said, "and I know you set the security system on it. I won't be able to get inside and return to my time without your help." The Time Policeman paused to smile another gut-wrenching smile that showed gums resembling the ridges Jackson had seen in fishes' mouths when Gran'pa

Jack had taken him fishing when he was small. The kind of smile Jack Nicholson had worn in the ancient Stephen King holo that had frightened Jackson as a boy. "Assuming it's the same kind of set-up we have, all I need is your face and hands to get myself in. And you don't even have to be alive for that."

The stick came off the shoulder faster than Jackson believed possible, turboing toward him so quick it seemed to grow larger as it closed in on his face. There was no reasoning with the madness driving Paulson, he realized as the animal part of his mind that controlled personal survival screamed from the dark cave he had forced it into. He watched himself move, a captive of the involuntary will to live that burned inside him, shrilling along his synapses.

His fingers curled along the surface of the stick.

Absorbed the kinetic energy.

Redirected.

Stepped outside the arc of the blow as blood beat wild bongos in his head.

The movement was graceful, as true as any chord he ever played on Odar'a.

Then he was under Paulson's swinging arms, setting himself up for what he hoped would be an incapacitating blow that would allow him to flee. Once he was running, he was sure he could easily outdistance the man, bionic enhancements or not. He cocked his right hand back and down, shooting it forward toward his attacker's chin.

Jackson felt the Time Policeman's arms close about him as his palm exploded into the man's chin. A wet, popping sound came from the suddenly closed jaws, partially shutting off a cry of pain.

But Paulson didn't go down. The Time Policeman

swayed uncertainly, true, but remained standing. His arms swept around Jackson and locked him within a prison of maddened flesh.

How strong was a Time Policeman? The question bounced off the walls of Jackson's mind as he struggled to find leverage to get away. His breath was crushed from him, and spots danced before his eyes like a faulty holo. He wondered if he would live long enough to know the answer.

Chapter Nine

"Does she know who I am?" Brelmer asked the female technician sitting beside him.

"No, Colonel," the technician said as she continued to make notes on the pad beside her on the computer console.

Brelmer leaned forward, placing his chin in his left hand as he opened his crystal eyes up to further allow the dim light in the room to illuminate the papers in his other hand. He scanned the notes quickly, absorbing their contents as he did every report that crossed his desk. Except that these notes were different, more personal than any had been before. Thoughts of Voxner and his damned hypothesis—that someone of considerable rank in Temporal Projects was leaking secret information to the media—ate at the fringes of his analytical mind.

But the information he held was in black and white, thoroughly documented and cross-referenced. Temporal Projects didn't employ anyone but the best. As long as their politics are right, Brelmer thought grimly as an image of Voxner flashed into his mind. Even the Time Police, men like Laszlo Slye, were the best to be found. It took a certain aggressiveness in men and women filling out the ranks of the Time Police that was lacking in ordinary citizens. A certain aggressiveness and just a grain of loyalty, coupled with a healthy dose of greed, of course. Voxner scraped those individuals from the bottoms of penitentiaries throughout the Republic and rolled them into the hospitals where they were transformed.

Brelmer shook his head free of the extraneous line of thought and returned to the problem at hand.

Lifting his head, he peered through the heavy pane of one-way crystel housing the captured time rebel.

She sat in the center of the room in a lotus position, her delicate forearms resting lightly on her bare knees. The defiance in the set of her body and features was oddly disturbing to Brelmer, almost as if he knew them. Which, according to the reports he held, shouldn't surprise him.

Her golden hair cascaded down her bare back, contrasting with the black shift she had been given. She looked healthy, tanned and lean, despite the dark purple bruise that stained her forehead. That had happened when the girl, the time reb—must keep this in perspective, Brelmer ordered himself—tried to escape being put into the time machine in Texas.

But the puffed lower lip and dried blood in the corner of her mouth were new.

Brelmer folded the papers and stuck them in a pocket of his lab smock. "What happened to the girl's mouth?"

"She tried to escape again at her noon meal, sir," the technician responded. "Henshaw had to restrain her."

Brelmer noticed the woman did not look up. "Her present condition wouldn't be due in any part to the prejudice this project seems to harbor toward the time rebels, would it?"

"Not that I'm aware of, sir." She looked up now, reacting to the harsh tone he had chosen.

"I certainly hope not, Tech-Corporal, for your sake as well as the Republic's. That girl is a very valuable piece of property at the moment, one whose true worth has not been mined even superficially. I want you to keep that in mind as you work your shifts."

The technician nodded.

Brelmer looked back at the captured girl, focusing on the dulled blood on her face. "Furthermore, I want you to find Sgt. Henshaw and have him sent to my office."

"Yes, Colonel."

Brelmer left the room without replying, slamming the door to the observation post for a final effect, knowing the time reb wouldn't be able to hear it through the detention cell's soundproofing.

Inside he was a mixture of emotions, each spinning and slamming into the others while clawing for purchase to collide again. He paused outside the detention cell's door, trying to regain the control he needed to be who he was. Never, never would he have expected something like this. What were the chances of something like this happening?

He pushed the question away, knowing it created still more questions, some of them so personal he dared not even admit their existence.

Stiffening his posture, Brelmer thumb-coded the door open.

The girl remained sitting, never turning to look.

The door closed behind Brelmer as he took a seat on the immaculate bed. Had she been sleeping on the floor as well? he wondered. Or had she been sleeping at all? He would ask the tech staff later.

He cleared his throat, not trusting his voice. "I want to talk to you, young lady."

She answered without opening her eyes. "That's great, because I don't want to talk to you."

The words stung, sounding so familiar, filled with the familiar anger. Responsive chords tuned to high-C tweaked within him, and he had to hurry to get a grip on the standard replies he had always made in the past. "Why?"

"Because you're the enemy, old man. Or hasn't anyone told you that yet?"

"I've never talked to anyone from the future before now."

Her eyes snapped open, filled with angry green fire. "Maybe that's because your policy of opening fire on anyone from the future prevents that."

"My group didn't start the action back in Texas."

"It didn't start there, damnit. It started here, with those time trips you and Voxner initiated to control history. You declared war on us."

"You must be joking. We have done nothing except insure our own present. If your group lives, then how can you say we have done anything to endanger you?"

Her eyes were positively feral when she looked at him, filled with raw hate. "We live, old man, but just barely. Each day we survive is a miracle. But not a miracle without cost. People disappear on a much too regular basis. Chaos is the rule rather than the exception."

"What would you suggest we do?"

She shook her head, sending her blonde mane flying. "There is nothing you can do now. The foundation for the war has been set, and only the twists of the timewinds will decide what will become of us all. What you have succeeded in doing is establishing the way for an entropy that may destroy all we ever knew of ourselves.''

Brelmer tried to take her words in, listening intently to the fervor with which she spoke. "How can I believe what you say is true? For all I know you are from an untrue future, an alternate time that would never existed had it not been for the time machine's invention.''

She smiled without mirth. "You have your convictions. I have mine. They will never meet." Abruptly, she forced herself to her feet, turning away from him to face the wall with the one-way crystel. "I could feel you watching me from there," she said in a quieter voice. "I know this room is constantly monitored and there is a team of people on the other side of this wall waiting for me to say anything at all about the future I come from.''

Brelmer waited. He shifted on the bed to find a more comfortable posture and heard the papers crinkle in his pocket, bringing back those impossible questions he had been lost in since arriving at the tech post. "It is important that I know about your time.''

She remained standing, facing away from him. Her back was tense with restrained emotion.

How many times had he seen Suzanne stand just so? "If you do not give me the information willingly," Brelmer said, "then I shall have to take it any way I can.''

She spun like a dancer, placing her hands on her hips. "Then do it, damnit, and don't tell me what you're planning to do. I fought beside people who died for their right to live. Don't expect me to hand my world over to you willingly.''

"The ways we have of extracting information are not pleasant," Brelmer said in a soft voice. "However, they are effective.''

She said nothing.

"Maybe you've discovered better ways in your time."

"Taunt me all you want, you soulless bastard, but you won't get anything out of me. We've been conditioned against everything you could use on us. Hypnos, chems, everything. We're all conditioned before they send us out. If you try any of those, I'll die. My heart will stop beating, and I'll die on whatever table you have me strapped to, in whatever chair I'm secured in. Torture me if you want, but my pain threshold will allow me to reach a certain point, and death will take me anyway."

Brelmer believed her. There was no doubting the revelry of defiance in her. The purple bruise on her forehead and the streak of blood on her cheek only underlined the emotion evident in her compact body.

"You exist at a very fortunate space in the scheme of time," the girl said in a lower voice. "If you consider time as a straight line, your present, your world, occupies the position of a fulcrum under the lever of time. At one end lies the past. At the other, the future. All because the invention of the time machine happened in your now. Time can't spin and change around you exactly the same way it happens to us. Sure, you see shadows splinter off occasionally, a few people disappear here and there, but no one important, because your staff makes sure of that. History is a playground to you, a mixture of equations you can alter whenever the whim strikes you, because it only makes subtle differences in your world. But the future, the future, how many future nows have died while you play your games? For all I know mine may have faded into nothingness when we jumped back from Texas. Do you know what that feels like? The not knowing?"

Tears sparkled like shattered diamonds in the girl's eyes. Her lip trembled. How familiar it all was, Brelmer thought to himself. He pushed himself up from the bed and moved slowly, making sure his movements couldn't be misinterpreted as threatening. "Surveillance out," he commanded, and watched the amber light built into the far wall wink out obediently. Now they were closed off from the tech post. This room was his world now and privy to no other eyes or ears. The intercom connection broke at his command and the plasteel one-way opaqued to a gray cloud.

Brelmer came to a halt in the center of the cell. "We are alone now; all the listening and visual devices have been shut down. What we say now is for us alone. Do you understand?"

The girl nodded.

Feeling the anticipation and excitement mount within him, Brelmer asked, "What is your name, girl?"

She did not answer.

"Come, come, girl. Surely you know about genetic coding? Geneticists even in our time can track DNA back to the original gene pools, to the ancestors you have. I had such a report worked up on you. Do you want me to tell you what it said?"

"What year is this?"

An inaudible sigh of relief emptied Brelmer's lungs. Could it be this easy? "2250."

"Then your report will show you that one of my ancestors is Suzanne Brelmer," the girl answered, meeting his gaze levelly. "Your daughter."

Brelmer entered the outer room of his office lost in

thought, not noticing the Time Policeman sitting in one of the reception chairs until the larger man snapped to attention.

"Sgt. Henshaw," the Time Policeman barked, keeping his eyes directed at the ceiling, "reporting as ordered, Colonel."

Brelmer nodded as he passed the man, holding the cold knot of anger around his heart in check. "I will send for you momentarily, Sergeant."

The man remained at attention.

Halting at his secretary's desk, Brelmer picked up the notes from the IN tray. There had been three calls from Voxner. He glanced at his secretary, watching the man squirm under his gaze. Was it merely that the man knew him well enough to know his present state of mind, Brelmer wondered, or was it something else? Damn Voxner and his suspicions. Soon he would be dodging shadows.

"Cancel whatever appointments I may have this afternoon, Guthrie," Brelmer said, "and hold my calls."

The secretary nodded and started punching keys on the computer beside the desk.

Brelmer entered his office and breathed a sigh of relief. The holoscreen came on automatically, building three-dimensional shapes filled with color in the center of the room. The holo was set on a news station 24 hours a day, interspersed with information programs on topics Guthrie, the secretary, thought would interest Brelmer. The show on now had something to do with laser surgery, and normally Brelmer would have been interested in the minute detail it showed.

He cleared the holo and sat behind the large mahogany desk, not yet calling for the lights, content with the placid darkness.

There had been nothing more gained from the girl after the disturbing confirmation that she was a descendant of Suzanne, even though Brelmer had tried every trick he knew. He had commanded, wheedled, stopped short of begging, but only because he felt it would have only heightened his feelings of inadequacy in dealing with the situation.

Now.

Now he didn't know what to do.

He was sitting on a powder keg and had a lighted match in each hand.

If Voxner found out about the time reb's lineage it would only serve to confirm the senator's thoughts about the leaks at TP. And if Brelmer resigned, he would be in no position to protect his daughter if Voxner found out later.

He was trapped and he knew it.

Trapped just as surely as the girl in the cell.

Maybe he should call her his granddaughter, however many generations removed.

He had considered killing her, removing any lead to Suzanne. But how could he destroy something that came from his daughter? From himself? And she looked so much like Suzanne. It would be like killing Suzanne herself.

Wearily, he considered his options, finding them alarmingly few. He had to find the damned leak in the operation and keep the knowledge of who the girl was from Voxner, that much he was sure of. But how much time did he have?

As the thought passed through his mind, he laughed bitterly. A man in command of the flow of time, he realized, and still fearing the passage of it.

Luckily, he had squelched the report on the girl's genetic coding investigation before it reached more than the technician he had spoken with before the interrogation. He had inserted new data in the comlink frame, which stated no ancestor for the time rebel could be found among the files the Republic now had access to. The technician had been sent to an office in Grenada, with a nice bonus and a warning.

"Lights."

The room lit quickly, and Brelmer adjusted the brightness by voice, settling for a dim setting that would enhance the mood he wanted to generate. Then he leaned forward in the old-fashioned swivel chair and thumbed the intercom, telling Guthrie to send Henshaw in.

The sergeant looked out of place in the office. The gray and white and black of his uniform clashed with the wood-hued somberness of the room. He looked uncomfortable to Brelmer, lost in the largness of it. Books lined one complete wall of the office, and the colonel was willing to bet Henshaw had never seen a book before.

"Sgt. Henshaw reporting, Colonel." The man saluted stiffly.

What prison did you come out of? Brelmer wondered as he stood and made his way around the desk. He sat on the edge of it, his right hand straying to the heavy marble nameplate sitting there. Suzanne had gotten it for him, he remembered. "At ease, Sergeant."

"Thank you, sir." The man's crystal eyes never met Brelmer's.

"I imagine you're wondering why I summoned you here, Sergeant?"

"Yes, sir."

"It's about the girl, the one we captured and brought back from the Texas operation."

A twitch started under Henshaw's right eye. "Yes, sir."

Brelmer stroked the marble nameplate, nurturing the cold dispassion filling him. "It appears she had an accident today, during her noon meal."

Henshaw looked at him, an uncertain light flickering in the crystal eyes. The twitch had spread to the sergeant's right ear, jerking the elongated tip back into the man's shaven skull. "Look, sir . . ."

Curling his fingers around the nameplate, Brelmer smashed it into the man's face, feeling the flesh and bone give quickly.

Henshaw fell, automatically reaching for his holstered weapon.

Brelmer lashed out with a foot, catching the sergeant in the throat and knocking him over. He stepped forward, resting enough weight on Henshaw's throat to keep the man down.

Henshaw gagged.

Leaning down, Brelmer whispered conspiratorialy. "If she has any more 'accidents' I will hold you personally responsible, Sergeant. Do you understand me?"

Henshaw could only croak weakly but Brelmer took it as an affirmative.

"I don't care if you have to watch her twenty-four hours a day, Corporal Henshaw. Agreed?"

A gurgling croak was the reply.

Brelmer removed his foot. "Good, very good. Now get to the infirmary, Private, and tell someone about your accident before you bleed on that very expensive carpet."

The Time Policeman was slow in getting up, holding his face in one hand.

Brelmer ignored him, feeling a little better, a little more in control of things swarming around him. He seated himself behind the desk again after Henshaw left the room, and thumbed the intercom. "Guthrie?"

The secretary was slow to answer.

"Guthrie!"

"Yes, Colonel?"

"Send for my daughter."

"Yes, Colonel."

Settling back in the swivel chair, Brelmer breathed in through his nose and out through his mouth, relieving still more of the stress he felt. The savagery with which he had dealt with Henshaw was not new, but it wasn't an everyday thing either. The violence of it was unsteadying, to say the least, but it had been necessary. Violence was a tool that every great leader used. And Brelmer fully intended to lead Temporal Projects.

But how to handle Suzanne? That was something he had never really been any good at.

Chapter Ten

Jackson Elgin Dubchek's life seemed to skate by in a schizophrenic panorama in his mind, flickering images that belonged to a torn holo tape, as his lungs begged for air. The thing that bothered him most was that his years no longer followed a regular pattern. Periods of history interacted wildly with what he considered to be the "real" time, till he was unsure exactly where, or when, he was.

Until his eyes snapped open and he stared into the burnished orange glare of the insane Time Policeman. As Paulson grunted with the effort of squeezing him to death, the madman's mouth twisted in a strained grimace.

Jackson was sure the next sound to reach his ears would be the ascending octaves of his ribs cracking beneath the unbelievable pressure. How strong was a Time Policeman? More than strong enough, Jackson's body told him. He twisted in the incredible grip, seeking purchase to use for leverage, breathing space. His left arm was free, and he used it to claw at Paulson's face. Then he slipped his thumb into the man's eye and started to shove inward, willing himself not to be sick because he thought the nausea would be just enough to allow his insides to be crushed.

The crystal eye felt hard, resilient, alien.

He pushed harder as unseen oceans roared in his ears, climaxing in sixty-foot swells that threatened to carry him into the darkness of unconsciousness.

The hardness darted against the ball of his thumb, trying to blink free, and he was surprised at the lack of moisture in the eye. How could any eye remain so dry and not be irritable all the time? Buddha, please let it be irritable now. He increased the force, sure his brain would relax its hold on life at any moment and the effort would have been in vain. But there! He felt a weakness, a giving. Would his thumb penetrate the crystal eye, or possibly slide under it to plunge into the socket? He tasted bile at the back of his throat but was unable to get it up any further.

Paulson's roars changed in pitch, from a maddened and hoarse yell to a bellow of agony. But the iron bands across Jackson's chest stubbornly refused to loosen.

Concentrating on his remaining strength, summoning it greedily from the other parts of his body, Jackson pushed with renewed vigor, spearing his thumb into the orifice. For a moment, amid the flickering cartoon drawings of his life, he saw Suzanne Brelmer staring at him with a softness in her gaze that he had missed over the last long months.

"Damn you!" Paulson yelled as he tried to shift away from the thumb.

Jackson felt the man's grip loosen. Not much, but enough to allow him to free his other arm. His lungs sucked in air greedily for only a second or two before Paulson clamped them shut again. Through tearing eyes, he raised his hands to either side of the Time Policeman's head, watching a trickle of red blood reluctantly worm its way down Paulson's face below the eye. The pupil sat crooked now, a darker color than its twin. Was it broken, or had he blinded the man? Jackson wondered. The thought of either possibility increased the sick weakness inside him.

Mustering the last ounce of his strength, Jackson clapped his hands as hard as he could over the madman's elongated ears, willing to rupture and destroy if it meant drawing only one more breath.

Paulson staggered beneath the blow and Jackson repeated it, striving to send the man to his feet.

Fall, fall, Jackson's mind screamed wordlessly because there was nothing left in his lungs to do anything with.

He clapped again, like an organ grinder's insane monkey performing before an appreciative audience. His eyes closed involuntarily. He felt the wet warmth of blood staining his palms as wild blackness reached out for him with hooked talons and a soul-shredding soundless scream.

Then he was falling, sure he would never wake again.

"You goddamned bastard!" Paulson yelled.

Jackson forced his eyes open after only absently noticing the jarring he received from hitting the ground. He saw the sky first, still filled with the gray clouds, and realized he was lying on his back. His lungs burned when he breathed, as if the oxygen had somehow been transmuted to alcohol.

A hand clamped onto Jackson's left ankle, and the enormous strength told him who it belonged to.

He twisted, rolling over in an attempt to get his free

foot under him. Buddha help him, he couldn't let the Time Policeman reestablish his hold. He didn't have the strength to escape a second time.

Failing in his attempt to pull his captured foot free, Jackson flipped and flopped in Paulson's grip, turning to face the man. The broad grin on the man's face showed only insane pleasure. Blood leaked from both pointed ears, running down Paulson's neck. The Time Policeman's muscles showed striated tissue in stark relief from the exertion. The crystal eyes held a lambent ruby glow even darker than the blood.

Almost, almost Jackson managed to evade the man's left fist, twisting his head to one side in the attempt. The fist exploded beneath his jaw and skidded under his chin. He felt himself being forced back into the wire mesh of the gate as the Time Policeman started to cover him with his cadaverous body. The man's breath stank of death, and foul spittle dripped on Jackson's face.

"Get away!" Jackson yelled, almost not recognizing the strained voice as his own.

Paulson's grin only grew larger. The Time Policeman maintained his hold on Jackson's ankle and pressed his thin and bony chest into Jackson's.

Swinging wildly, Jackson pounded his fists into Paulson's sides, hoping to dislodge the man and escape. He levered a hand under Paulson's chin and tried to force the man away but couldn't. The Time Policeman was melding so closely to him that Jackson was sure he could feel every bone in the man's body. There was no meat to batter and bruise, precious little musculature to paralyze. The Time Policeman was a walking skeleton of reinforced bone and ceramic joint supports.

A hand gripped Jackson's throat and started closing.

He struggled but only managed to rock his shoulders free of the muddy ground for an instant.

Then the pressure faded from his neck. Through his swimming vision he saw Paulson sit up, still resting his weight on Jackson's chest. The bleeding from Paulson's ears had slowed but the madness had not dimmed from the hollow eyes.

"You'll die too fast that way," Paulson croaked, "and we've got all the time in the world, you and I." He laughed loudly at his own joke.

For a moment Jackson wanted the Time Policeman to kill him. It would end all the suffering, end all the confusion he had about the past/present/future, stop the endless questions about who was right and who was the enemy and who had the right to live. Now, damn you, he wanted to tell Paulson, but couldn't force the words from his bruised throat, kill me now.

"They're gone, Jackson," Martin Dubchek's voice reminded him from the hollows of his mind. "Ana and Bobby and Larisa are gone. My neighbors think I'm crazy. They tried to have me committed. Someone else is living in the house that belonged to Ana and me. The kids' swing set is gone. I need help, Jackson."

Martin, his big brother. Tough Martin, the big brother who refused to let him cry in front of his friends when they were both small. Big brother Martin who, though he didn't show it directly to Jackson, was proud of the little brother who walked in his footsteps. They had shared secrets all their lives, and it had been Martin who helped Jackson put his life back in some semblance of meaning after they lost their parents in the Great Plaza fire by making Jackson stay with him and Ana and the kids for the week following the double funeral.

Only now Martin needed help. Help that, according to Irene of the Mnemosyne, only Jackson could give.

"They're gone, Jackson."

Jackson threw his body against Paulson's with renewed vigor, shifting to reach behind him for the knife at his back. The blade came away in his hand as Paulson reached for his throat again. The haft felt warm, right, deadly in his palm.

"Now you're going to die like a gravy-sucking pig, qwerk," Paulson promised, leaning forward to use both hands.

Controlling the nausea he felt over what he was about to do, Jackson shot the knife around and forward, turboing it into the Time Policeman's solar plexus. He felt it skid, then skate as it threaded through bone and muscle, seeking something softer, more vulnerable. Slicing. Killing.

Paulson stiffened immediately, rocking his bald skull back in a throat-ripping cry of agony. The hands shook as the fingers trembled and loosened.

Jackson gulped air, swallowing great handfuls of it, not caring that it splintered down his throat and ignited in his lungs.

The Time Policeman's head swiveled downward suddenly and the crystal eyes, one light and one dark, struggled to focus on him. Paulson opened his mouth to say something. A bloody froth spilled out to collect on the knobby point of his chin. His arms lifted, slithering painfully toward Jackson's face.

Jackson twisted the knife, grimacing at the thought of what the sharp weapon was doing inside his attacker's body.

Paulson groaned almost inaudibly.

For one frightened moment, Jackson didn't think it

would be enough. He damned himself for waiting, for putting Ana's life and the lives of his niece and nephew in jeopardy, while another part of his mind rebelled against what he had done.

Then Paulson fell forward, spilling as if in sections, to become a loose, cadaverous-limbed sack of disjointed bones.

Hoarse screams died at the back of Jackson's throat. His body felt drained of all strength, and it was a seemingly impossible task to slide from beneath the corpse. He was unable to get to his feet immediately as nausea spasms wracked his body, yanking his stomach empty as forcefully as any trip through time had ever done. He leaned forward on his hands as the sickness gripped him, feeling his fingers sink into the cold mud. After a moment, when it seemed that everything inside him was starting to settle, he wet his palm in a small collection of rainwater and tried to wipe his face.

"Are you all right?" Skeleton's voice asked.

Jackson looked up, feeling tears from the emotional physical reaction to his battle on his face.

Skeleton stood in front of him with the help of his friends. A huge knot clung to the side of his head where the stick had hit him and strings of drying blood hung from a torn patch of scalp. "You have never killed before?"

"I have," Jackson corrected, thinking of Laszlo Slye. "Once. But it was in the heat of a battle, and I wasn't really sure of what I was doing till it was already done. It wasn't like this. It wasn't so . . . wasn't so . . ."

"Personal?"

"Yes."

Skeleton shook his head, then held a hand to his temple as if the movement had been a mistake. "This is war, young friend, and that man would have killed you and enjoyed it. There are warriors and butchers in every war. A warrior kills because it is war and there is no other choice, but he feels the death because he is a man as well. A butcher, like the man lying there, kills because he enjoys it."

Jackson listened, wishing he could find some salve in the gaunt man's words, knowing he would have to live with what he had done today for a long time to come. Cautiously, he levered himself to his feet as his head tried to swim in circles around him. His stomach rumbled threateningly. "I'm afraid I don't make a very good warrior."

Skeleton smiled. "Yet here you are still alive."

Pulling the woolen coat the Mnemosyne had given him tighter about his shoulders, Jackson nodded in agreement and turned to make his way back to the time machine, a cold numbness filling him as he watched the gray skies wash over the deathland he walked through.

"Wait."

Turning, Jackson found one of the thin men trotting toward him, loose rags that had once been a jacket of some kind flapping around him like shredded wings.

"You forgot this," the man said when he reached Jackson. He held the knife out, bloody streaks still showing where it had been wiped at unsuccessfully.

Unable to think of a way to turn the knife down without affronting the effort spent to return it to him, Jackson took it, holding it loosely in his right hand, unwilling to slip it casually back into his sheath. He mumbled a terse thanks to the man and went back along his way.

The time machine sat beside the barnlike structure,

undisturbed. He pressed his face and hands on the ident plate of the crystel windows, then pulled the door open. After the door shut back, he leaned back in the chair for a moment to collect himself, wishing he had Martin there with him to make him feel more human. Or Suzanne Brelmer. Jackson envied her because she seemed to be so strong, so willing to accept whatever responsibility life laid on her shoulders. His shoulders felt bowed.

He put the knife in one of the woolen coat's pockets and punched in the destination date and coordinates, amazed at how his fingers shook. Then he buckled in and put his mask on, wondering if his stomach had anything else to sacrifice. He engaged the power and was swept away in an atomic blast of cat piss and burned coffee grounds.

Giant hands clapped, squeezing oranges, adding gusting dollops of industrial strength ammonia, twisted, rolled, smashed, until the mixture was a seething volcano of beautifully spiralling lights, fountains shooting upwards, downwards, spinning in a varying radius around him, glinting off the crysteel windows.

The time machine jerked to a stop, changing directions suddenly as if it had hit something. Dull, metallic clanging filled Jackson's ears as his stomach tried to parachute out into his maskbag.

He pried his eyes open as a light electric shock rippled along his synapses, finding only darkness. Panic seized him in a cold-sweat grip and shook him out of the seat's harness. Where the hell was he? He thumbed the servomotor that controlled the polarization of the crystel window, lightening it as much as he could with little result. The only thing it helped him discover was that the time machine had settled next to a concrete block wall.

Scratches from the machine's impact scarred the gray blankness of the wall, looking fresh against the antiquity of the building blocks. An eery familiarity clung to the dark shadows gathered around him, but Jackson couldn't put a name to the place. He was at the bottom of a building, of that much he was fairly sure. But at what time? What year?

Where was Irene?

Had he somehow homed back in on the Landers Auditorium basement instead of the second-floor room he had left from earlier?

He switched on the time machine's exterior lights, still feeling weak from the fight with Paulson and the time trip. A dull gleam rippled from the multi-colored bullets parked in the huge space around him.

Wherever he was, Jackson thought as he pushed the time machine's door open, it was for certain that he wasn't back at the Landers. His first thought was that he had somehow been caught in the Wheeling Loop again, but the bullets told him he was in the present. His present. He wavered uncertainly on the steps of the time machine, trying to blink his vision into a better clarity.

It was just as well he hadn't arrived back at the home base of the Mnemosyne, Jackson told himself as he stepped down on the smooth concrete floor of the parking area. Irene wouldn't have let him rest, insisting on assembling whole parades of questions for him to answer, then would have tried to pour some chicken soup down him and convince him he needed to make another trip for more research.

But first he had to get the time machine to a place of relative security, even though every fiber of his being wanted to set the coordinates for Wheeling, West Virginia

1968 and hope the damned thing rusted there with everything else he had seen there.

Except for Martin. It was so hard to remember Ana's name, as if he was reaching for it through fog. How long would it be before he was totally unable to remember it at all?

He shivered. How close had he come to being displaced and having the same thing happen to him? Yet, if it weren't for the sense of responsibility that plagued him, wouldn't that be an ideal way to evade Friz Brelmer and the Time Police and the Mnemosyne? Pick a time he would feel comfortable in, where his abilities either as a linguist or with Odar'a would serve to give him an occupation and a means of earning a meager living, then simply fade away.

Wearily, he climbed from the time machine, knowing he could never do that. At least not until he had solved the situation Martin was in.

Scuffing noises let him know someone was approaching at a quick pace.

Jackson flattened himself against a wall on the other side of the time machine, wishing he could pull the darkness of the parking area around him like a cloak.

"What happened to the goddamned lights?" a voice bellowed.

"Beats the shit out of me, Sarge. I just came on shift."

"Where's Clancy?"

"Here, Sarge."

"What the hell happened to the lights?"

"Couldn't tell you, Sarge, I was just going off shift."

"Shit. Can either one of you guys find your ass with both hands?"

"Hey, Clancy, I got a flashlight if you need it."

"Don't bother. Clancy's ass is big enough he won't need no help."

Weak cones of yellow light shot into the darkness, spreading into nothingness before they reached the first line of bullets.

Peering around the corner, Jackson saw five large shadows converging on him, surrounding the pillar the time machine had rebounded off of. In the bouncing glare he caught a glimpse of the security uniforms the men wore. Not all of the letters could be seen but his mind filled in the missing ones for him. Stark and crisp, emblazoned on a red field of black lightnings, the ID patches marked the men for Temporal Projects Security Force.

Booted feet thudded on concrete as the security guards came toward him.

Jerking his head back around the corner as a beam raced down the wall toward him, Jackson cursed the unreliable time machine and wondered how the hell it had appeared in the parking area of TP. More important, though, was how he hoped to get out of the heavily secured area without having to explain the time machine.

He pushed away from the concrete pillar, intending to try to lose himself in the parked vehicles, when a bullet flashed its lights on and shot toward him. Pinned between the twin beams, Jackson knew he would never be able to avoid the bullet before it was on top of him.

Chapter Eleven

Even as Jackson steeled himself for the coming impact, hoping to miss most of the force by sliding over the smooth back of the vehicle, the bullet's tires screeched as they locked up. The turbo drive whined like a cat with its tail caught in the spokes of a gyrobyke as the bullet shook free of the concrete floor and skidded sideways. It came to a rocking rest only inches from Jackson's belt buckle.

With an electric hiss, the passenger door of the bullet winged open. A small light over the console flickered on for a moment before a hand snapped it off, allowing Jackson only an instant to identify the bullet driver. Paress Linnet, Temporal Projects' costume designer. There was no mistaking that long face creased with the wear of many smiles, nor the darting periwinkle blue of the woman's eyes.

"Get in, Jackson," Paress ordered. "They'll be on you in seconds."

What the hell was Paress doing there? Jackson wondered. Then realized she had more right at TP than he did. She still worked there, with Suzanne, and wasn't an outcast the way he was. An outcast who had agreed never to time-travel or come anywhere near TP again, he reminded himself.

"Somebody's helping the qwerk escape, Sarge."

"Get those damned lights back on!"

Jackson threw himself inside the bullet, burrowing low into the seat to avoid the shots he knew must surely come. The servo-motors in the passenger seat ratcheted as they tried to adjust automatically to the false information his outstretched body was feeding them.

"Hold on," Paress said as she reversed polarity in the magnetic drive. She looked over her shoulder and aimed the car backward.

Shots crackled, muted slightly when the passenger door hissed to a perfect seal. Jackson watched the headlights skim across the handful of security guards assuming positions in front of them like a formation for an impromptu shooting gallery. Only the windows in the bullet weren't crystel the way they were in the time machine. He sat up, holding himself in place till the passenger seat could make the needed adjustments and strap him in.

The bullet skidded backwards, the front end floating sickeningly as Paress jockeyed the small vehicle through the rows of parked bullets. Big bullets, little bullets, red bullets, blue. Jackson saw them all blur by.

A security guard broke cover as they wheeled into another row, holding his weapon before him in both hands. Jackson saw orange flares spill from the machine pistol's muzzle as sparks scattered before Paress's bullet, tracking them at a velocity that would overtake them in seconds, leaving pock marks scarring the floor.

Just as Jackson was sure the next burst would rupture the bullet's windshield, Paress cut the wheel again, losing them in another dizzying spin that left them on the outside perimeter of the parking garage. He felt the bullet float free again as it broke the ties of gravity for a moment. The vehicle came almost to a complete stop before the costumer slammed it into forward cycle again. The magnetic turbine whistled threateningly before it locked into gear. The tires spun and shrieked, then finally grabbed a fistful of unsure traction.

A flashing neon EXIT sign hovered over them, but in the clinging shadows that filled the underground garage Jackson wasn't sure if an exit tube was there or not. What if they hit a solid wall or the tube doors were closed? The bullet was frail. It wouldn't survive the impact, and neither would they. The security guards would administer the *coup de grace* if they did.

"Where are we going?" Jackson asked.

"Out. Anywhere. Does it matter?"

The bullet shot into the darkened tube, bouncing crazily as it hit the upramp too fast. The undercarriage connected roughly with the concrete, and Jackson saw sparks scatter in their wake.

"How did you know I was there?" Jackson asked.

"I didn't." Paress touched a button on the steering wheel. The gate at the top of the ramp started upwards and Jackson found himself wondering if it would be open enough in time. "I was just leaving work when your time machine phased into the garage and wrought havoc with the electrical system. At first I didn't know what was going on. I thought maybe one of the experiments in the TP Research Center facilities had gotten screwed up somehow and dropped a time machine through the building."

The bullet skated through the gate just as the lights in the underground garage splashed on and a red SE-

CURITY SHUT-DOWN read-out fed through the monitor beside the gate, causing it to shoot down at a bolt-wrenching pace that missed them only by inches.

Jackson shifted in the seat, wincing when the servos adjusted to a position that stressed the injuries he had received in the fight with Paulson three hundred five years ago. He watched the costumer check her rearview mirror as she took a haphazard course away from Temporal Projects, weaving a trail that took them closer and closer to the downtown area of Kansas City. Stars twinkled overhead in a clear sky and he observed them with interest. It reminded him of the nights he had spent lately in Branson, when he had shared a tree and a mood with Odar'a, letting his fingers and his subconscious find the right strings to echo the emotions he felt but couldn't put words to.

Buddha, how he wished he was back there, working through a rendition of "Missouri Violets" or "Sweet-Cakes and a Pound of Butter." He closed his eyes for a moment to clear them of the irritating dryness that plagued them, then forgot to reopen them. Questions about how he had reached the underground garage instead of the Landers Building in Springfield and what he was going to do next demanded his immediate attention, but he evaded their touch with a mental alacrity he did not find echoed in his body.

He thought back to the last night he had spent in Branson, before Martin had called and he had gone in search of the Mnemosyne. It had been breezy then, almost to the same degree of chill that Paress's bullet blew around him. He had held Odar'a in his lap, loving the dulcimer as his fingers traced the familiar hour-glass shape of her, listening to her sweet voice as if he had never heard it before. There had been stars that night. Whole handfuls of them thrown indiscriminately against the canopy of complete blackness overhead. He had purchased a mixed bucket of cashew cat and chicken earlier and had worked through half of it before taking Odar'a out of her case. He had nibbled occasionally, more for the taste than any hunger.

His brain fuzzed in the middle of the memory. Lethargy filled him and he couldn't feel the turns of Paress's bullet any more. He hadn't been alone that night, had he? He pictured himself under the spreading limbs of the oak tree again, holding the dulcimer, suddenly so sure he hadn't been alone. A shadow leaned forward in his mind to kiss him, the scent of the woman exotic and mysterious, yet known to him. He had felt her lips on his then, hadn't he? A part of his mind tried to warn him, to scream that he had been alone and that this was all a trick. Lips. Yeah, he could feel her lips against his, sense the heat of her as his temples throbbed in anticipation. The woman who had been/hadn't been there broke away from him, her laughter like silver bells. The female Tysonyllyn. He felt anticipation rise within him at the memory. But hadn't he met her later, after Martin's call for help? He ignored the question as he did all the others and reached for her. She evaded him in the dream, holding out a hand. He looked down and saw the bloody knife in her stained fingers. Horror gripped him, slammed him over the edge of consciousness as the lumbering cadaver of the Time Policeman approached him from a wintery forest of naked and clacking limbs. The small fire he had set to keep him warm changed swiftly to the head of Laszlo Slye, came apart in fiery flinders as he remembered how the pistol had chugged against his palm in Prague . . .

"Jackson?" Paress called from the other side of the door.

He ignored her, standing under the warm needle spray of the shower, wanting nothing more than to collapse on the bed of the newly rented motel room she had reserved for him. As long as the nightmares stayed away. He looked down at his hands, making sure the blood was finally gone. He could barely remember the costumer shaking him awake in the bullet, saying he had been screaming and trying to escape the seat belts in the passenger seat. Only vague snatches of visual or audible memory remained of the trip to one of the outside bungalows of the cheapside motel. He had leaned on the older woman the whole way, he remembered. How the hell had she managed to get him to the room and stand him under the shower? Had she undressed him too? He wasn't sure.

"Jackson?" The bathroom door opened and a shadow fell across the shower curtain.

He felt lightheaded from the sickness of time traveling, and from the emotional vortex that had tried to suck him away in the fitful nap he had unwillingly fallen into in the bullet. The heavy vapor of the hot water cascading down his body seemed to starve the oxygen from the air.

"Jackson?" A hand started to pull the shower curtain back.

He clutched Paress's fingers reassuringly. "I'm okay. Really. Just more tired than I thought."

"Okay. I didn't want you drowning during the time I was gone."

"You were gone?" For a moment a panicky feeling wrapped itself through his intestines, leaving cold spots where the emotion's tenacles touched.

"I went to buy you some clothes. You can't wear

those things you were in. I disposed of them down the room's incinerator.''

"How long have I been in here?"

"Long enough to wrinkle, dear."

Jackson smiled in spite of himself and released her fingers.

"I also picked up something for us to eat. If you hurry, you'll get it hot."

"Thanks, Paress."

He heard the door close behind her and turned his attention back to the bar of soap he had been using. The soap had shrunk three sizes since he had been using it, feeling small and frail in his fingers, unequal to the job of making him feel completely clean. But would anything give him that feeling again? He was afraid to answer himself.

He shut the shower off and pulled the towel from the bar overhead, disdaining the warm air dryer that could flood the cubicle and dry him in less than two minutes. He wanted the feel of the towel, a final scrubbing before he put new clothes on.

The mirror, partially unfogged now, showed him the scattering of bruises and abrasions Paulson had inflicted on his body. A necklace of purple coins dangled around his throat just under the skin. When he touched it, though, it wasn't as tender as he thought it would be.

The clothes Paress had bought reflected her profession as costumer at Temporal Projects. They weren't exactly standard issue, but neither were they terribly expensive. He wondered how he was going to pay her back. Being a pick-up dulcimer player in Branson hadn't exactly filled his coffers. The vid-call he had made to the Mnemosyne had been collect, and they had had to arrange fare to Springfield for him. He missed having the walking-around money he had enjoyed while working at the New Ninevah Library, missed having a place of his own for the last year. Most of all, though, he missed the books he had saved for and purchased over the years. Some of them he might not ever be able to replace. Unless he used the time machine to obtain original copies of them.

His mind shuddered away from that thought as he stepped into the fringed, parchment-colored leatherette pants Paress had brought for him. There would be no more time-traveling after he got Martin's situation squared away, he promised himself as he shrugged into a royal blue skintite shirt with ruby sequined hawks sewn across the back. He was amazed at the fit, then realized the costumer had to be very skilled at her trade to be working for Temporal Projects. A pair of off-white boots and rustic brown catskin gloves completed the ensemble. He tucked the gloves in a rear pocket of the pants, unsure if his swollen hands could tolerate even their slight pressure.

He used the toiletries he found in a small plasak next to the clothing, skipping a shave for now because he didn't care to see any more blood for a while.

Paress was seated on the bed when he found her, watching the room's holo with rapt attention. In 3-D, complete with stereo sound, a sports anchorwoman introduced a film clip about the night's basketball game, narrating as the Kansas City team played to a close victory. Jackson hated watching sports holos, preferring to see them on flat-screen monitors. With the 3-D effect of the holo, he was never sure if he was about to be hit with the ball or not.

The costumer had moved the room's small desk in front of the bed to use as a table. Jackson took the narrow chair that came with it, sitting across from the woman. An array of pasta delicacies adorned the napkin-covered table.

"You found a Pizzamax?" Jackson asked in disbelief. He forgot much of the pain and discomfort his body protested against with every move when he slid his fingers under the first piece. Buddha, how long had it been since he had been able to find junk food like this? Branson had not had one within walking distance of where he stayed.

Paress smiled as she popped the tab on a Cherry Coke and handed it to him. "This is Kansas City, Jackson. We're not totally without culture here, despite the vicious rumors circulated in the suburbs."

The plastin container felt cold and wonderful in Jackson's hand. He sipped it carefully, but it still burned its way down his throat and up his nose. Tears came to his eyes, but he bit into the heavily garnished pasta anyway.

They ate in silence as Jackson put away fully three-quarters of the meal. He felt guilty for having eaten so much, even more so when Paress asked him, with seriousness, if it was enough.

"The last I heard," Paress said as she cleared away the unedible remnants of the food, "was that you had resigned from the time-traveling business for good."

Jackson hesitated, not knowing how much he could tell the woman. True, she had saved him from Buddha knew what back at TP, but how did he know that wasn't part of a far larger scheme to gain his confidence? Friz Brelmer was a brilliant and vicious man. Jackson had experienced both aspects of the Praetor Centurion Lieutenant Colonel for himself.

As if guessing his thoughts, Paress said, "Suzanne

told me what happened back in Prague. I'm the one who told her about Rosita Alvarez being displaced. Of course, she never told her father, or I would have been fired. So, see, we are comrades of a sort.''

''Something happened,'' Jackson said after a moment. He had to trust someone. There was no way he could continue the hunt for Martin's wife without help. The time machine the Mnemosyne had let him use was out of reach now. Unless he wanted to face them and their needs again so soon. He still trusted Suzanne and, since she had trusted the costumer, it seemed that he could too.

''What?'' Paress resumed her seat on the bed, giving him all of her attention.

''My brother's wife disappeared. Her and their two children. My niece and nephew. Buddha, I even have trouble remembering their faces or names. I can't even imagine what it must be like for Martin.''

''Was she displaced?''

Jackson shook his head. ''No. There was no reason to do that. She was a housewife. My brother works at a civil service job in Weatherford, Texas. I don't think he's even heard of Temporal Projects.''

''How did he know to call you?''

''It wasn't a matter of knowing. Martin and I are all we have left of our family. Our parents died in the Great Plaza Fire three years ago.''

''I see.''

''There's no other explanation for their disappearance, Paress. Martin said none of their neighbors remember Ana or the children and someone else is living in their house. I don't think I would remember them at all if it wasn't for Martin.''

''So what do you plan to do?''

He let his eyes drift to the silent holo scattering life across a 25-inch space in the air. "I don't know for sure. Find out what happened to make her not exist and change it, I guess."

"That doesn't sound easy."

"Standing by doing nothing is harder."

Paress took his hand in hers and squeezed gently. "If someone changed time somewhere, you can be sure they're not going to take kindly to having it changed back."

Jackson nodded. "I have a contact with the Mnemosyne. They've been researching the problem for me. In exchange for my services."

"Which is how you came by the time machine?"

"Yes."

"And have they done anything for you?"

"They believe something was altered in 2074 or 2075, but I can't remember what went on in those years."

"I can tell you what people were wearing, but I've never really gotten into history for anything other than clothing designs."

Tenatively, as if afraid a too rapid approach would scare the possibility away, Jackson asked, "Do you think Suzanne would be willing to help?"

Paress patted his hand and smiled. "Of course she will. She likes you, I can tell. But I don't know if she'll be able to help much. Her father is intending to demote her this afternoon, according to scuttlebutt around TP. I haven't had the chance to talk to Suzanne. From what I've heard, though, her authority is going to be seriously curtailed. She will no longer have free access to the time machines."

Inside his bruised chest, Jackson's heart sank.

Chapter Twelve

Suzanne swept past the empty desk where her father's secretary usually sat like an ornamentation and tapped lightly on the door to the Praetor Centurion's office. She felt nervous. Partly because she was late and it was her fault she had left her pager in her office instead of carrying it with her as she was supposed to, and partly because she didn't know the nature of the meeting with her father. Had he somehow found out about her mother's addiction to Capricorn? She didn't have the slightest idea and knew better than to torture herself with the endless questions that kept cropping up. Her father had taught her that when she was a girl. Stress was a wasted emotion that would never reach fruition. Even anger, when channeled properly, often achieved desired results.

"Enter."

Pushing the door open, Suzanne followed it, putting away all the feelings of fatigue and frustration. So far she had been unsuccessful in obtaining any kind of medical relief for her mother, despite the hours spent in the chem section of the research library downtown. She hoped this impromptu meeting with her father would be more pleasant.

As she sat in one of the plush seats before his desk, he didn't look up, busily writing on an old-fashioned pad with one of the antique Bic ink pens he had refilled regularly.

How often had she sat like that? she wondered, trying to feel any difference between the eight-year-old girl she had been then and the twenty-five-year-old woman she was now. Both phases of herself had sat just so, watching quietly as Daddy finished putting down whatever stray thought or developed theory he was currently working on. There was one difference in the seventeen- year span, though, she told herself. At least now her feet reached the carpet.

"Suzanne," he greeted her when he laid his pen aside.

"I came as soon as I got your message, Father," she replied. Damnit, why did she sound so servile toward him? She had proven her worth several times over. Even in her close professional relationship with him at TP, she had never let familial obligations interfere with her work, and often put up with being shunted aside professionally while her father worked on other interests.

He waved her apology away, leaning back in the swivel chair with his steepled fingers making a ledge for his chin. "The time is fine, Suzanne. I had to stay late anyway. Security found a time machine that returned to the underground garage less than an hour ago."

Suzanne felt her heart skip wildly, then resume beating at a more frantic pace. For a moment she wondered if it might have been Jackson, then dismissed the idea almost instantly. Jackson Dubchek had seemed to vanish from the face of the Earth after the trouble in Prague. She still missed him from time to time when she reflected on the things they had shared while discovering some of the unsavory undercurrent flowing through Temporal Projects. She had discussed him with Paress Linnet a few of those times, and found the older woman more willing to listen than her own mother. "Do we know when it was from?"

"No. Somehow when it phased into our time continuum, the power surge tapped into the lower building's electrical circuits and knocked them out for awhile. Security saw someone leave, but they didn't get close enough to get an ident. Apparently someone else was waiting for the machine, because whoever brought it here left with an associate immediately."

"But why bring a time machine here?" Suzanne saw her father's brow furrow in perplexity, knowing the look was mirrored on her face. Like father, like daughter, her mother had often said about her mood swings and some of her habits. The petulant look that confusion generated was one of them, and Mrs. Brelmer had often shared an imitation of that look with her when they were alone, in an effort to push Suzanne from one of her somber moods.

Brelmer sighed and spread his hands in front of him, pushing away from the desk. "I don't know, Suzanne. Maybe it was to draw attention to Temporal Projects. The lower garage is declassified, you know. Half a dozen media people got there to take pictures of the time machine before it was disassembled and taken away. Those people are still in the public relations office waiting to hear how a time machine materialized from nowhere."

"They don't know we didn't have anything to do with it?"

Brelmer shook his head. He stood and crossed the room to the wall behind him, leaning against it so his face was partially concealed in the shadows.

Suzanne knew then that there was more to the meeting than just the problem of a misplaced time machine. When it came to anger, her father had always been something of a showman, choosing to reveal it in stages, just as a ringmaster would draw attention to the different acts. Hiding his face so his emotions couldn't be easily read by those who knew him most was one of the first steps. What was going on?

"I couldn't tell them that," Brelmer said. He crossed his arms across his chest. "The general populace doesn't need to know that the time machines we've developed often replicate themselves at the arrival dates if enough power is available. The media hype makes them think all we're doing is opening a doorway. They don't know we're often building a doorway at the other end too."

"And they don't know about the time rebels either."

"Exactly. Can you imagine the kind of panic that knowledge would create in the average person?"

"Yes."

"There would be a rush to laser this building to the ground."

"I know."

He pierced her with a hawkish gaze, dim light glancing ebony off his crystal eyes.

What had he looked like before having the new eyes implanted? Suzanne asked herself as she watched him. It had been less than two years ago, but she still couldn't remember.

"Do you, Suzanne?" His voice was definitely accusatory.

Suzanne, stung by the apparent hostility in his words, looked directly back at him, feeling her jawline tighten defiantly. "I think we both know the answer to that."

"I don't." He uncovered his chest and shoved his hands into his pants pockets.

"What are you talking about, Father?"

Pushing away from the wall, Brelmer paced in front of the wall of books. Suzanne noticed he was careful to remain partially in seclusion at all times. "Senator Voxner brought something to my attention that I had not really been aware of. It appears the media's information on Temporal Projects has been growing by quantum leaps the last few weeks. Even the stories the foodmarket mediamags are carrying are striking ever closer to the truth."

Suzanne felt a freezer coil wrap itself around her spine and tighten, almost taking her breath away. Mother? Had he somehow found out about Mother's indiscretions? "I don't think that's entirely true," she said, wondering if he could hear the unsteady tremor in her voice. "Just yesterday I saw an article entitled, 'I was a Teen-Aged Time Bandit.' "

"Our continued research depends for the most part on the secrecy we are able to maintain. Once the knowledge, the very idea of what we've been able to do here, becomes available to the masses, I'm afraid public opinion will force us to abandon the project."

"But wouldn't the senators realize how important what we are doing here is?"

"When they're confronted with all the facts, Suzanne? And I do mean all the facts, not just the ones we choose to tell them. How would you feel if you were a layman and you were told that people we have sent back in time have sometimes come back with diseases that are extinct in our century but could possibly wipe out a large percentage of the populace? Or that we seem to be experiencing an invasion from OUR future that wants to wipe out much of what we are doing? And many of us as well? Would you believe you were acting in the people's interests by allowing such experimentation to go on?''

"We have learned so much, though."

Brelmer nodded. "You don't have to convince me of that, Suzanne. I've been here. I know we have a lot of things to learn yet. I'm trapped by the excitement of it just as you are."

"The problem isn't just the time machine from nowhere and nowhen, is it?" Suzanne asked, knowing she had cored through to the crux of her father's argument in one of those intuitive bursts that she also knew he found extremely annoying. "It's something else."

"Yes."

"What?"

"Someone has been feeding the media information about TP."

"Who?"

His return silence was completely damning.

Suzanne felt her anger rise to the boiling point immediately, throbbing at her temples. She forced herself to remain in the chair and keep her voice at a temperate level. "You think I'm the one, is that it, Father?"

"It doesn't matter what I think, Suzanne. What matters is that the integrity of this project is maintained. If much of what we do here hits the mediavid, our relationship is going to draw a lot of attention. We may be in for senatorial hearings the likes of which have not been seen since ancient Watergate. Are you ready to stand in the spotlight and endure something like that?"

"Father, you should know by now that you can trust me, and that I will stand by you no matter what happens."

He fixed her with his crystal gaze, and for a moment it seemed to Suzanne that he could see through her. Just as the foodmarket mediamags testified that Time Policemen could. "You can say that, Suzanne, after the way you helped Jackson Dubchek return to Prague? You can sit there and tell me that after that little maneuver of yours cost Slye's life, and almost mine as well? You expect me to believe that without any reservations?"

"That's unfair, Father, and you know it. Jackson saved your life then."

"Jackson Dubchek was the reason I was shot in the first place. If you and he hadn't forcibly taken the time machine I would never have been in any danger."

"Nor would you have known of the games Voxner is playing with history behind your back. You wouldn't have known about Rosita Alvarez, or about the treachery Slye was capable of. Don't kid me or yourself, Father; the Time Police may act under your commands, but their loyalty does not belong to you. At least not all of them."

"Damnit, Suzanne, you're going too far!"

"No, I'm not. The trouble is you know it but you won't admit it. This whole job, containing and controlling the chaos Voxner has made of history, has become a driving force for you. Mother was right about one thing, and I've been so caught up in events around here that I couldn't see it. You don't take time out of your day for either of us anymore." She felt hot tears well up and threaten to stain her face, keeping them back by force of will alone.

Her father exhaled in a long, low breath.

Suzanne could hear her heart beating in her ears,

waiting as if she were a child again and, having just seen the lightning flash, knew the thunderclap couldn't be far away.

His voice was carefully measured when he spoke, stripped of emotion but so violently held back that the absence was highlighted just the same. "Our discussion is over, Suzanne. It was never meant to be that in the first place. I just wanted to notify you of my decision to remove you from your position as reports officer. Your access to the upper floors and to the time machines has been restricted. I want you to take a few days off, then report back to the historical verification offices. You will be replacing Helen Droi, who is retiring."

A million questions raced through Suzanne's head as she tried to pick her father's face out from the shadows. Surely this was some kind of cruel joke. She had never envisioned herself as anything other than her father's right-hand person. How many times had they sat in this office and nitpicked theories and ideas until they both felt they had a workable design? How many times had he used her as a sounding board for a problem or a speech? Damnit, it wasn't fair.

Without speaking, Suzanne got up from the office chair and crossed the room.

"Suzanne."

She stopped halfway through the door, not looking back, knowing her father's voice held no lessening of his resolve.

"I'm sorry it had to come to this now. Maybe later it will be different. Perhaps the things going on around us will be better."

She glanced over her shoulder as the first tears spilled from her eyes. She felt so damned incompetent, as if she were somehow to blame. But wasn't she? Hadn't it been she who had recruited Jackson Dubchek in the first place? Hadn't it been she who helped Jackson go back to Prague? Hadn't it been her fault her father had been shot and almost killed? How could she hold herself so blameless and disagree with his views on the matter? If the roles were reversed, would she do anything different? Her voice sounded brittle when she spoke. "I hope so, Father, I really do. I love you, you know." Then she hurriedly pulled the door shut before he could respond, leaving her subconscious to find whatever fantasy absolution for her it could later.

She half-ran to the elevator, not wanting the night security guards to see her looking so disheveled. She was the praetor centurion lieutenant colonel's daughter. Her father's only child. And a woman in her own right. She would not let them see her cry. Damnit, no one would see her cry over this.

Blinded by tears she couldn't stall any longer, Suzanne reached out and thumbed the emergency stop button, feeling the elevator cage freeze in place. She sat on the floor, her forehead resting on her bent knees as she let the emotion run its course in gasping, racking sobs that she knew would leave her empty and drained.

Chapter Thirteen

Jackson watched Paress Linnet punch in the coordinates for Suzanne's private line at Temporal Projects, adding her employee ident when the security computer broke on-line. They'd tried Suzanne's condo earlier and left a message, but it had gone unanswered.

He felt tired, wanting nothing more than to return to the rented hotel room and collapse on the broken springs of the bed. Only that wouldn't bring Ana back. Nor were there any guarantees that the nightmares wouldn't stalk him till he spent the night awake anyhow.

Stifling a yawn, he sneaked a look over Paress's shoulder as the security computer read-out zig-zagged across the screen so no illegal vid-snooper could penetrate its defense and raid personnel files.

Cold, artificial light from the 7-11 they stood before oozed over his shoulder to splash on the flattened drink tins and fasfood cartons that littered the ground around his booted feet. He didn't like the neighborhood they were in. But Paress hadn't had the time to be choosy, had she? And he had certainly been in no shape to ask at the time.

He yawned again, feeling the ache from the battle

earlier settle even more deeply into his bones. He put his hands in his pants pockets to help keep them warm against the October chill that swept through Kansas City. The knife, thoroughly cleaned and disinfected, was a weight of conscience taped to his left ankle. It brought the unpleasant memories into sharper focus with its every touch, but the feelings of protection balanced that in Jackson's mind. At least for now.

Especially in this neighborhood.

A low-slung bullet hissed by, scattering riffs of a heavy-metal jam over two hundred years old. Jackson watched it for a moment until it faded into the darkness of the surrounding streets. The Second Republic made sure its citizens wanted for nothing to eat or a place to sleep, he knew, but this was a city like any other in history for all that. And predators roamed the alleyways in Kansas City more freely than they had in Branson. He had had a couple of altercations in Branson that had ended once with him outdistancing the mugger that attacked him and once with him losing the meager amount he had made playing Odar'a all day.

He wouldn't be able to run tonight. Not without his skeleton falling completely apart and leaving him nothing more than a bag of flesh.

The vid-screen cleared as the call was pushed through.

"Come on, Suzanne," Paress Linnet whispered.

Jackson felt the urgency in the older woman's voice echo inside him. They were taking risks with TP's security if the guards had spotted her bullet as the one that had rescued him from the underground garage. How long would it take for a police bullet to get here if the security computer had already notified the dispatch? He glanced at the chronometer suspended above the head of the Hawaiian-shirt-clad store clerk. 20:39. Buddha, how he hated the waiting.

"She's there," Paress hissed excitedly.

An odd emotion surfaced inside Jackson as he realized he was about to see Suzanne Brelmer again. How many times had her face floated around inside his head at odd moments? He had visualized her in dreams, during favorite snatches of melodies while playing Odar'a alone as well as during shows. The sweet corn blondeness of her hair, and the small pout of her full lips.

"Suzanne, it's Paress."

He had told her a year ago that she was the most fascinating woman he had ever met, and had meant it. Just as, in the very next breath, he had meant that he never wanted to see her again. Her world lay with Temporal Projects and the Time Police. With her father. Jackson considered them to be nothing more than government-regulated butchers and liars.

"I know, Suzanne," Paress was saying. "No, I wasn't told about it. You know how the office grapevine is. Guthrie isn't exactly tight-lipped either, you know."

Jackson strained his ears, trying to hear the reply. He had thought he remembered exactly how her voice sounded, but now he was unsure.

"I've got someone with me," Paress said, motioning for Jackson.

He started to step forward, then felt a heavy hand drop on his shoulder. Time Police? Jackson wondered as he spun around. Or Republican Patrol? He held his hands up in front of his face, so the move could be mistaken as submission if it came to that, rather than the defensive one it was.

Three teenagers, dressed in syntho-leather with hand-painted feathers braided in their hair, confronted Jackson. Dark tattoos stained their faces, emphasizing the skeletal structure beneath the blotchy skin almost to the point of caricature. Burning hollows gleamed dully in their eyes, letting Jackson know there would be no compromising with them. Capricorn addicts. The telltale maroon glow at their temples, goat's horns as they were called on the streets, gave that away.

The one in front was the largest of the three young males. A looped chain of silvery plastel dangled in four strands from his shoulder to hip, giving him a chingle-chingle to his movements. The grin he gave Jackson was totally without mirth, without warmth. Purple and pink feathers fell across his right eye, leaving only the dulled inky blackness of one to stare with.

"Who owns the bullet?" the biggest youth asked, lifting an arm toward Paress's vehicle. The movement was so slow it seemed to articulate every muscle involved.

Keeping his hands up, Jackson shifted, placing himself directly between the youths and Paress. He wanted to tell the costumer to run for the bullet, but that would have cancelled whatever small chance the surprise move would have given them.

"Go away," Jackson said. "We don't want any trouble."

The leader grinned even larger. "We don't want any trouble either, qwerk. We just want whatever spare Fed-credits you happen to have on you." A small gun materialized in his hand from the depths of the loose-fitting syntho-leather vest. He used it to illustrate his words. "And the bullet."

Heart churning at a furious pace, Jackson weighed

his chances of getting to the gun before it could be fired, surprised at his own desire to take command of the situation. Wouldn't it be easier to give in to their demands and let them have whatever Paress had? Had his trips for TP and the Mnemosyne affected his logic and unhinged his mind? Or had he been operating in a survival mode so long that he feared relinquishing the bullet and its opportunity for escape more than he feared death?

"It's okay," Paress said in a frightened voice behind him. "They can have it. The insurance will cover the loss."

Jackson kept his eyes on the dulled one showing in the leader's face. Paulson's and Slye's faces kept flashing through his mind as a kaleidoscope of pulsating images. The cold and artificial light from the convenience store helped wash the rest of the humanness from the trio's features.

"Didn't you hear me, Jackson?" Paress said. "Let them have the bullet."

The man on the leader's left moved up suddenly, grabbing his partner by the elbow. "Hey, Ristin, it's him. Jackson. The guy the lady paid us to put down."

Before the second guy's words had time to die away, the pistol in Ristin's hand was tracking onto Jackson's mid-section. "Can't be, Moone. This guy looks too young, and he's got both arms."

"It's him, Ristin. Look at the damned picture again. This is the qwerk the woman paid us to do."

What woman? Jackson's frenzied brain tried to follow the events before him. Maybe this was all a mistake induced by the Capricorn high. It had to be. Both arms?

Ristin shoved a bone-thin hand inside the syntho-leather vest and pulled out a crystal-coated photograph that fit neatly in the palm of his hand. He shook the hair out of his face to see better. But the gun never moved.

Behind him, Jackson could hear Paress whispering frantically into the vid, the words lost somehow in the flux of emotions warping out of control inside him. Buddha, was everyone out to kill him? And the woman, who were the three talking about? Irene? Or, possibly, Suzanne Brelmer acting to defend her father's post at Temporal Projects?

Ristin smiled wickedly; the artificially too-white teeth revealed gleamed against the dulled yellow of his skin. The maroon glow at his temples deepened color, seeming to roil like angry fires under the skin. "You are Jackson, aren't you?" He pointed the gun directly at Jackson's chest. He held the crystaled photo forward for Jackson to see. "This is you, isn't it, qwerk?"

"The arm must be a mech," the third man said, taking an illegally electrified baton from a loose sleeve. The end shot out at his touch, adding another eight inches of dulled gray crystel. "Wonder how much a mech arm will go for on the black 'market, Ristin?"

"Run, Paress!" Jackson bellowed as his fingers knotted in the mediamag rack behind him.

Paress Linnet bleeped off the vid and scrambled for the bullet. Jackson knew the bullet's security system would keep their attackers away long enough for her to escape if he could keep them from her.

Swinging the mediamag rack, Jackson ducked to one side at the same time, hearing the flat crack of the pistol Ristin held. Something tugged at the billowing sleeve of the skintite and for a moment he thought he had been hit. Then the rack smashed into Ristin's face. The force of the blow spread up Jackson's arm, reawakening all the old hurts from the earlier battle.

Ristin went down with a shrill cry of rage and pain, wrapping his arms around his head.

Still holding the rack, Jackson fended off Moone, then hurled it at the guy holding the electrified baton. Sparks shot up as it connected with the weapon, sizzling like bacon in a frying pan. A flesh-burning stench filled Jackson's nose, taking him back for a moment to Buchenwald. Then he was on his knees, scrambling for the gun Ristin had dropped.

Moone made another grab for him, but Jackson held him off with a kick to the groin that felled the punk as quickly as if someone had yanked his feet from under him.

Jackson had had enough of fighting. Enough of killing. But the survival mechanism that had saved him before beat a wild aria inside him. He felt his fingers close around the gun, his sense of feel so sharp he could tell the difference in the weapon's plastic and metal parts through tactile ident alone.

He thumbed the hammer back as the baton-wielding youth shoved up from the litter on the sidewalk.

Jackson could feel his hands shake as he trained the muzzle on his attacker. The baton crackled menacingly. The goat's horns on the youth's temples had turned black, and Jackson could see the adrenalin rush throbbing through the skin.

"Back off," Jackson said.

Moone started to move.

"Stay down," Jackson told him, shifting the pistol. He wondered if the quaver stayed out of his voice enough to let him sound in control. Or would it frighten them more if they thought he was out of control? That he might fire at the slightest move they made?

Still moaning, Ristin pushed away from Jackson, as if afraid he might be the first target.

The crystaled photo lay abandoned next to a McPlankton Double carton.

Fisting the pistol in his right hand, Jackson retrieved the photo and shoved it inside a pocket. "Who told you about me?" he asked Ristin.

Ristin groaned weakly and shook his head.

Centering the muzzle of the pistol on the baton-wielder's crotch, Jackson said, "Tell me about the woman or you're going to be checking the black market for a mech dick." He couldn't believe the harshness in his voice, or that he had made the kind of threat he had. But that kind of violence was the only coin the punks dealt in. He had no choice but to present possibilities they would understand. Even if it made his stomach queasy to envision actually having to carry the threat out.

"I don't know. She was just a piece of quiff. At least that's what I thought. She found us in the bar down the block. She told us you'd be here tonight and gave us five thousand Fedcredits to off you. Said she'd pay us another five thousand once we did the job."

"What was her name?" Panic clawed at Jackson's intestines. What if this new threat didn't belong to the Time Police or the Mnemosyne? Who else could know about him? Then he thought about the list that Laszlo Slye had recovered, that had named him as a subversive against Temporal Projects. The list that had been the reason the Time Police had first displaced him in New York of 2183. And then there had been the female Tysonyllyn.

She had known about him too. She had been from the future, where he had been some kind of hero. From *a* future. What if there were futures where he was considered to be a menace? The possibilities were staggering. He felt a worm of nausea grow in the pit of his stomach. Where would he be safe if that was true? Or perhaps he should be asking *when?*

"She didn't give us no name."

"But she named me?"

"Yeah. Jackson. That's all she told us."

"Did she tell you why she wanted you to kill me?"

"No."

"You didn't ask?"

Jackson saw perspiration bead down the punk's face. "It was five thousand Fedcredits, then and there, qwerk," the youth answered belligerently, "and she didn't want no driffin' question and answer session." His eyes batted like too-quick metronomes, as if afraid he had overstepped the thin line of survival he teetered on.

Anger lashed inside Jackson like a summer storm. He had to force his finger steady, to keep from pulling the trigger convulsively. He breathed out through his nose to control the emotion. He waved the pistol and told the two standing punks to get down on their stomachs. Keeping his eyes on them, he moved backwards toward Paress Linnet and the waiting bullet. He fitted himself under the gullwing door and allowed it to seal. Paress nearly popped his head out of socket as she powered the magnetic turbine in a tight U-turn that slid them out of the convenience store's parking lot into the sparse flow of night traffic.

Thumbing the window down, Jackson tossed the pistol out, never looking back to see it hit. Only then did he give himself over to the muscle-wrenching shakes that shivered up and down his frame. Buddha, Buddha, how close had he come to killing another?

"Jackson."

He recognized Paress's voice but closed his eyes and pushed himself away into his mind.

"Jackson."

He made himself answer, biting his tongue as his jaws tried to chatter. "I'm okay, Paress."

"You don't look it."

"I don't feel it either, but at least we're still alive."

"Did you know those people?"

"No."

Paress harumphed. "They seemed to know you."

"Someone hired them to kill me." He couldn't believe he could make the statement so matter-of-factly.

"Who?"

"They didn't know."

Paress slid around another corner. Jackson watched her flicking quick glances in the rearview mirror, expecting her to warn him of an approaching Republican Patrol car at any moment. "So what do we do now?" the costumer asked.

"What did Suzanne have to say?"

"I told her I had you with me and you needed to see her. She told me to meet her at TP."

Jackson started to ask why there but realized in the same instant that Suzanne would know any reason he had to see her would involve the time machines. The thought that she would believe him to be using her stung him. The Suzanne Brelmer he had met and gotten to know deserved better than that from a part-time dulcimer player. "How is she doing?" he asked as he fumbled the crystaled photo from his pocket.

"She sounded like she had been through the nine hells and back again."

"Because of her father?"

"She didn't say."

It's none of your business, Jackson told himself as he tried to scan the photo in the darkness of the bullet. You couldn't spend time with her or help her if you wanted to.

Both arms. The punk's words kept rattling off the insides of Jackson's brain. What had he meant? *Both arms.* He reached overhead to flip on the travel light. Soft light bathed the photo, and a ragged scream caught at the back of Jackson's throat.

Chapter Fourteen

Moving through the darkness of the research library, Suzanne tried to visualize where she was from memory. Were the vid stacks on current history here? Or here? Paress had been in such a hurry at the end of their short conversation she could barely remember the year the costumer had given her. Somewhere between 2072-2082. But there was a lot of history in that decade. Especially when you considered the history of the world, and not just the North American sector of the Second Republic.

What could Jackson Dubchek possibly want from her? Access to the time machines, surely. Paress had agreed to that all too readily. Her thoughts turned back to her father's meeting, to the time machine that had materialized in the underground garage. She felt certain that Jackson had been manning that machine and just as certain that Paress had helped him escape.

But why?

Had Paress been in contact with Jackson and not told her?

Suzanne loved the old costumer as a friend. Ever since Paress had opened her eyes to the displacements that had been going on for years at TP, she had shared a bond with the older woman that replaced much of what she had lost in both her father and mother. She had talked about a lot of things with Paress, including her confused feelings about the interpreter.

A chill shot through Suzanne as she trailed her fingers down the computerized display vid at the end of a row of vid 'ssetes.

Could Paress be the informer her father was searching for? How much had she told the costumer over the past few months? How much was the woman privy to anyway? Suzanne was sure the costumer had her own network of information set up at TP. Paress had been there too long not to have.

She tapped the display button and the listing of vid 'ssetes obediently pulsed out its information. WLD HST 2070-2075. Okay, this was a row to start with, but what the hell was she looking for? Paress hadn't mentioned that. She turned the corner and used her magnetic ident plate to key up the viewer.

And why had Paress been in such a hurry? At first she had seemed to want her to see Jackson for herself. She could still remember the unsure 7-11 sign flickering in the background of the area open to the vid.

A door hissed open against the south wall, and Suzanne's heart seemed to stop like a dropped glob of gelatin flattening against the floor. She snapped off the viewer and stepped to the shelter of the heavier shadows of the 'sseteracks, the green letters of the index seemingly imprinted on her eyes till they quickly faded away. Paress? Or one of the Time Police checking up on her activities at her father's request?

"Suzanne."

Paress. She stepped from the 'sseterack and called the costumer's name.

Two figures trailed hand-in-hand across the open area of the stacks. Jackson! A warm feeling spread through Suzanne, and she hurried to quell it. He had already made his intentions about her known. She would only be beating her head against a wall by wishing it were otherwise. Anyway, did she really care for him, or was it his unavailability that made him such a challenge?

Suzanne switched on a small study light on a nearby desk and studied Jackson. He looked older, as if their time apart had been longer than one year. Worn and haggard, with less spare flesh on his body than there had been before. Not fat to begin with, Jackson had thinned out to the point of being wiry and wolfish. A two- or three-day growth of beard stained his chin. And were those bruises around his neck? Suzanne had to firmly grip the maternal feelings she was experiencing.

"Suzanne," Jackson said, reaching out to take her hand.

She felt the calluses crossing his palm. Those were new too. The Jackson Dubchek she remembered had been a linguist working in the New Nineveh Library, with hands soft from working a keyboard occasionally. These hands belonged to someone who had done a lot of manual labor. What had life been like for him since she had last seen him? Suddenly a thousand questions filled her head, and she steeled herself not to ask even one. He had already told her what he thought about her involving herself in his life. As the kind of woman she expected herself to be, Suzanne was determined to honor that.

"Jackson," she responded, letting go of his hand with more regret than she had anticipated. Chances were it was the confrontation with her father that made her seem readier to let herself go in the arms of the only other man she had respected. Despite his feelings for her father, Suzanne knew Jackson was more like her father than he knew. Both were strong-willed when events forced them to be, and neither could avoid what they considered to be their duty.

But what had stitched those pain lines across his face, almost erasing his youthfulness?

"I just keyed up the files on 2070-2075," Suzanne said as she brought the viewer to life again. "What are you looking for?"

Jackson joined her at the viewer while Paress sat at the small desk. Suzanne was conscious of the fact that the costumer was giving them as much time alone as she could, which made it even more apparent that Jackson was not planning on staying long. She only hoped she could help him as much as he evidently thought she could. She was also conscious of the fact that he was taking pains to make sure their bodies in no way touched.

"I don't know," Jackson said.

She watched his fingers hesitate over the keys as he operated the computer-assisted viewer, as if they were suddenly reawakening to a world they had all but forgotten.

Jackson talked as he traced events, brown eyes darting along the lines of 'ssete script. He told her about his brother Martin and the disappearance of Ana, his sister-in-law.

Suzanne felt a growing knot of horror form at the back of her throat. "What you're saying doesn't make any sense, Jackson. Father wouldn't allow anyone to tamper with the past enough to alter the present."

"It's been done before. Remember the translation I was initially to do for Temporal Projects in 2183? The Persian ambassador was assassinated when I was there."

"But not according to our history. Father made sure that was taken care of so that nothing reflected in our time."

"But who knows what else has been covered up during the time Temporal Projects has been operating under Voxner? The whole world we're living in now could be the result of just a few events being changed along the way. You haven't experienced displacement first hand. I have. We only know what we see around us, and small changes aren't even felt. Lester Wu's disappearance struck a chord in me because I was really close to him. Martin and Ana I have seen only occasionally and already I was doubting her existence. I can't remember conversations I may have had with her. And I'm sure there were some. Do you know what that feels like? Can you imagine the pain my brother must be suffering?"

Watching his fingers peck at the keys in impatient anger, Suzanne sensed there was more to Jackson's current emotional state than he was letting on. She wished she had had a chance to talk to Paress first.

Without warning, Jackson slapped the viewer. Veins stood out along his neck as he closed his eyes. Suzanne could see the visible effort he made to regain control of himself, noticing the dark blush encircling his neck for the second time.

"Damnit," Jackson said in a harsh whisper that barely reached Suzanne's ears. "It's here somewhere. I know it is. But what the hell is it?"

"How did the Mnemosyne figure out the time period?" Suzanne asked. She stepped in front of Jackson, taking the keyboard away from him. For a moment she felt the heat of his body against her back, then he shied away.

"I don't know."

Suzanne bypassed the old televid listing, lists of top 10 books and records, shifting the search out of the cultural into the political. "Logic would dictate," she said softly, "that if any changes were made, they would of necessity be ones that would affect our present-day government. Fortunes could be made and lost easily by knowing which horse won what race or what team won what game in any century you care to choose. Father believes that time can be tampered with to that degree without knocking events out of kilter." And political changes affecting the present-day would be the only thing her father would allow. Or ones that Voxner would order. Could her father have been responsible for Ana Dubchek's disappearance? And how would he react if he knew? Her mind skipped across that question and turned more to the problem at hand. "What was Ana's maiden name?"

Her fingers poised over the keyboard as Jackson wrinkled his brow in concentration. "It would be so much easier to ask Martin these things."

"We don't have Martin here," Suzanne said softly, "and I don't know if I'll be able to get you in here again."

"Sommers," Jackson said after a moment of thought. "Her father's name was Lamont Sommers. They lived in Dallas. Martin was going to college there when he and Ana met."

Cross-referencing the viewer to family histories, Suzanne keyed in the name and watched the vid quickly fill with connecting lines indicating family trees. She found

Lamont Sommers's name and focused the screen on it. "Lamont Sommers," she read, "married Abby Cravey and they had three sons. No daughters."

"Which may mean Ana's mother was never born either." Jackson studied the screen.

"What was her name?"

"I can't remember."

"Damn." Suzanne stared at the blinking cursor, willing it to draw her attention to the information they were lacking. How long had they been at this? How soon would it be before a security guard on a regular round discovered them? And, if discovered, what would her father do?

"Something," Jackson said as he tapped the vidscreen with a forefinger. "Something important. Something Ana was so proud of. Buddha, help me sort this out."

The note of helplessness in his voice stung Suzanne. Jackson had been so happy-go-lucky when they had first met, so excited about the research Temporal Projects was doing. But then, so had she, and she had not been hounded by the Time Police the way Jackson had and still she found herself torn unknowingly from both her father and mother.

"Her great-grandfather," Jackson thought out loud. "Ana's great-grandfather. She kept his picture on the wall. Franco. Miguel Franco. He was one of the men who signed the Second *Plan de Iguala*. She was so proud of that."

Suzanne saw the smile on Jackson's face and she knew it was from triumphing over whatever barriers the confused time had erected between him and his brother's family. She returned to the POLITICAL section, geo-graphed Mexico in particular, then brought up a copy of the Second *Plan de Iguala*. There. Down at the bottom, in a rich and flowing script, was the name Miguel Franco.

"If his name is there, what happened?" Jackson asked.

Suzanne could hear the panic welling up in his voice and for a moment she considered the possibility that Ana Dubchek might be so lost in the twisted threads of time that no amount of researching would unearth her. "Wait," she said with more confidence than she felt. "Let's follow this and see what happens." She brought up Miguel Franco's file from the BIOGRAPHIES section and scrolled through it.

According to the information there, Franco had been 23 when he signed the Second Plan. He had had four brothers and two sisters. Unmarried at the time. The file ended much too abruptly. The bottom line showed that Franco died on March 19, 2074. The same day the Second Plan had been signed.

"He never had a family," Jackson whispered hoarsely. "Why?"

Suzanne noticed the crazed light that had entered his eyes, making them look glassy and vacant under the soft green glow of the vid. Deciding against caution and against her better judgement, she put a hand on his, squeezing gently. "Take it easy, Jackson. There has to be an answer."

"Find it."

Tapping the keyboard, Suzanne called up more reference files on Miguel Franco but found nothing amiss. According to what was listed in the libraries of Temporal Projects, Franco had mysteriously died the same day he signed the Second Plan and had never fathered the grandmother of Ana Dubchek.

"Someone else changed time," Jackson stated quietly.

"What makes you think that?"

"If your father or the Time Police had been involved in it, the whole file would have been closed off. No, this is something small in our present, yet it obviously reaches greater proportions in someone's future."

"Someone's future?"

"Yes. Damn, I get headaches thinking about all the paradoxes of this thing." Jackson reached out and blanked the vid. He walked away from her, stumbling wearily through the 'sseteracks, away from her, away from Paress.

Hesitantly, Suzanne followed.

Jackson halted at the end of a long row, standing with his back to her.

"Paradoxes are a natural outgrowth of time travel," she reminded him in a soft voice. "Even in truly observational modes, we make changes in people, in events. But time is a river, it flows ever onward in its course despite whatever flotsam is thrown into it."

"Martin's wife isn't flotsam, Suzanne."

"I know that." She inched a step closer to him, wanting to put her arms around him and console him. "There's only one way to find out what happened to Miguel Franco. We have to go back and see for ourselves."

He turned to face her. "Not 'we', Suzanne. Me. I have to go back. Chances are the Time Police of this year, maybe even of this century, are not involved in this. Your father hasn't noticed any changes, or you would have known about it.''

"That isn't necessarily true. I don't know if Paress told you, but I was demoted today. That's how I came by the keys to this library."

"That wasn't until today. Ana has been missing for almost a month. Your father would have noticed it by now if it was going to make a difference in this time line."

"You think someone from our future is responsible?"

"What else is there to think? You and I both know about the time rebels. How many different futures exist right now? How many of them are being born and how many of them are dying even as we speak? And Ana. She is a part of her great-grandfather's future. Even if we succeed in bringing her back, how can we really if she doesn't exist?"

"Quantum physics," Suzanne said automatically.

"I'm a linguist, not a scientist."

"It's a theory Father holds to. Basically there are two foundations for the theory. One states that nothing exists. The other, that everything exists. Father and I believe that in time, everything exists, at all times, but there is only one true time line and all others are nothing more than shadows and imperfect reproductions. Assuming that the latter theory is true, Ana exists because she has always existed, and all we have to do is find a way for her to exist in this time line again."

"But what do you believe, Suzanne? The evidence clearly states here that Ana was never born, that Martin never married her, and they had no children. Which sets of evidence am I supposed to believe?"

"What do you want to believe, Jackson?"

He sighed tiredly, like a helium baloon with a slow

leak, deflating and sagging. "Do you know what it's like, Suzanne? Only a couple days ago, I met a woman who helped me research some information for the Mnemosyne in return for their aiding me in finding Ana. She was from the future. A future. Hell, I don't know. At any rate, she helped me. Said I was a hero to her people. Yet, tonight, when Paress was calling you on the vid, three street punks tried to kill me. They said a woman hired them to assassinate me."

"The same woman?"

"I don't know. They didn't know anything about her. She even gave them a picture of me so they wouldn't make any mistakes. It's me, Suzanne, but a future me. A me that doesn't exist now." He handed her a crystaled photo and she couldn't miss the shaking of his hand.

She turned the photo over and raised it to capture the meager light stemming from the desk.

"It's a picture of me that I will not ever let exist," Jackson said vehemently. "Even if it means death at my own hand."

It only took a moment to see the tortured flesh hanging from the man in the crystaled photo and to see that it was Jackson, then Suzanne sagged against the 'sseteracks as her stomach twisted.

Chapter Fifteen

Jackson took the crystaled picture from Suzanne as she tried to regain her breath. He slipped it into a pocket without looking at it again. The image of him, only a year or so older at most, with his right arm amputated just below the shoulder and some kind of burn scars criss-crossing his face in a starburst that originated just below the blackened stump of his right ear, would undoubtedly remain in his memory for years. Or, at least, until it happened and became gruesome reality.

"That can't be you," Suzanne said weakly.

"But it is, and we both know it." Jackson turned away from her, unable to fully control the anger and fear surging inside him. How different his life would have been had he never met her. No horrors of time-traveling, of killing, of seeing himself as he might become.

"It could be a fake."

"Why? What could anyone hope to gain by doing something like this?"

"To scare you away, back to wherever you were before your brother brought you to the Mnemosyne."

"All I want to be is left alone." He whirled suddenly,

feeling the hot emotion seethe over the edges of his being. "I don't want to be involved in anything Temporal Projects is doing. I want to stay as far away from your father as I possibly can."

"But you're here now, Jackson."

"To help Martin, not because I want to be."

"I know."

He stared at her through the darkness, feeling a desire stir inside him that seemed to come from nowhere. He envied her the composure she appeared to regain so easily after being confronted with the picture. It had been long moments of mind-numbing disbelief before he had been able to show Paress in the bullet.

"You said yourself this is only a possible future, Jackson. It doesn't have to happen."

"You don't understand, Suzanne. I'm not a gambler. I don't want to take the chance that this might happen. I don't want to end up like that picture."

Her voice assumed a harder edge. "If you don't want this to happen, then why did you come here tonight?"

"To help Martin."

"You're willing to risk that future to aid your brother?"

His voice caught in his throat. "Martin is my brother, Suzanne. I don't have a choice."

"Yes, you do. You could easily call him and tell him there's nothing you can do for Ana."

"But that's not true."

"Maybe it's not true. Don't you see that? Just because we found an inconsistency in history as we perceive it doesn't mean we're going to be able to patch things up. Have you ever changed the flow of history before?"

"No . . ."

"Then how do you know you can help anyone?"

Her words made him feel like a rat with its tail caught in a trap. "I don't, but I've got to try. For Martin's and Ana's sakes."

"And for your own peace of mind?"

"Yes."

Her face softened in the darkness and she reached to touch his cheek. Part of him wanted to recoil from her, wanted to disavow the intimacy she offered, but he let her fingers trail across his skin, rasping over the two-day-old stubble. He was surprised at the comfort he felt. How long had he kept all that he had been through bottled up inside himself? Irene only wanted him for the information he could gather; he was sure the old woman had some feelings for him, but the survival of the Mnemosyne and of history itself was the underlying motivation in her relationship with him. Brelmer wanted him dead, or would after the praetor centurion lieutenant colonel found out Jackson had piloted the time machine into the underground garage of TP. Paress was willing to help him, but she, like Suzanne, was totally off- limits.

In the past year, there had been no one Jackson could talk to. He had fooled himself, thinking he could sweep the past events away so easily. Instead they were all there, gathered in the front of his mind like so many pieces of broken glass. Sharp and threatening.

Suzanne pulled her hand away but didn't break eye contact. "Don't you owe yourself the same chance you're giving Martin? The chance to set things right for yourself?"

"What's right, Suzanne? Our history seems to be falling into a shambles. There are no guideposts to mark our way, and every step we take may be a dead end."

"No." The vehemence of her reply surprised him. "I won't believe that. Things may be altered or changed, but I can't believe they are so muddied over no one can find them again."

How many times had he thought the same thing? Jackson wondered. He had tried to put the idea of time-traveling out of his mind for the last year, but every so often, while playing Odar'a by himself or in those scattered few moments before dropping off to sleep, the possibilities had ricocheted from the logic panels of his mind. But history, and the future, he supposed, were constructed like spiderwebs: pull one strand and how many others shake as well? Everything that was changed reflected somewhere else with just as much force.

"Have you wondered why it wasn't until tonight that an attempt was made on your life?" Suzanne asked.

Jackson shook his head.

"Maybe whoever was behind the assassination attempt did not have a record of you until tonight."

"I can't believe that. My record of birth, my job history, all those are on public file."

"But what if they aren't in whatever future we're dealing with? What if the files they have access to are just as spotty as the ones we have concerning the Second Plan de Iguala?"

Jackson turned the theory over in his mind. Sure, it could be true. Even the world wars that weren't mentioned in the present constitution—they had happened but there were no records of them. The Mnemosyne hadn't even known of them. Memory of the Mnemosyne's vocal record of history troubled him. Somewhere in their human history books, there had to be a listing for Jackson Elgin Dubchek. Could it be the information Irene and her followers committed to memory that was causing his current problems?

He shrugged away from that for the moment, realizing the Mnemosyne had surely not changed the history concerning Ana and her grandfather. None of the people they had sent back in time had returned.

"It's also probable that what you've done with your life up to this point has been important to whatever future the woman was from. Maybe they couldn't have existed without you returning to Prague of 1968."

Without his inadvertantly causing the death of Rosita Alvarez, Jackson amended.

"Perhaps the constitution you recovered for the Mnemosyne was another hinge that helped bring that future into being. You have no way of knowing."

Jackson nodded, feeling a little better. At least Suzanne had agreed with his present line of thinking, proving that he had given sufficient consideration to every nuance he could lay mental fingers to. She was wrong about one thing, though. The flow of time wasn't really a river anymore. It was a dark and angry ocean, and he was going to have to have faith in himself to chart his course for any hope of restoring Ana to Martin.

"Think things out before you try to hide yourself away, Jackson. If you remain stationary, you'll be a target for whatever forces are searching for you."

"Besides your father's Time Police, you mean?"

Her shoulders stiffened.

Jackson immediately wished he hadn't said anything. She had problems of her own, big ones according to Paress Linnet. What right did he have to snap at her that way after she risked more than her professional career to help him? "Look, Suzanne, I'm sorry. I didn't mean that."

He wished he could put his arms around her. "It's just that every time I get involved in time- traveling, things seem to be even more complicated than they were the last time."

"That's because they are," Suzanne replied. "Even for me. I still don't understand exactly why Father pulled me out of the active end of the project, but I don't exactly buy his story that it was because he suspected me of leaking information to the media. I think he's just as confused by everything as we are but he can't admit it. Not even to himself."

Jackson remained quiet, letting them both assemble their thoughts. The crystaled picture was a sharp edge in his pocket, and he decided to get rid of it at the first opportunity. Let it fade, he told himself, like the memories of Paulson and Slye; let it fade and become a nightmare he could deal with at a later time. Suzanne was right about one thing, though: if he remained in one spot he would be easier to trace. At least if he let his name and location be known. "They knew I would be at the convenience store tonight," he said as the realization struck him.

"The vid is automatically copied for every call coming into and going out of the building," Suzanne said.

"Which may mean whatever future tried to kill me tonight may be directly connected to Temporal Projects." For a moment an image of Suzanne Brelmer only a few years from their present dropped into his mind. Could she have been the one who paid the street punks the 5000 Fedcredits to kill him? Yes, but a future Suzanne, his mind argued, not the one standing in front of him. Jackson's head hurt as the tangents and possibilities attracted and repulsed each other with dizzying frequency. A dark ocean. Chart a course and follow it unerringly. He had to at least attempt to save Ana.

"Paress said your father had banned you from the time machines," Jackson said.

"He deactivated my key to that floor," Suzanne said with a grim smile, "but I'm not locked out. Yet. He taught me a lot of things when I was growing up, not the least of which was always to set up your own systems for things. I can get us in."

Jackson felt a mixture of relief and panic flux inside of him.

"We'll need a vid keyboard from here to get in." She turned and walked back to the end of the 'sseteracks.

Jackson lifted the keyboard up and held it as she pulled loose the quick-disconnects on the unit. Then he wrapped the wires around the keyboard.

Paress stood at their approach.

"We'll need clothing," Suzanne said, "suitable for wear in Mexico in 2074."

The costumer produced a small notebook and an electric stylus that hummed low as she flicked it on. "Casual dress?"

Suzanne smiled and Jackson liked the effect it had on her face. "We're going to be attending a formal political function."

"Where do you want me to meet you?"

"I don't want you to meet us anywhere. Get us enough things to last a couple of days, along with the right papers and some currency we can use, then tube them up to the time machine area and get out of the building. Chances are when I open the doors on that floor, a security team is going to be en route."

"You're not going," Jackson said as the costumer hurried off.

Dark and angry fires glinted in Suzanne's green eyes. "You're going to need my help, Jackson. You're almost dead on your feet now. How much further do you think you're going to be able to push yourself?"

Jackson started to argue despite the reasonableness of her observation. He had no right to ask her to endanger her life, and already she was helping him break into one of the tightest security installations in 2250. Part of him held back because he didn't want to face another trip through time alone.

"I also don't like the idea of staying behind as target practice for the cretins operating security around here."

Jackson still wanted to say something, but quickly noticed it would have been wasted on Suzanne's back, because she was already moving through the darkened library away from him. He hurried to catch up, carrying the keyboard under his arm like a piece of luggage.

He caught up to her at the elevator as the door slid open after recognizing her ident. The hallways sounded eerie and hollow despite his best efforts to move quietly. Inside the elevator, Suzanne had manually diffused the cage light so it didn't disturb the dark shadows lining the hallway. He could feel his heart slow-thud in his bruised chest as the elevator hissed upwards at a stomach-loosening pace, conscious of the possibility that a Time Policeman could seize the elevator at any time and bring it to a halt long enough to fill the cage with bullets. But would a member of the Time Police do that with Suzanne with him? He was sure the answer would be yes and that apologies would be extended to Brelmer for the execution of his daughter.

Catching Suzanne's eye, Jackson said, "Thanks."

She looked unsure of herself. "I want you to trust me, Jackson, and I know that's probably impossible with the circumstances being what they are. But I feel responsible for you, for your involvement with Temporal Projects."

The opening doors of the elevator interrupted her and she quickly clapped her hand over the light control, extinguishing the fluorescent glow.

Jackson led the way out into the darkened hallway, waiting for Suzanne to debark. He strained his eyes against the shadows but barely made out the walls that confined them.

Suzanne took the lead again, hurrying now.

"Where is everyone?" Jackson asked as he trotted in the attempt to keep up.

"At a party Senator Voxner is giving. Father didn't want to go, but the invitation was one that couldn't be refused. The whole development team is there as well, which is another thing Father thought should not happen." She reached a double door and slipped the wires from the keyboard, jamming them under the plate guards on different sectors of the computerized ident-lock. "Now be quiet. I've got to get this just right. There are monitors along this whole floor that are manned 24 hours a day. Someone has already seen us get this far and knows by now that we're not authorized here."

Jackson held the keyboard steady as she worked, frequently glancing over his shoulder, knowing the rapid thunder of approaching feet would fill his ears in seconds. If he was recognized, they would shoot first and ask questions later. An overimage of the crystaled picture in his pocket spread across the blackness of the hallway.

"Damnit!"

Swiveling his head back around in a painful snap, Jackson saw Suzanne sucking on a finger.

"Broke a fingernail," she said apologetically.

Jackson turned back around to watch the hallway. Security lights popped into life, flooding the corridor with lambent ruby glows. He felt Suzanne keying the board to life in his hands and wondered if the jury-rigged set-up was going to electrocute him before the Time Police could arrive.

"You remember *King Lear?*" Suzanne asked as she continued tapping. "It's a play by William Shakespeare."

"I can't really recall it right at this moment," Jackson answered truthfully. There. He could hear them now. Footsteps. Running footsteps.

"I entered my own code in the lock on this floor," Suzanne said. "Actually two of them, one of which Father did not know about. In *King Lear,* it is his children who ultimately betray him. I knew that if I ever had to use the special circuitry I added, the reference would be fitting. So, when I finish typing in King Lear's children's names, we should be in."

The ruby glow of the hallway made it hard for Jackson to judge distances, especially when he was squatting on his haunches the way he was. How far away was the opposite end of the corridor? The first Time Policeman came into view just as the security door behind him lisped open.

"Come on, Jackson!"

He felt Suzanne pulling at his sleeve, felt the material fray in her frenzied grip, and tumbled over. He forced himself back to his feet as the first scattering of shots whined off the security doors. Then he was running for all he was worth.

Suzanne had opened the door of the first one and was reaching to pull herself inside.

"Halt, qwerk! Halt and we won't shoot any more."

But you won't shoot any less, either, Jackson wanted to say if he had the time. He bounced off the hull of Suzanne's time machine, angling toward the mini-tube, which had a package sitting on the shelf in front of it. He hoped it was the clothing Paress had arranged for as he threaded his fingers through the string binding it. Slipping awkwardly as he changed impetus, he forced his body back across the intervening distance separating him from the time machine. He hurled himself inside just as the Time Police tripped the security lock and the double doors swung open.

The explosions of the automatic weapons dropped in intensity as Suzanne closed the door. Jackson tried to get himself strapped in before the machine rocked to life, managing to pull a helmet and face-bag into place just before he was slammed across the two back seats.

It felt like he was being torn apart.

Old wounds broke open, spilling him through lacerated flesh and letting cold energy invade him.

New wounds seemed to warp his body from every imaginable direction and then some.

There was a stink, a belch, a misfire of oranges and ammonia, a squeezed mixture of citrus and cat juices. Then a raucous Death with an iron-plated tankard bonged him forcefully between his eyes, and Jackson spilled into a black abyss as cold as the frozen north.

Chapter Sixteen

The party was in full swing when Praetor Centurion Lieutenant Colonel Friz Brelmer arrived, but he didn't delude himself for one moment that it was an innocent function, as Voxner had protested that it was.

Brelmer stood at the massive and ornate double doors, looking over the huge ballroom floor tiled in meter-wide squares of glossy white and black. Dozens of people congregated on the dance floor, decked out in clothing in a multitude of brilliant colors. The women's clothing ran the widest gamut of styles, though, ranging from the Oriental and Elizabethan baroque to dress that revealed all but the essential ingredients of femininity.

Beside him, with her arm looped through his, his wife straightened slightly, and he knew she was trying to ease the pain that she lived with constantly.

"Are you all right?" he asked her, patting her arm.

The look she gave him was scathing, but Brelmer knew it wouldn't be readily apparent to those around them, not even the broad-shouldered doorman who came to take their coats. June Brelmer had learned to be the perfect corporate executive's wife during their last thirty years together, despite the pain that hounded her continually. Whatever their feelings toward each other in private, they never showed in the public eye.

"I'm fine, Friz, don't you worry about it. I've been taking care of myself and my needs for quite some time. There's no reason for you to begin worrying yourself at this point." She undraped her wrap and gave it to the obsequious doorman.

Brelmer followed her example and left his hat, automatically noticing the bulge under the doorman's arm that had to be nothing less than a mini-Matthews. Was Voxner expecting trouble then? his military mind reflected. And the thought of that angered him even more. The cream of Temporal Projects' crop was here tonight in force. What if a squad of time rebels were to appear here tonight? By what right did Voxner feel he could call something like this?

His wife immediately snubbed him by going directly to the little cadre of other political wives gathered in one corner of the room. Brelmer knew she was aware of his discomfort every time he got around those women, and that he refused to go there.

His mood already dark over Voxner's breach of security, Brelmer made his way through the milling throng to the bar in one of the other rooms. Only a few of the men had dressed, as he had, in full military uniform, preferring the exotic instead.

The bar only held a handful of people, most of them men huddled in small groups and sharing small glass-topped tables. Artificial and carefully groomed real plants adorned the walls and windows, occupied corners, and seemed to creep from every spare bit of space. Uncomfortable images of the last mission to Texas 1836 clunked into view in Brelmer's mind and increased the unease he was already feeling.

The bartender gave him an artificial smile that echoed the flora in the hanging basket above the counter in its total lack of life and vitality. Brelmer seated himself on one of the high- backed chairs and felt it mold itself to his posture, maxing out for comfort and support.

"Praetor Centurion Brelmer," the bartender greeted, and a little warmth seemed to taint the man's waxy lips. "You'll be wanting an old-fashioned screwdriver with cubed ice, not crushed. I'll have it for you in just a moment."

For an instant, Brelmer was taken aback, then remembered how thorough Voxner could be when entertaining. The senator had probably had the staff handling the food and beverage preparing for this night for a month or more. Photos and stats regarding personal taste would have been provided for everyone attending. Keep everyone happy and overwhelmed by the service and attention they received, and gradually their defenses and inhibitions would dissolve. Brelmer thought it was a good plan but knew it wouldn't work on him. Voxner knew he could, and did, handle his drinking.

The party had to be a fishing expedition for Voxner. There was no other explanation. But who was the fish?

When the bartender brought him the drink, he swiveled the chair around to survey the activity on the dance floor. What could Voxner be hoping to discover tonight? Mentally, Brelmer reevaluated his estimate of the time in which Voxner could have set the party up. Conceivably, with all the information the senator had at his disposal, and acting through the large staff he maintained, Voxner could have arranged for the party in one day. The invitations had come over the government vid at Temporal Projects that afternoon. Voxner knew he carried weight and that all of TP's employees would show up.

Would Suzanne be in later? Brelmer was uncertain if his daughter even knew about the party. His thoughts locked on her for a moment, and he reexperienced the sour taste in his mouth he had gotten when he demoted her. Suzanne was a very proud girl. Woman, he corrected himself. Sometimes it was so hard to not think of her as the little girl he had played with. She had been his release after all the hours at his job earning each progressive promotion. June had been wrapped up in her pain and under sedation much of the time then. Suzanne, little Suzanne in her pigtails and braces and hugging her latest teddy bear, had been the highlight of so many of his evenings at home. Even when he had gotten home too late to visit with her, he sometimes spent half an hour just watching her sleep.

What must she be thinking of him now?

The bartender brought him his drink, and he swirled it around a few times before taking a sip. It went down smooth and warm, with a bitter citric aftertaste. For all of Suzanne's life he had been instructive rather than critical, developing her abilities toward a logical bent. He had been so damn proud of her when she started following in his footsteps. He had never thought of having children when he was young, had never thought of having a son, did not even know June had been pregnant with Suzanne until his wife was in the second trimester, due to his assignments abroad. Even when he had helped June convert the second bedroom into a crib-and-comforter affair, the impact of actually holding a child that was his had not really hit him. Then Suzanne came along. With tiny red fists, an angry cross-eyed look, and a squeal that sounded so strained and low that it seemed for sure that she would never be heard.

But now things were different. Suzanne was no longer a wriggling, red-faced double-handful that seemed to be constantly wet at one end or the other. No longer the little girl with pigtails and braces. No longer the college student who had seemed to constantly challenge her professors till they were exasperated and amazed by her brilliance.

She was a woman.

And he had demoted her from a job she had put a lot of time into, in the hopes he might be able to keep her from conceiving a child that would carry her line and convictions into the future till it reached the descendant that he now held captive in TP's security rooms.

What would Suzanne do if she knew?

Weariness soaked into him, and he drained the glass, leaving the broken, icy skeleton behind. The bartender brought a fresh drink without being asked.

He studied his reflection in the ornately stained mirror behind the bar, staring past the ghostly pattern of the ancient Roman bathhouse where toga-clad men were attended by women slaves of statuesque beauty. His bare skull gleamed in the low-intensity lighting, barely highlighting the scar just above his forehead. His black beard seemed to jut out in proud defiance.

He wished he could take Suzanne into his confidence. That way maybe he wouldn't feel as lonely or as trapped by the project as he seemed to be now. Suzanne had a way of understanding him that even June lacked at times. June was a part of him, true, and even though her pain often kept her distant from him when he needed her most,

Brelmer looked to his wife during many personal moments of indecision, using her example and bravery as something to push him onward when it seemed he had nothing left to give. In fact, it had been June's single-mindedness about living her life and caring for her family despite the pain that had helped him with the decision concerning Suzanne's future.

Voxner just didn't understand the Pandora's box that had fallen open with the discovery of time travel. Not unless it touched his life. And the senator had appointed Praetor Centurion Lieutenant Colonel Friz Brelmer to make sure that never happened.

Without a word, the bartender placed another drink in front of him and took the empty glass away.

Brelmer toyed with the glass, making damp circles on the teak surface that intersected and looped within one another, mentally assembling and disassembling a Moebius strip that time could pass on. There had to be a way, logic told him, that the flow of the centuries could twist and turn through the loops of time passed into time yet to come that would mark history on one side only. Yet, with what they had discovered so far, every venture into the past left indelible footprints.

With everything so confused, how could anyone be sure of what had happened? Or had it already happened and was only now being acted out? Maybe everything they had learned about history up to this point in time had been false, waiting to be altered as they seemed so incapable of not doing.

Paradoxes.

And no control in sight to measure all the variables against.

"Penny for your thoughts, Praetor?" a feminine voice said.

Looking over his shoulder, Brelmer found Assistant Undersecretary of Culture Sarah Hadenforth Elgin standing quietly behind him. She wore a small smile that seemed tainted by a secret sadness, and held her guitar case with both hands in front of her. The semi-transparent dress she wore made Brelmer remember years past when he was still at the Academy and women were frail things waiting patiently for a soft conquest.

"I'm afraid you wouldn't be getting your credit's worth tonight," Brelmer said.

"I don't know, Praetor. The few times I've had occasion to speak with you, I've found you to be both informed and persuasive."

"You'll have to remind me of what we were talking about one of these times." In a lot of ways, Elgin reminded Brelmer of Suzanne. A milder, more experienced in the ways of the world Suzanne.

"Would you mind company?" she asked. "Or were you enjoying a brief bit of solitude?"

Brelmer waved to a chair.

She placed the guitar carefully beside her chair and climbed aboard, placing unclad elbows on the bar and lacing her fingers to make a platform for her chin.

Brelmer started to call for the bartender's attention, then noticed the man was already on his way with a drink in his hand. He watched the bartender sit the glass in front of Sarah, turn on a brief smile that wasn't all window dressing, then leave them alone.

Brelmer said, "Voxner's certainly got his staff on their toes tonight."

Sarah raised an inquisitive eyebrow, arching it demurely in a way that seemed to accentuate her sensuality. "You would expect any less of our illustrious Assistant Secretary of History?"

"No. Not really. But you have to admit he does have a certain flair for pompousness."

"Which is an affordable luxury on the budget his department commands since you have taken over Temporal Projects."

"I'll take that as a backhanded compliment, Miss Elgin."

"It's no secret that you've been a good administrator, Friz, and it was certainly expected in light of your past achievements. The only secret that seems to remain is exactly what your people are doing over there."

For a brief instant Brelmer felt threatened, as if Elgin's questions were meant to encourage answers he was not permitted to give. Was this a test, then? Arranged by Voxner? The senator certainly knew he appreciated the woman's music despite his usual preference for rock 'n' jazz. He sipped his drink to give him time to consider.

Without waiting for his reply, the woman swiveled on her chair to survey the dance floor.

Brelmer echoed the move, for a moment entranced by the flow of limbs, clad and almost-clad, that lifted sinuously to the slow beat of the music. "Why aren't you out there?" he asked.

She chuckled without looking at him. "Let's just say that I received an offer better refused. My no-thank-you wasn't well received."

"And you presumed a military uniform might better serve to deter the young man?"

She smiled at him brightly, her eyes flashing in the semi-darkness. "To put it bluntly, Praetor, yes."

The sense of entrapment evaporated within Brelmer, and his stomach became less tense, less ready to twist and turn painfully. "Call me Friz, please. I spend a lot of long hours immersed in protocol every day."

"All right, Friz." Her voice was warm and soothing.

"Have you played yet?" Brelmer asked, indicating the guitar case.

"Earlier, but the crowd seemed more ready for the dance music the band had to offer."

"That's because they don't appreciate music the way it was meant to be appreciated."

"Now I'll take that as a backhanded compliment." Brelmer smiled in spite of his mood.

"Has Voxner interrogated you yet?"

"What do you mean?"

"I've noticed him with a handful of Temporal Projects' department heads so far tonight," Sarah said. "So far, not many of them have seemed pleased with what he has to say."

Searching for the information leak, Brelmer wondered, or exercising a more personal influence among the department heads so they didn't get so involved with their research that they forgot under whose thumb they worked so diligently? He noticed he had finished the third drink without knowing it and started to set it back on the bar, then decided against that and held on to the glass so the bartender wouldn't be as tempted to replenish it.

If Voxner was playing the fox in the henhouse tonight, Brelmer knew it would be better to play his role with a clear head. He wondered where Suzanne was, wishing she would show up at the party, knowing her absence would be damning in the senator's eyes.

Chapter Seventeen

The time machine seemed to shuttle through the decades like a stone skipping the surface of a lake. Nausea gripped Jackson and squeezed him dry, tugging him into the lining of the two back seats. An echoed retching sounded from the front seat, and he knew Suzanne was being seized by the same forces that held him in a viselike clutch.

Had the heavy bombardment the Time Police gave the time machine as it broke through the time barrier had any affect on the machine's abilities? What if one of the bullets had broken some vital piece of circuitry that would pitch him and Suzanne endlessly through the centuries? Or if it had been damaged in some way so that the machine materialized outside the Earth's orbit, maybe as little as an hour behind the planet's yearly cycle around Sol? Would the time machine survive the rigors of space until they could set new coordinates? If they could set new coordinates.

Jackson raised his head to peer through the vacuum of color that swirled around them. Suzanne's blonde hair seemed to be the only bit of reality in view.

Then the time machine seemed to flip.

Plunge.

Spin and twirl.

Like the Tasmanian Devil that pursued Bugs Bunny in the ancient vidtoons on Saturday mornings.

There was an impact, slight, as if they had passed through a spiderweb that had almost held them. The spinning came to a gradual halt that left Jackson's mind still revolving and a weakness in the pit of his stomach. Then he was crunched through the padding of the time machine's interior, rebounding with bruising force from the unit's metal skeleton. A dry groan knifed through his lips before he could stop it.

Bright sunlight flooded the inside of the time machine, making Jackson's vision brittle and fogged. He closed his eyes, trying to curl up into a fetal ball till the pain passed. Unconsciousness reached for him with grease-coated talons, pricking his mind as it sought to drag him away from whatever now he was presently lodged in. Electric fire seemed to dance up and down his spine.

Fingers wrapped around one of his ankles and pulled.

Jackson came up screaming as bitter memories killed the peacefulness he was trying to sink into, his hands knotted into fists.

Suzanne recoiled from him with a scream of her own.

Jackson made himself relax, slowing the eighth-notes of his heart inside his chest, forcing himself back to where he was and what he was doing there. Martin and Ana. The stink of bile flooded his nostrils and he tore the face mask away.

When he opened his eyes again, he saw Suzanne staring at him with a frightened look on her face. For the first time he noticed the trickle of blood from her nose smudging her upper lip. He reached forward to touch her face gently, ashamed at the way she flinched away from him. "Are you all right?" He traced her nose with a forefinger, not finding any new bumps or swelling that would indicate it was broken.

"Yes. Are you?"

Jackson nodded. "I haven't had much sleep for a long time now." It amazed him that he could so easily forget how long it had been since he had left the Mnemosyne to research the Buchenwald prison camp for them. Had it been a day? Or had it been days? It could be both, he realized, depending on when he left and when he made the time window back into his present. He took a handkerchief from his pocket and dabbed the blood from Suzanne's face, relieved to find that the bleeding had already stopped. "Where are we?"

"According to the instrument panel, we arrived at the correct date and year of the signing of the Second *Plan de Iguala*."

Jackson peered through one of the crystel windows at the hollow the time machine had settled in. Broken rocks burned white by a desert sun littered the cracked and parched earth around them. Even as he asked himself how hot it must be outside, he heard the time machine's internal cooling system kick into action, and felt the cooled air push doughily into him. Overhead, lost at times in the blinding glare of the sun, a pair of large birds flapped lethargically to glide and dip in the thin desert air. "Is the machine fully operational?"

Suzanne turned around to give the controls her attention.

Resting his aching head on a forearm braced against the crystel window, Jackson watched her movements, surprised at how much he trusted her after all he had been through. Surprised, too, at how much comfort he felt, just having her there so he wasn't alone.

"Everything checks out fine," she said after a few more minutes of clicking through check-out modes of the time machine's internal computer. Jackson was amazed at the number of schematics that had come up on the small vidscreen built into the time machine's console. He had been taught the basics of the machine for his initial journey to 2183. He hadn't even known the full extent of the machine's capabilities. As if time travel itself wasn't enough.

"Can you tell where we are?"

The vidscreen blurred, looped back in on itself, then regurgitated information Jackson hoped Suzanne would find useful.

Suzanne consulted a travelog foldmap that was secured under the console in a cavity Jackson had not known existed, linking the hand-held mapping processor to the console computer via thread-thin circuitry. "Less than ten miles from Mexico City," she said after reading the information from the foldmap.

"What is the local time?"

"Thirteen-eleven."

"The signing took place when?" Jackson strained to remember.

"According to the information TP had, the Second Plan was signed at a public forum at fifteen hundred hours."

Ignoring the ache that pervaded his body, Jackson forced himself from the back seat, edging past Suzanne to pop open the passenger door. Desert heat slapped him across the face, sucking the oxygen from his lungs. Heat waves shimmered across the bleached desert sand. Despair filled him as he thought of the distance, limited by the time, and his hope of success was as barren as the land that surrounded him.

Still, he had to try. For Martin and Ana. For himself.

Maybe if Chrys Calvino had been there, Jackson told himself as he dropped to the sandy desert floor, maybe she could have reached the capital city in time on foot. She had a penchant for running, for all things physical. How often had she left him behind, straining to catch up, too exhausted for the sex she always offered afterwards?

Turning his mind from the negative thoughts, Jackson reached into the back seats and took out the package Paress Linnet had prepared for them. Feeling the beat of the sun on his bare head, he hoped she had had the foresight to send hats.

"What are you doing?" Suzanne asked as she stepped from the time machine.

Jackson seated himself cross-legged on the sand with the bulky package before him. "I'm going to try to make it."

"Jackson, you can't be serious. You're not up to travelling through the desert for that kind of distance. Especially considering the shape you're in."

"I am serious, though, Suzanne."

"We can try the time machine again and hope we get closer."

He looked up at her, squinting against the sun. Was the concern on her face genuine? He shook the question from his mind. One problem at a time, Dubchek, and even then you may be overloading your capabilities. "Suzanne, I don't even pretend to understand time travel the way you do. So far I've survived on the basics. I know that you can go back, that things can be changed, and that you can get very, very dead if you don't watch yourself at all times. I also believe that the past as we know it is in a state of constant flux. It's possible to travel back to a time that never existed, to an event that never happened. I think that's already happened to me." He gave her a brief explanation concerning Vice President Fosdick. "What I'm not sure of is that you can return to the same past twice. Not even in the Wheeling Loop. I was there at different years, surrounded by different histories. I know I am here now, in the proper time line until I find out differently. What I don't know is if I can hop in that time machine and return to it so easily." His voice softened. "This may be the only chance I have of saving my brother's past and his wife and children. I've got to try."

"You won't do him any good by killing yourself in the attempt."

He looked back at the package in front of him. "I'm not going to kill myself," he replied stubbornly.

Without another word, Suzanne turned and walked back to the time machine.

For a moment Jackson thought he had angered her enough to leave him in the desert to his own devices. He wanted to call out to her, to ask her not to leave him, but didn't trust the strength of his voice. Buddha, why did things in life have to be so complicated?

Instead of clambering into the machine, Suzanne seemed intent on freeing something from under one of the seats, pulling at it angrily till both feet lifted from the ground.

Focusing on the task at hand, Jackson freed his knife and started to saw on the plastic strands binding the package. The polished blade glinted brightly in the sun. Images of Paulson, the Time Policeman, impaled on its sharp tip strayed into his mind. He forced them away. Not a weapon, he told himself as he fought to keep from throwing the knife away. Not a weapon. A tool. A tool that would fit in with any society, no matter how advanced or how primitive. His tool.

The plastic strands parted easily at the knife's touch, and Jackson somehow kept from thinking how the deranged Time Policeman's intestines must have done the same.

By the time he flipped the cover off the package, Suzanne had returned, carrying a small metal box and a canteen. It wasn't until he saw the canteen that Jackson realized how thirsty the nausea had left him.

"It's not cold," Suzanne warned as she uncapped the canteen, "and it won't taste as good as water from a natural spring, because it's been seeded with electrolytes and other chemicals to help return a flagging metabolism to some semblance of norm."

"Thanks." Jackson took the canteen in both hands and tilted his head back to take a sip. It wasn't as bad as Suzanne had led him to believe. It was liquid, lukewarm from the coolness still locked in the time machine, and had a faint metallic aftertaste. Still, it slaked the emptiness in his stomach.

It was hard to tell which costume was for a male and which was for a female, and Jackson doubted he would have been able to choose if Suzanne hadn't been there. But then again, if she hadn't been there, Paress would have sent only one set of clothes.

Both costumes were white and loose-fitting, complete with open- toed leather sandals and wide-brimmed straw hats. Jackson tried to recall what he remembered of Mexican history and found it painfully inadequate. Until its acceptance into the Republic, the economy of Mexico had remained impoverished for centuries.

"You don't have to go," Jackson told Suzanne as he handed her the sandals that outfitted her costume. "You can wait here."

"I'm not a person to sit on the sidelines, Jackson," she said with a smile. "I thought you would know that by now."

He nodded and moved away, wondering if that wasn't why he involved her in his search in the first place. On the other side of the time machine, he exchanged the clothes Paress Linnet had given him to wear in 2250 for the ones she had given him to wear in 2074. In the tepid air that flowed through the open fangs of the hollow the time machine had settled into, he could hear the rustling of clothing on the other side of the machine and knew that Suzanne was changing as well. Desire stirred inside him, surprising in its intensity, but he capped it quickly, willing it to wither and die. He stored his clothing inside the machine, seeing the soft swell of one of Suzanne's breasts through the crystel windows for just a moment before the white blouse she held overhead dropped down to cover it.

He closed the door quietly so she wouldn't know he had seen her.

Buddha, why were there so many temptations in life? So many inconsistancies? He wished he could have been a better student in the religious training his mother had insisted he have. Maybe then there wouldn't have been so many questions or so many indecisive moments. But even that would not have made Suzanne any less the daughter of a man who would kill him once Brelmer's crystal eyes locked on him.

By the time he walked back around the time machine, Suzanne was going through the metal box she had retrieved. "Here," she said, handing him a plastic tube. "This will help shield you from the ultraviolet rays."

Jackson squirted some of the tube's contents in his palm and smeared it on the exposed parts of his body. It felt cooler just having it there. Suzanne sighed impatiently and took the tube from him, stepping behind him to smear it on his neck and behind his ears.

Then, after printing the time machine's security system with both his and Suzanne's idents, Jackson checked his chronometer. Less than an hour and a half remained before the signing ceremony was to take place.

Struggling over the lip of the baked earthen wall that hid the time machine from casual view, Jackson led the way into the heat of the desert. He breathed as Chrys Calvino had taught him to during the infrequent times she had coaxed him onto a running track with her, in through the nose and out through the mouth. And each breath seemed to sap the moisture his body needed to survive. He hastened his step after noticing he had not exceeded Suzanne Brelmer's limits. Probably, she was in better shape than he was. She looked like a woman who took care of her body and took the time to look good. She wasn't a public librarian and linguist like him, who seemed to be Buddha-blessed with a metabolism that never let any of the cashew chicken or pizzamax he consumed show.

Perspiration gathered in his eyebrows as he forced himself forward, falling in drops that sometimes stung his eyes. He kept his head down, watching the cracked earth constantly, aware that any misstep might cost him a twisted ankle and whatever chance he had of correcting history. So immersed was he in summoning every erg of strength left in his body to the next step, he didn't hear the excitement in Suzanne's voice the first time.

She grabbed his arm and forced him to look at her.

"A road, Jackson. Look." She pointed.

Jackson squinted in the wavering distance and saw it. A thin, alabaster bone that cut through the yellowed sand of the desert in a straight gash that disappeared over the hills to the north.

"Someone's coming," Suzanne said.

Jackson shifted perspectives and till the large plume of dust coming from the south came into view. He followed Suzanne down the hill, both of them croaking through dry throats and waving their arms.

"Thank you, Jesus," Jackson said in Spanish as he helped Suzanne step from the interior of the old prospector's four- wheel-drive truck.

Jesus was an old man, white-bearded, with two front teeth missing and a way of smiling that told Jackson the man was self- conscious about them. He looked like a dwarf atop the huge, open- topped truck, stained wine-dark against the bleached skin of the desert he professed to live in. The old man had been very much surprised to find two Norteamericanos so far from civilization, but had stopped for them just the same. Judging from the numerous scars that twisted around the man's heavy forearms and from the machete scabbarded on the driver's door, Jesus was also a man with considerable experience.

With final wave, Jesus drove the large truck away, rattling over the cobbled streets.

Jackson checked his chronometer and started in the direction of the crowd at the other end of the plaza.

"How much time?" Suzanne asked.

"Only minutes."

"But we made it, Jackson."

"I hope so." He was amazed by the architecture surrounding them. True, 2074 was indeed far removed from his present, but the archaic design of the buildings, their sheer immensity, spoke of times centuries before. The buildings towered over them, trapping a square of blue sky over their heads. The stone floor of the plaza rang beneath their feet.

Frustrated with the crowd gathered before him and grimly aware that whatever time he had was ticking away second by second, Jackson grabbed Suzanne's wrist and pulled her after him, bulling his way through the people. Scathing invective pursued his almost-stalled flight, embroidered in Spanish and English.

By standing on tiptoe, Jackson occasionally got a glimpse of the speaker's stand and the nineteen men and women seated with him. Behind the stand a large and ornately designed fountain spewed water into the air from a large fish. The returning water splashed from the naked shoulders of the three stone mermaids seated around the fish.

Which one was Miguel Franco? Jackson asked himself as he shoved by a fat man. He heard Suzanne squeal in panic, and turned to see the fat man holding her by the other wrist. The fat man spat at Jackson's feet. Giving up the thought of peaceful reconciliation, Jackson lashed out with a foot and kicked the fat man in the groin, watching the man topple to the ground.

Then he was moving again, forcing his way to the forefront of the crowd with renewed vigor. How long would it be before the fat man got to his feet and pursued him? What was going to happen to Miguel Franco?

Aerial news cameras recorded the incident, hovering over different points of the masses.

An angry yell reached Jackson's ears from behind. "Jackson!"

Not turning to heed either the yell or Suzanne's warning, Jackson collided with the people standing in his way, apologizing automatically in Spanish, begging passage because it meant life or death.

Why hadn't he taken time to review the event at the research library at TP? That way he would have known from what quarter to expect an attack. Would have known what the attack was. But strategy wasn't something a linguist would have need of and he knew it. He wasn't a warrior. He was a librarian.

His lungs ached and he felt the knife, sheathed under the loose cotton shirt, beat against his chest.

Just as he had almost reached the front of the crowd, he saw a look of horror flicker through the speaker's face. The man held his hands up before him and tried to back away.

He heard Suzanne scream his name as he watched all hell break loose in front of him, then felt her body crash into his legs and bring him to the ground. He tried to get up but Suzanne clambered on his back and pinned him, screaming something in his ear that he couldn't recognize.

An ear-splitting screech of autofire hammered an aria into the plaza.

Jackson could tell the assassins were on one of the upper stories of the buildings around them, but not which one. Who? Why?

Bullets ripped into the speaker, spiking through his palms to penetrate vital organs. Blood mixed freely in the waters of the fountain behind the signers of the Second *Plan de Iguala* as bodies tumbled into it, staining even the fish's breath that broke across the mermaids' backs.

Jackson watched helplessly till tears blurred his vision.

Chapter Eighteen

The little glow of satisfaction that had been building in Senator Ronald Reuel Voxner reached its peak when he saw the Brelmers arrive at the party. He sat in a cushioned chair behind the console of the hidden observation post he had had constructed above the dance floor. From this point the floor looked like a huge chessboard.

A chessboard that was covered with his pawns, Voxner told himself, each of them hoping someday to achieve a position of power. Voxner dashed those hopes daily and enjoyed it.

He settled back in the chair, the servos barely audible as it hummed to accomodate his movements. So far this evening he had blatantly threatened three people to make them monitor Brelmer's moves more closely, the same threat implicitly to five other people, and had pulled in a couple of debts owed from people in departments not directly under his control. Influence didn't stay intradepartmental if you knew what you were doing, and Voxner worked the system to his benefit.

Forcing himself up from the plush chair, the senator made his way to the door of the observation room and knocked once. When the answering knock sounded, letting him know no one was in the hallway, he thumb-printed the door open and passed through. The Time Policeman standing guard there was a big man, and Voxner only reached the man's shoulder. Knudsen had been with him for years. How many Voxner wasn't sure, but he had been one of the first to undergo the surgery necessary to create a Time Policeman. The man was a flesh-and-blood juggernaut. But Voxner owned this particular juggernaut, just as he owned everyone he did business with in one way or another.

Even Mrs. Friz Brelmer.

But the woman didn't know that yet.

Voxner was on his way to introduce her to that particular line of thinking.

Once the door shut behind him, it was indistinguishable from any other part of the expensively crafted wooden wall. At his nod, Knudsen walked away to begin patrolling the upper floor of the mansion. With the powerful laser constructed into the Time Policeman's left arm, coupled with the still experimental but effective tracking system that read out through the man's crystal eyes, Voxner felt completely safe moving within the crowd of people writhing across the black and white floor. It only took a touch of the small box implanted under his left thumb to signal for Knudsen's immediate attention. The system had saved his life on two occasions, and everyone assumed the Time Policeman was just a bodyguard who had luckily been in the right place at the right time.

Voxner took the winding powered staircase to the floor and was met at the bottom by a waitress in an all-but-transparent shift. Her smile was sugary-sweet and the senator made a note to have the girl brought to his chambers after the party.

The smile he gave his guests was false but felt comfortable. It was the same one he had been using for years while moving through the political circus of the Second Republic to gain the power he wielded so effectively. Just as he broke the hopes, dreams, and aspirations of those who served him, he also broke the careers of beginning senators whose views would ultimately bring them into conflict with his own.

With all of Friz Brelmer's expertise at sorting through data and new thinking, the praetor would have been an able politician had the urge so moved him. Thankfully, though, the motivations that powered the praetor through this life were of a different bent. So different, in fact, the Brelmer's engines and natural curiosity trapped him in his present position.

If it hadn't been for the damned Mnemosyne and their constant prying into the affairs of Temporal Projects, Voxner would have been a much happier man. Still, even with the information that was somehow leaving the walls of TP, nothing was leaked of the overall plan for Project Clio that Voxner was putting into place one brick at a time. Even Brelmer, for all his practical mind, so attuned to looking for patterns in everything he dealt with, would not guess what Voxner was truly doing until the praetor was walled within the maze he had helped construct.

Voxner stopped to sip his drink and verify his bearings. The dance floor seemed so much larger now that he was a part of it. Which was why he never made a personal foray into the games he set up and conducted with such orchestrated precision. Plans only worked if the planner remained above everything. Untouchable.

The women with whom June Brelmer had taken refuge from the party turned their heads at Voxner's approach. How quick they were to realize their husbands' jobs might hinge on the way they conducted themselves. Voxner's smile felt more honest.

"Ladies," he said with a small inclination of his head. After allowing time for proper response, he looked at June Brelmer, singling her out. "Mrs. Brelmer, I know of your interest in the artists of the Renaissance period. I wonder if I might trouble you to look at a new acquistion I've recently made."

"Really, Senator Voxner, my interest is only a personal one. I've had no schooling for it."

Voxner easily recognized the falsity of the woman's smile, just as he noted the quick flutter of her eyelids as she tried to figure out how he had known of her passion for painting. "I've no reason to doubt the veracity of the painting, Mrs. Brelmer. I would just like your opinion on what would be the best setting to display it. And there is nothing like a woman's touch." He held out his hand for her to take.

The other women in the political wives' clique made encouraging noises that Voxner knew June Brelmer could not ignore. He felt the reluctance in her grip as she took his hand.

Voxner led her across the outer fringes of the dance floor, knowing Brelmer could not see the senator with his wife. The senator knew Brelmer had slipped into the quiet bar for some solitude, just as he had been certain June Brelmer would snub her husband. In fact, if it had not been for Friz Brelmer's penchant for bars and Voxner's need to speak to June Brelmer alone, the bar would not have existed tonight at all.

"I have several more paintings at my home in Moscow," Voxner said to fill the quiet silence that trailed after them, "but the ones I have collected here suit the mood of this large house."

"I've never been to Moscow."

"You'll have to come with Friz someday, then. He visits me there frequently on business. I'll have to have you up soon for a purely medicinal purpose." Voxner watched to see if she would give any sign of noticing his term "medicinal." He was disappointed, but quickly realized June Brelmer was a woman used to dealing with the pain that often tempered her emotions.

He led her down a short hallway into another room of the mansion. The senator felt naked for a moment, knowing Knudsen was now further away from his signal than he had been all night. But so was the crowd he feared.

With a grand gesture, he indicated the new painting he had recently purchased, satisfied with the glow that lit June Brelmer's eyes. She loosed his hand and stepped forward to observe it more closely.

Voxner was not really taken with the picture. It had been purchased for its ability to impress people he wanted to impress. His own private art treasures he kept in a security-controlled underground vault in Moscow, and ranged through a more lewd collection of paintings as well as ancient photographs. One of the premier assignments of Temporal Projects and the Time Police had been to acquire vintage sets of both PLAYBOY and HUSTLER magazines. It amused him from time to time to think of different agents acting under his direction to travel through time each month to gather the magazines.

The picture was of a feast in a lavishly furnished dining hall, complete with a cheery fireplace.

"This is magnificent," June Brelmer said. She did not look at him, too taken with the picture.

Or avoiding him? Voxner wondered. The woman was good at playing games. She had to be in order to keep her mind turned away from the pain that was her constant companion. "And in true Renaissance style. Note the dark shadow barely discernible on the lower right hand corner of the window."

"The representation of Death." She nodded approvingly. "Many of their paintings included symbolism like this. A constant reminder that even amid all the trappings of richness and luxury, Death was waiting to claim them all."

Voxner stepped around to her side so he could face her easily. "A role you're not entirely unaccustomed to, Mrs. Brelmer. True?"

She whirled to face him, indecision carved into the tight features.

"You have your own representation of Death dogging your footsteps, don't you, Mrs. Brelmer?"

"What are you talking about, Senator?"

"Let's not fence, Mrs. Brelmer. I know far too much about you to play games of that nature."

Wordlessly, June Brelmer turned to leave.

For a moment Voxner was stunned. When was the last time a woman had so flagrantly violated his authority?

June Brelmer opened the door.

Voxner breathed one word. "Capricorn."

June Brelmer's spine stiffened, and she seemed caught on the threshold.

"Capricorn," Voxner repeated.

The woman's hands trembled as she closed the door and turned back around.

Voxner chose to hold his place rather than to move forward and intimidate her. Already she was aware of the tenuous ground she occupied. Any further pressure on his part might frighten her into flight. And that was not what the senator wanted. He had a use for her.

"What are you talking about?" June Brelmer demanded. Absently, she massaged a shoulder, wincing as if the movement hurt.

"To put it succinctly, my dear woman, I own your doctor. Just as I own the Capricorn he has been giving you to fight your constant pain."

He blocked her denial with an upraised hand.

"Don't fight me on this, Mrs. Brelmer, please. I'm too thorough to let negotiations reach this point without hard evidence of some sort. I have the visits you've made to Dr. Gerard on 'ssete."

"You can't get me convicted for using Capricorn without implicating yourself, Senator."

Voxner smiled, enjoying how the woman's mind had fled so quickly to the obvious rather than the more sublime. Most of his victims outthought themselves rather than needing much finesse on his part to knock them completely off-balance. "I have no intention of showing the 'ssetes in a court of law, Mrs. Brelmer. I was thinking more along the lines of your husband." He paused to let that sink in. "How would Friz react if he learns his wife is taking an illegal drug?"

June Brelmer's lower lip quivered and her eyes looked wet.

"Let me examine the two extremes for you," Voxner said. "On the one hand, Friz can be totally horrified that you would even consider doing something like this, and would leave you. Or he can be so sympathetic he resigns his politically appointed post, thinking that someone as undeserving as he should not occupy such a position. And without some function in life, I cannot see your husband remaining the man you fell in love with. Neither is a pleasant alternative."

"Damn you!"

"We're all damned, my dear woman. Only some of us appear to be so more than others."

Her fists clenched and unclenched as she stared at him.

"Or there is another possibility."

"What?"

Voxner walked to couch in the center of the room, situated to afford the best possible view of the paintings on the walls. "I find your husband a most irritating man, Mrs. Brelmer, just as I'm sure you have upon occasion. Though, I'm sure, for quite different reasons. Friz is a man thoroughly lacking in any ambition politically. He seeks to achieve something of himself that I don't understand, a certain level of himself just because he believes it to be there. Do know what I'm talking about?"

"Friz is a perfectionist about things."

"Yes, but there is more to it than that. A perfectionist I could live with. They manipulate just as easily as anyone else I've met. No, with Friz it's just enough knowing that he could do whatever he sets his mind out to do. That's what intrigues him so much about Temporal Projects and the idea of time travel. It's like being given a perfectly round ring and being told to find the end of it. Friz believes it to be there, so he will search until he finds it."

"Or until he believes it doesn't really exist after all."

"So you do understand what I am talking about."

"He can be a very difficult man."

Voxner felt more secure about the emotional web he was weaving now that the woman was sympathizing with him. He would never trust her, no, but be able to use her, that was another matter. "Exactly. He is hooked by the possibilities that lie within the walls of the project buildings. I want a man like that working for Temporal Projects. The problem is that I don't think Friz always tells me what he is working on or what he has discovered."

June Brelmer remained silent.

Voxner knew she understood her role now, just as he knew he would have to spell it out for her. "I want you to let me know if Friz stumbles onto anything you think might interest me. Just in case he forgets to tell me immediately."

June Brelmer's voice was bitter. "Surely you have other spies watching my husband, Senator."

"Yes. Many. But Friz is a very close-mouthed man. I'm sure you appreciate what I am saying."

"Yes." But the reply seemed strained.

"It will all be for the best, Mrs. Brelmer. Really. All I am doing is exchanging your freedom from pain for my freedom from ignorance." Voxner reached into his pocket and produced a caplet of Capricorn, holding it on his outstretched fingers.

Timidly, like a wild animal in the old Walt Disney vids he had had resurrected, the woman approached and accepted the drug, quickly gulping it down dry.

"You have made a good bargain, Mrs. Brelmer, one that will benefit all of us." And his smile toward her was as honest as they got.

Brelmer took the vid in the corner of the bar, bringing his drink with him. He wondered who would dare disturb him at Voxner's party, thinking briefly of Suzanne. He thumbprinted into the vid's circuitry and the monitor cleared, showing him the round face of Reg Bowles, the night security chief at TP. Bowles looked agitated, gnawing anxiously at the thick mustache he wore.

"What is it?" Brelmer snapped, knowing Voxner would have had all the vids in the mansions tapped and taped.

"Your daughter, sir," Bowles said.

For a moment a cold flood of icicles shot through Brelmer's intestines. Had Suzanne done something to herself as a result of the demotion? "What about her?" he asked hoarsely.

"She broke into the time machine lab and traveled back."

"To what year?"

"They don't know yet, sir. The techs are still trying to blueprint it. Most of the research team are at the party tonight."

"Damnit, Sergeant, I know that."

"Yes, sir."

Fingers rested lightly on Brelmer's shoulder and he looked up to see Sarah Hadenforth Elgin standing beside him.

"Is anything wrong, Friz?" she asked.

"Yes. Could you find my wife for me? I'm going to have to leave immediately."

She nodded and walked away, carrying the guitar case protectively through the crowd.

Brelmer returned his attention to the Time Policeman.

"She took someone with her, too, sir."

"Did you get any kind of ident on the other person?"

"Not yet. We're still searching through the security vids. We do know it was a man approximately the same age as your daughter."

Dubchek? There was no way, Brelmer told himself. The librarian had been only too glad to step away from Temporal Projects. And Suzanne wouldn't put her job on the line for such a loser. She had more sense than that. Didn't she? Damnit. He hated the loss of control he felt more than anything. "I'll be there in minutes, Sergeant. Make ready a team." He blanked the vid without waiting for a reply, then pushed away from the small table.

He couldn't believe how quickly the problems seemed to pile up and almost consume him. His stomach knotted and felt like it was being pierced repeatedly by needles. The information leak at Temporal Projects, the great-great(?)-granddaughter he had captured back in 1836 and now didn't know what to do with or how to feel toward, and now Suzanne's insubordination. What the hell was he going to do? And where was June?

Chapter Nineteen

As rapidly as it had begun, the crackling of automatic rifles died away, pinging final notes from the mighty columns that supported many of the structures around the plaza.

Jackson looked up, tasting dirt and feeling it caked in the wake of his tears of helpless rage. Bodies of the signers of the Second Plan lay shattered everywhere, their blood staining the plaza floor and already drawing big black flies.

A mourning wail rose from the assembled crowd as they got to their feet and found more dead amid their own ranks. Jackson felt numb inside from the violence, the hopelessness of it all. He watched in dumb horror as a peasant mother tousled the hair of a young son in an attempt to wake the boy from death, heard her first screeching cries echoed inside the emptiness of his chest.

Who would do this? Why?

"Jackson, get up."

He felt the tugging on his arm but ignored it. Someone stepped on his lower legs, wrenching his ankle painfully.

"Damnit, Jackson, we've got to get out of here before the authorities come."

The tugging turned into real pulling, and he reluctantly got to his feet. He closed his eyes against the swimming sensation inside his head, sure he was going to vomit again but realizing there was nothing to disgorge.

"Come on, Jackson," a voice coaxed.

He looked down to see Suzanne holding his arm across her shoulders to support him as she forced them in lurching steps away from the death and violence. He noted the hard set of her face, the smudged dust shadowing the milky paleness of her skin. Didn't she understand what had just happened? What they had been forced to be witness to? He wanted to ask her but couldn't remember how to make his voice work. A last glance over his shoulder showed him that one cluster of bullets had shattered the lips of the stone fish, turning the smooth stream into an unshaped torrent of water.

Closing his eyes to lock out the reality of what had happened, he let Suzanne guide him, forcing his legs to mirror whatever movement she wanted. Minutes or hours later he felt a swirling of sluggish air only a few degrees cooler than the air in the plaza.

Blinking, he let the visual impressions flood in on his mind, imprinting a melange of color and shapes he found no solid connections for. No memory. Fans rotated overhead with a loud humming. The ceilings in the building Suzanne had led them to were tall and far away. Alabaster. For a moment it seemed that the yellowed design worked into the rock held blood stains. Then his eyes closed in a slow blink, erasing the image.

"Is your husband all right, *señora?*" a man's heavily accented voice asked in English.

"Yes." It was Suzanne's voice.

Jackson clung to the audible anchor, focusing on it to keep from being blown away by the tides of strained physical and psychological storms that raged inside the shattered pieces of his mind. Slye, Lester Wu, Alvarez, Lance Paulson, the signers, they were all in the storm with him, waiting for a cessation in their own small boat of memory as he rode out the watery turbulence, rocking up on each swell to catch a glimpse of their overfull craft. Suzanne. Think of Suzanne. She needs you to help get to a place of safety.

He fumbled away from her possessive hold, assuring her he could stand on his own.

"Are you sure?"

"Yes." Too angrily, he told himself, then repeated the affirmative in a much softer voice. "Yes. Thank you."

"Do you need some help with your husband, *señora?*"

"I don't think so, but thank you for asking."

"You were in the plaza?"

"Yes."

"Madre de Dios. It is a wonder you still live."

Suzanne took the key offered by the small clerk and Jackson felt her take his hand in hers, leading him away from the desk. Other people came in from the plaza as they made their way to the elevator. Crying women shook and wailed as stunned men hunkered down by the inner wall of the hotel. Sirens sounded just outside the door and Jackson saw one police car thread cautiously through the mass of hysterical people. The gay decorations that hung across the street announcing the signing looked empty, their bright colors lost somewhere in the din of confused emotion.

The elevator door closed and swept the sight from Jackson's view. He sagged tiredly against the wall of the cage, staring at the rectangle framing the door and trying to make sense of it all. The assassination had happened. He could still feel the death rattle of the hidden guns echoing inside his body. He had seen it. So what, then, of the future? His future? The one in which Ana had lived? With Lester Wu and Rosita Alvarez, the Time Police had used displacement to lose them in time. But this was different. According to the history he now faced, Ana had never lived. Even if he had somehow managed to rescue her and restore her to the present, his present, where had she been until then? Was there some sort of netherworld for the souls of those lost in the shifting centuries? Or was time some endless circle and the past event somehow destined to come true?

Jackson's head hurt from thinking about the random possibilities. And there was still the crystaled picture of himself to consider. There was no easy way to file any of it away.

"Jackson?"

Unwillingly, he looked up at Suzanne. Her hair was disarrayed and fell in blonde strands across her face. Mascara ran in lines down her cheeks and he knew she had been crying too.

"Are you all right?"

"No." He took a deep breath and blew it out, feeling a release of the tightness inside his chest. He braced his hands above his knees and bent forward as he breathed deeply again, feeling the blood surge to his head.

The elevator came to a gentle stop on the fourth floor. Jackson saw Suzanne check the key in her hand before leading him out into the corridor. A dozen people wandered aimlessly through the hallway, conversing in strained Spanish, wailing over the assassinations.

Jackson studied their faces but they were all unknown to him. Only the pain was familiar.

"We still have the time machine," Suzanne said as she opened the door to their room.

The room was modestly furnished with a bed, a small bathroom, a television, a nightstand and an accompanying lamp shaped like a rearing bull.

"That may not make a difference," Jackson said. He couldn't believe the dulled, defeated voice that was his. Walking stiffly, feeling the pain of the wrenched ankle, he came to a stop at the room's only window. He placed his hands on the window, thinking that if he could just pass through the glass, all his problems, all the impossible questions that demanded his constant attention would be erased forever.

"Jackson?"

Ignoring Suzanne, he stumbled back to the bed and fell on it. Blackest darkness swarmed over him, pulling him into a thick, swampy miasma where the nightmares crouched, waiting with broken fangs.

Suzanne sat on the bed beside Jackson, watching as the man's labored breathing finally evened out into regular exhalations. What had he been through? Gently, she traced the deep purple collar of bruises around his neck. Terrible things, she was sure. Did he hold any of it against her? But it was a worthless question because she thought she knew the answer to it.

More tears came to her eyes then, followed by racking, coughing sobs that seemed to come from her very center. Visions of spinning men and women being torn apart filled her head. Prague hadn't even touched her this deeply. The city had been at war, and violence was a medium she and Jackson had been forced to travel through. But this. This had been something else entirely.

And how much had Jackson seen of such things since they had parted a year ago?

Enough to rob him of the youthful and carefree look on his face that she had remembered so well.

Moving slowly, she slid away from the bed, holding back the emotion inside her that threatened to shatter her completely. How much of what he was going through was her fault? She had recruited him for Temporal Projects because she had liked the way he presented himself, the easy way he smiled. There had been a spark inside Jackson Dubchek that kindled something inside her when she met him. Something that had been missing from the infrequent affairs she had with men. But there had been no desire for Jackson then, just an urge to get to know him better. But there had been no time. The mission he had been sent on had been a rush operation, as everything connected to TP seemed to be. And, afterwards, all their lives had been changed by his experience.

She undressed in the small bathroom, washing her clothing out and hanging it on the shower rod to dry before stepping under the cleansing water herself. She luxuriated in the shower, drawing as much comfort from it as she could. She enjoyed the smell of the small cake of soap as she washed her face, relished the feel of the needle spray pelting into her face, making her body tingle all over. She found a tube of shampoo and used over half of it in the attempt to wash the dust from her hair, ignoring the guilty feelings that plagued her for squandering it.

As she showered, she closed off the emotions that tried to break out. She had to be strong. Like her father.

In control. If you were in control of yourself, you could be in control of the events that tried to drag you under. Jackson needed her to be strong right now. A help rather than a hindrance.

She had to be strong for her mother as well. While she had control of a time machine, she fully intended to go back to the 1960s in an attempt to find a drug that would ease her mother's pain. The research library she had immersed herself in had made much mention of the pharmacologically active era in old North American history. Surely there was something in that time frame that would help her mother. And, according to the 'ssetes she had searched through, Woodstock was just the place to find it.

A cry of trapped pain knifed through the hissing of the shower.

Suzanne recognized Jackson's voice immediately. She cut the water off and ran to the bed, grabbing at a towel but missing.

Jackson writhed on the bed, held prisoner by some memory. His face knotted in agony as he clutched the sheets in white-knuckled hands.

Leaning over him, Suzanne tried to restrain him, to bring him gently out of the nightmare. She was dimly aware that she was dripping water on him.

After a moment, Jackson opened his eyes and looked at her blankly, as if unsure where, or when, Suzanne supposed, he was. He relaxed, slumping weakly back into the comfort of the bed. Only when he looked at her body did she remember she was naked.

Embarrassed, she took her hands from her shoulders and started to move away, looking for something to put on.

"Suzanne." Jackson's fingers on her hip felt warm.

She turned back to face him. "You were having a nightmare," she explained.

Jackson's fingers dropped away.

She had felt the unwillingness in herself and Jackson to have the tactile connection broken. She saw the uncertainty in his eyes, felt the uncertainty echoed by the trembling of her own body. Wondering if she wasn't just making one more complication for herself and him, she placed a knee on the bed and leaned forward.

He caught her in eager arms and she could feel the ragged gasps of his breath darting across the back of her neck as he held her. She closed her eyes and gave herself over to the sensuality that swelled within her.

His hands moved under her, keeping her atop him, as if the pressure of her weight was a comfort. Warm fingers found her nipples, and she held herself up on her arms so he could use both hands. Warm lips nuzzled at her breast. Her own breath became hurried.

He touched her gently, in a loving exploration of all her body's secrets, forging their twin desires into something more than themselves.

Suzanne let herself go and fell onto him, pressing her lips against his, trying to free him of his clothes. Something hard pressed against the softness of her breasts, and she looked down to see the knife he had sheathed there.

Without saying anything, Jackson released the makeshift sheath and, unlike the clothing he had dropped carelessly to the floor, placed the knife between the mattress and boxsprings, as if afraid of being without the weapon.

Then they were both naked, sliding against each other as he rolled her over on her back and slid into her slowly. She felt him fill her up, stretch her into a bliss that she hadn't known for a long time. He moved against her, tentatively at first, then harder as the lust overcame the caution. He kissed her and hugged her fiercely. For the first time in months Suzanne felt safe and wanted, not even feeling strange that it would be in a hotel room so far removed from home that the return journey seemed impossible. The first climax seized her in strong, soft fingers and lifted her incredibly high, dashing her on the dulled reefs of ecstasy before sweeping her up again.

Suzanne woke, and the bed was empty in the room's darkness. For one panicked moment she thought Jackson had left her. Then she saw his silhouette against the lighter pane of the window. She lay still, watching him look out the window at the darkness of night beyond, wondering what thoughts raced through his head. The post-coital euphoria had left her feeling drained of the fear and uncertainty that had filled her after the assassination.

She sat up on the bed, arranging the sheet so it covered her.

"Did I wake you?" Jackson asked, turning from the window. He had pulled his pants on, Suzanne noticed. The moonlight slicing into the room softened his face, making him look more like the old Jackson she remembered.

"No."

"I tried not to."

"How long have you been up?"

"Not long."

Suzanne felt uncomfortable. It would have been so much easier to talk to him now if what happened this afternoon hadn't occurred. Now it sat there between them like an unshaped piece of clay, waiting for an acknowledgement to give it form and substance.

"I've got to try to go back, Suzanne," he said.

She wished she could see his face better, wished she knew what to tell him. A part of her wanted to abandon everything and everyone and simply stay here with him in this time. But it wouldn't be that easy. What they had shared this afternoon could have been nothing more than a weak moment for both of them. And she could not shirk her own responsibilities any more than Jackson could. She was too much her father's daughter. "I know."

"Time has been changed before," he said. "And it has been changed back to correct whatever mistakes were made. The Time Police did that in 2183 with the Persian ambassador. Maybe I can do that here. Yesterday."

"When are we going?"

He shook his head. "Not we, Suzanne. I can't accept the responsibility for you in this."

"It's not entirely your choice."

"Yes, it is."

"You can't stop me."

"Suzanne, please." His voice sounded tired.

She immediately felt sorry for challenging him.

"Don't make this any harder than it already is."

"What are you going to do?"

"I'm not sure. I walked downstairs earlier and got a paper, sat in the local tavern and listened to people talk. The assassination team disappeared without leaving a trace. Does that sound like anyone we know?"

"Time travelers."

"Either the Time Police or someone from one of our futures. But I've got to go back to see if something can be done."

"But if nothing was done the first time around, what makes you think your attempt will be successful?" Suzanne hugged her knees and tried to ignore the cold chill spilling down her naked back.

"Maybe I can make this past an alternate one that has no bearing on our present. Like the past I discovered back in Wheeling. Maybe it's already been done and we just haven't found our way into that timeline yet."

"Why can't we go together?"

"Because I want you clear of this thing, Suzanne. I care about you a lot. Maybe more than I realized. Maybe as much as I wanted to the first time I met you."

His words made her feel warm but the strings attached scared her. How many sides was she playing already? Double-crossing her father to help Jackson, trying to find help for her mother while keeping her addiction to Capricorn secret, trying to find some semblance of herself in the whole tangled mess. She felt that he wanted her to say something back, to acknowledge the reciprocity of feelings. But she couldn't. Not yet. Not until she could make other decisions that would allow her a wider freedom of choice.

The silence that stretched between them seemed oppressive, and Suzanne wished she knew the words to break it. Her voice was strained when she spoke. "When will you be leaving?"

"In the morning." His short answer told her that he had been expecting her to say something else. He went back to staring out the window, and Suzanne rolled over, seeking the sleep that would anesthetize the problems and the questions of loyalties that pulled at her with sharp teeth.

Jackson purchased a beat-up Volkswagen from a rotund teenager minding his father's car lot not far from the plaza. He gave generously of the money Paress Linnet had included in the package she had made for him and Suzanne.

The car had a transmission that the teenager had to explain to Jackson, but after a few minutes of playing with the clutch and accelerator, he got the hang of it. He followed the main roads out of Mexico City, conscious of the way he tried not to look at Suzanne, conscious, too, of the way she tried not to be caught looking at him.

Buddha, why does my life have to be so screwed up?

The lack of conversation between them made the trip back to the time machine seem like it lasted hours. The uneven power driving the small car only increased the illusion.

Images of Suzanne's naked body striving against his the way it had the previous afternoon played across the glare on the dusty windshield, shimmered in the morning heat waves. Had it only been a mutual need for comfort? Jackson asked himself. Or had it been something more? Perhaps those questions were only wishful thinking on his part, though. He had been comfortable with the idea of Chrys Calvino as a sometime sex partner. Why couldn't he fit Suzanne into those same parameters?

Because he didn't want to.

He gripped the chipped steering wheel more forcefully as he tried to channel his mind back to the highway and his chosen course of action. Was Suzanne right? Had he already made this trip once and found only death waiting?

"There." Suzanne's voice interrupted his reverie.

Jackson followed her pointing finger and saw the ridge where they had left the time machine. He pulled the Volkswagen to the side of the road, and they left it.

Desert heat sweltered around them as they moved

up the slight incline. Jackson's clothing became damp immediately and stuck to his body. The knife was a bar running down the left side of his ribcage.

As they had agreed over breakfast that morning in the hotel, Suzanne climbed into the time machine and strapped in. She powered up, setting the machine so it would replicate itself here for Jackson to use next.

As he watched her going through the routines of setting her destination, Jackson searched his heart and mind for some words to say that would soften the parting. He wanted to tell her that he would see her again. But he didn't know if he could if he wanted to, and wasn't sure if he wanted to. Seeing Suzanne meant taking the chance of seeing Friz Brelmer again, and Jackson wasn't sure if he would live through that experience.

He saw hesitation on her face, framed by the bulkiness of the crash helmet, but it was quickly covered by the mask bag she clipped into place.

Abruptly, the time machine seemed to shatter, filling the air with the scent of oranges and ammonia. It faded, then rebuilt itself in exactly the same spot.

Only now it was empty.

Jackson felt the loneliness surge inside him, amazed that the feeling could generate such power. Then he made his body function and opened the door of the time machine. He strapped himself in mechanically, knowing there was something he could have said to Suzanne before time swept her away and damning himself for not having the courage to say it. He hit the initiation switch and felt the machine yanked roughly into the uneven flow of the timestream, his brain shattering to dance wildly with rolling oranges, boiling coffee pots, and hundreds of images of Morris the Cat.

Chapter Twenty

The time machine shivered to an unsure halt and it was only after Jackson released his pent-up breath that he realized he wasn't sick. For a moment his mind played with the possibilities of that discovery. There had been another time he hadn't gotten the familiar nausea, but it was a struggle to remember when. So much had happened. The trip to 2205, he remembered. He hadn't gotten sick then. Why? Images of the dark- skinned female Tyson-yllyn rushed at him. Sex. That was the common factor between this trip and that one. Both times he had had sex within a twenty-four hour period before using the time machine. Could that be it? Maybe the increased amount of endorphins in the bloodstream was the trigger that held the nausea at bay.

For a moment Jackson felt like laughing, glorying in a discovery that not even TP had made, wondering if Suzanne had made the same connection. Then he noticed the complete darkness that surrounded him.

The irreverent joy that bouyed him up despite the desperation of his short jaunt back through time gave way to quiet panic.

He placed a hand on the crystel window and rubbed, thinking the darkness might be due to a film over the inside. His hand came away clean, and the darkness remained unmarred.

Had he somehow reappeared inside something? A foundation of one of the huge buildings that surrounded the plaza in Mexico City?

He slipped free of the restraining straps of the chair and shucked his helmet. He hit the toggle that opened the driver's door. Relief flooded through him when he saw and heard it unseal and unfold.

A cavern, he told himself as he stepped out of the time machine. The survival circuitry of the machine hadn't been damaged or somehow failed. He had traveled back into a small cave of some sort. He blinked, waiting for his night vision to clear as the luminous readouts faded from his eyes.

Gradually, his surroundings came into focus. Instead of rocky walls, he found the crushed bodies of automobiles and knew at once where he must be.

Wheeling.

Wheeling, West Virginia. In the junkyard.

And Wheeling, as he had already seen, was a hunting ground for Time Police forces of his present and more than one future. As well as for the two old men who owned the junkyard.

The time machine was sandwiched between the inner stacks of junk cars. A few inches either way and it would have fused with one of the metal corpses. But the circuitry had prevented that from happening.

State-of-the-art, Jackson could remember his instructor at Temporal Projects telling him with an unctuous smile. But the man had told him nothing of the Wheeling Loop or how the time machines often fell prey to that glitch in the system.

Reluctantly, already knowing what he would find, he returned to the time machine and inspected the power level, finding it too low to attempt another jump. The POES was out of the question at night. It would be morning before he could gather enough solar energy to make any attempt to shuttle forward to the past he wanted. For a moment he wondered if Suzanne was in the junkyard as well, stuck in another section. How large was the junkyard? He didn't know. Both times he had been there before he had been fleeing for his life.

Cautiously, he wormed his way through the stacks of broken and bent cars, seeing rats larger than his fists scurry away from him to fade into the darkness. He stepped carefully through the maze, aware that the old men who lived in the junkyard slept lightly, not wanting to accidently step on a rat the size of one of Wu Wing's cashew cats and have it swarm up his leg in an attempt to get away. He had seen a holo about rats as a boy that had left him shaking and scared for nights. Martin had made fun of him despite their mother's stern warnings.

Another turn brought him to a clearing that opened out onto one of the aisles of the junkyard. The red mud between the two masses of stacked cars was torn and stiff, scarred by the tires of some piece of heavy equipment.

He crouched at the opening, getting his bearings. No one appeared to be around. One end of the aisle swung back on itself and was lost in another maze of wreckage. The other end did the same, except that right at the bend there was a small shack. The pole next to the small building with the thick cable hanging down told Jackson that electricity was available there.

If he could find a way to make the connection.

A prickling sensation spread across his back as he left the protective shadows and trotted for the shack, tensed for the second someone would see him and start shouting.

The door was locked when he got there. He peered through the dusty window and saw shelves filled with parts, engine parts as well as body parts. Tools were scattered haphazardly around the small room, sitting on work tables or hanging from shelves. Tucked neatly under the corner of one table Jackson saw a rectangular red box on wheels with a handle that said Battery Charger. He wasn't sure exactly how to work the small machine, but knew from the way it was plugged into a nearby wall outlet that it could produce the 60-cycle power it took to charge the time machine.

He used the knife's heavy handle to shatter a small pane of glass in the door, surprised at the quiet way it tinkled to pieces then spilled silently to the ground. He reached inside and opened the door.

How far was it to the time machine?

The cord that came with the battery charger looked to be only fifty meters long. It would never be enough. Come on, come on, he urged himself as he began to search through the dirty and crooked cabinets of the shack. Buddha, help me. I can't get this close and fail.

A lower cabinet yielded coils of extension cord in hundred-meter lengths. Or close to it. Jackson thought North America, or parts of it, was still using the English measurements at this time. He removed two coils of the least frayed cord and moved off with the battery charger after plugging one extension cord into the outlet.

He moved slowly, trundling the small machine before him as he paid out the extension cord behind him, making sure it slithered into the shadows so it wouldn't be noticeable on the ground.

Just before he reached the aisle that led to the time machine, the first cord ended. He stopped a moment to hook the other one up, then continued.

The creaking of crickets sounded under the black hulks of the cars almost loud enough to interfere with his hearing. He froze as lights swept through the cracks between the wrecks, hoping the momentary flicker wouldn't be enough to reveal his position. When the light moved away from him, he sank back against the wall of ragged metal, feeling the talons of adrenaline thrill through him.

A rattling and squeaking vehicle veered into the aisle where the shack was. Jackson tracked it through the infrequent spaces in the wall of cars, watching it bounce and waver as it traveled over the red mud ruts. With a final clatter and an ear-piercing backfire, the vehicle's motor lapsed into silence. The lights winked out seconds later.

Jackson was moving again before he heard the truck's door open. Fratcher and the other man? Or possibly someone else looking for something salvageable from one of the wrecks. The vinyl-encased cord slid through his hand as he herded the battery charger on. What if the extension cord wasn't long enough? Uncertainty gnawed at him until the time machine came into view and he saw that he still had a few meters of extension cord slung over his shoulder.

Kneeling quickly, he placed his hand on the ident

plate near the external power port and waited for the time machine to identify him. Then the power port flowered open to allow him access, sparks of dulled blue energy cycling around the opening that let him know the security system was still operational. Anyone else attempting to tamper with the power plant would be summarily repulsed.

Jackson attached the clips of the battery charger to the power plant, knowing it wouldn't matter which clip went where as long as the energy cycle was completed. He opened the lid of the charger and read the almost indecipherable instructions with the help of a small hand torch cached in the power plant hull. He moved the selector toggle to QUICK CHARGE, hoping to get the time machine's power up in only a few minutes instead of hours.

Wisps of voices drifted into the hollow where the time machine lodged, broken conversations he could make no sense of. Crickets still chirped. His pulse beat in his ears. The only thing missing was the hum of activity from the charger.

Thinking the charger might be cycling at a decibel level too low for normal hearing, he touched the machine's outer hull, expecting to feel the operational vibration. It remained still and cold to his touch.

Exasperated, he tripped the toggle several times, to no avail. He used the hand torch to check the indicator built into the face of the charger. The needle remained in the off position, which Jackson assumed meant it wasn't getting the power it needed.

Men's voices rebounded from the stacked cars, echoing hollowly in the empty metallic bellies.

Wiping perspiration from his face with a shirt sleeve,

Jackson picked up the extension cord and began running it through his fingers, feeling for a cut or broken place where the wires weren't connected. He kept the hand torch off and stumbled through the darkness, waiting for the bite of electricity that he was sure he would feel if he accidently grounded the naked wires.

He reached the aisle without finding anything and knelt in the shadows, trying to find the men who had arrived in the ancient pickup. He could still hear their voices, more distant now, unhurried. Apparently they hadn't noticed the forced entry on the shack.

With his heart in his throat, Jackson left the security of the darkness and continued checking the extension cord.

He saw the reason for the power failure before he got to it. In the shadow left by the pickup, he could barely discern the unplugged ends of the extension cords. Had they come apart when he shifted shoulders with the second cord? Or had the driver accidently unplugged them when he got out of the pickup?

He dropped to his knees and picked up the loose ends, jamming them together and hoping it would kick the charger into operation. Just as he levered himself to his feet, a man's voice came from directly in front of him, on the other side of the pickup. Light sped dizzily across the hard-packed ground, falling momentarily across his fingers.

Grunting silently with the effort, Jackson spun and tried to flee, catching his foot in one of the petrified ruts and falling headlong.

"What the hell was that?" a man's voice asked.

Jackson scrambled up, staying in a half-crouch as he searched for somewhere to hide. How long would it take for the time machine to charge on the setting he selected? Surely no longer than minutes. But first he would have to reach it. And Fratcher and his partner showed no compunctions about using the shotguns they carried.

"I didn't hear nothing, Billy."

"Well, I sure as hell did."

Glancing beneath the undercarriage of the pickup, Jackson saw a pair of booted feet crunch around the front of the vehicle. He knew he could never reach the time machine's hiding place without being seen. And once that happened, discovery of the extension cords would follow within minutes. Sure, he would be safe from harm inside the time machine, but without power he would be trapped there. Fratcher and his companion, or the two unknown men who owned the pickup, would be able to starve him out.

If some of the Time Police contingent didn't find him first and figure out a way to circumvent the time machine's security system.

Moving quickly, Jackson lifted the tarp covering the rear section of the pickup and climbed under, holding his breath.

"Do you see anything, Billy?"

"No."

"Neither do I, so let's go grab a beer at the Red Dog and go home."

"There was something here, I'm telling you."

"It was probably the rats. Lordy, did you see how big some of them sumbitches were?"

"Yeah, maybe."

The footsteps halted at the end of the pickup bed, and Jackson had to force himself not to look. Then they faded away again. A shrill screech signaled the opening of the doors, and he felt the pickup shift under the settling weight of the two men. The engine popped and stuttered as it caught life. The drive train whined loudly as it took off in reverse, working back the way it came.

When the pickup came to a stop to reverse directions, Jackson got ready to throw a leg out from under the tarp and run for the security of the smashed vehicles. He stopped immediately when he recognized Fratcher's voice.

"Billy."

"Yeah, Mr. Fratcher?"

"Did you find that condenser?"

"Sure did, Mr. Fratcher. Daddy will be by first thing in the morning to pay you for it."

Trapped, with no way to leave the pickup without being seen, Jackson waited in the darkness as the vehicle gathered speed, taking him away from the junkyard. Taking him away from the time machine. How far would the two men go before stopping? How would he find his way back? The bed of the pickup hammered at him in tandem with the questions as the vehicle bounced across the rough road.

Chapter Twenty-One

"Colonel Brelmer."

The hushed call for attention turned Brelmer's thoughts from the carnage in the plaza. "Report, Corporal."

The man took another step forward till he was at Brelmer's side. "There's no sign of Jackson or your daughter, sir."

"You've checked all the motels?"

"Most of them, sir. The rest of the squad has sealed off the perimeters so they won't be able to leave the city without being spotted."

Brelmer fixed the younger man with a glare. "You mean if they don't use the time machine, Corporal? Or haven't used it already?"

The tips of the Time Policeman's pointed ears reddened.

"Keep searching, Corporal, and let me know the minute you find anything."

"Alabama, Colonel."

Brelmer watched the corporal expertly fade into the large crowd gathered around the assassination scene at the fountain, then turned his attention back to the victims. Loud wails still swelled from the crowd, echoed at a greater diatonic range by the sirens of the emergency vehicles clustered in the plaza. Even as he watched, another ambulance moved slowly through the mob of grief-stricken people.

Conscious of the stare one of the uniformed local law enforcement officers was giving him and knowing it was because of his lack of mobility and the look of dispassion on his face, Brelmer put his hands in the pockets of his pants and turned away.

Where the hell was Suzanne? Why had she brought Jackson back to this time?

Bits and pieces of emotion-charged Spanish threaded into his thinking, but did not bring comprehension with them. It was easy to see what had happened. But why? Was Jackson somehow involved?

He could see no other answers. According to a list Laszlo Slye had retrieved from a future rebel while on a mission in the past, Jackson Dubchek headed a number of people who made visits to the past in efforts to change things. Which was why the decision was made to dump Jackson in 2183 after he was first contracted to do the interpretation of the Persian ambassador's speech.

Despite the lighter-weight cloth his imitation 2074 costume was made of, Brelmer was still hot. Heat spread across his shoulders and made his shirt stick to his body under the hooded poncho. He kept the hood up as well, which increased the heat containment that was making him uncomfortable, but it also served to keep the sun from blistering his bare skull. The poncho gave him places to secrete various bits of equipment for information gathering as well as personal protection. The Matthews he had holstered across his chest felt reassuring and made the burden of the temperature easier to bear.

He followed the outer edges of the crowd, watching everything but making sure he didn't draw anyone's attention.

His immediate impulse was to travel back to a time just before the assassination, and intercept Jackson and Suzanne. But according to the information at TP, the assassination was something that was supposed to have happened. If he and his team of Time Police stopped Jackson from doing something he was supposed to do, what would happen as a result? No, the chances were too great to risk that. Not until he knew more about this presentpast situation.

Taking a small earphone from a specially sewn pocket inside the poncho, Brelmer inserted it into his ear and scanned the reports his troops were turning in. The dull dialogues and flat, monosyllabic answers occupied the conscious part of his mind and allowed the subconscious free rein.

He crossed the street behind the fountain, scanning the long scars that decorated the huge pillars of the buildings. Jackson could not have done this by himself. There was simply too much carnage, too much death.

Reaching the other side of the street, he watched the swirl of people around the fountain shift patterns till there were smaller swirls inside the larger whole. He wiped perspiration from his forehead before it dropped on any of the microcircuitry woven into the poncho. Most of it would be safe from heat and cold and moisture, but the openings for speaking and hearing allowed weaknesses in their systems.

If Jackson had help in killing these people, though,

why had he needed to get Suzanne involved? As a hostage? But couldn't the man see they had gotten away cleanly?

Except that Jackson knew as well as he did that Brelmer could navigate time till he arrived just as the assassination took place.

Was that where he would find Suzanne then? In the past, under a gun held by Jackson Dubchek?

Brelmer stroked his bearded chin, using the habit to bring his panicky thoughts under control. Nothing would happen to Suzanne. He would not allow it. Even if it meant warping his own time to go back and destroy Jackson Dubchek in infancy. No matter what the consequences of the act.

What use would Suzanne be to Jackson now? If he had her in the past, couldn't Jackson see that she could be released now? Suzanne would remain in the past event forever for Jackson to hold as a protective charm. Time had placed her there through Jackson's hands. Even if Brelmer returned home and found Suzanne safe in her apartment, didn't Jackson know that if Brelmer interfered in the assassination Jackson had so callously initiated or helped with, Jackson could still kill Suzanne? She would exist there indefinitely unless Brelmer found a way to free her.

Lifting the flap of the poncho where the microphone was hidden, Brelmer said, "Jameson."

The channel cleared of the extraneous chatter immediately. "Yes, sir?" Jameson's voice said in Brelmer's ear.

"Has Lanigan finished his interview with the local chief of police?"

"No, sir."

"When he does, I want you to patch Lanigan through to me at once."

"Alabama, Colonel."

Brelmer heard Sgt. Jameson's harsh authority crackle across the microwave frequency, issuing commands with alacrity. Apparently no one had thought their colonel would be interested in what they were doing. Only in results.

Possibilities presented themselves in staggering numbers to Brelmer. None of them were appealing. And none of them presented an immediate solution. With time at his beck and call, Brelmer knew he could jump back to any point in Jackson's past and kill the man before he ever got Suzanne involved in this. But . . . what would he change in a time so close to the present? Something so close to Now?

It was a contradiction to the theories Brelmer had advanced himself: that the far past could be changed in ways that would alter his present, yet not drastically so; that the immediate past was to be left strictly alone because the potential for change was much greater. The centuries between alterations would act as a buffer zone as long as nothing major was changed. Like someone infiltrating the Manhattan Project in the old United States and setting off one of the atomic bombs the scientists were working on.

Brelmer had seen gaps in security like that early in his association with Temporal Projects, and had taken steps to make sure installations like that were closely guarded by the Time Police. At the first sign of trouble, and there had been some, troops were deployed into the field. There had been two attempts on NATO countries in the 1990s by bands of future rebels, which had ended in failure because of Brelmer's tactics.

Brelmer watched a pair of uniformed men pull another body from the fountain, stirring the stained water as it came free. No, interference with the immediate past would be out unless as a last resort. Provided someone could find out where Jackson had spent the last year.

The stand-off Jackson had engineered would be played out in the past. This immediate past.

"Colonel?"

"Yes, Lanigan?"

"Wasn't much I could find out from the local guy, sir."

"He believed the credentials Paress fabricated for you."

"Yes, sir. No problem with that. But this guy didn't know nothing. Nobody saw anything, nobody heard anything. Until the body count started going up around here. He said his men covered the plaza and couldn't find a damn thing. Even with the helicopter team they had in the air only minutes after the shooting started."

"They should have had the helicopters already in the air."

"Yes, sir."

"Jameson?"

"Yes Colonel?"

"You looked at the research concerning this period of history?"

"Yes, sir, right before we left, sir."

"And according to our records this assassination took place?"

"Yes, sir."

"Stand ready to receive your orders, Sergeant, and relay them on to your troops."

"Ready, sir."

"We are going to make the trip back to only a few hours ago in an attempt to arrange my daughter's rescue and remove Jackson Dubchek from the world of the living. We are in no other way going to hamper the assassination. Is that clear, Jameson?"

"Yes, sir."

"Move your troops out slowly, Sergeant, so we attract no undue attention. No travel will be made through the machines until we are all present and accounted for at the target site."

"Alabama, Colonel."

Brelmer switched off and took the earphone out. He gazed at the bodies being lined up on the plaza floor, saw the tortured features Death had imprinted on them, saw the shattered bone gleaming white in the desert sun. Desperately, he grabbed for the inner control that had always been there for him when he needed it. Would Suzanne's body be there the next time this event looped through itself? Or was that why his men could find no sign of her or Jackson? Because he had gone back and succeeded?

He didn't know. For the first time in his whole, carefully organized life, Praetor Centurion Lieutenant Colonel Friz Brelmer wished for an omen that would show him he was doing the right thing. But he could not find one in the bloodied waters of the fountain, nor on the faces of the newly dead or the grieving.

Reluctantly, he moved out of the plaza area, on to an uncertain future in the past.

Flower power. Make love not war. The times they are a'changin'. The Age of Aquarius. Antiestablishment.

Communal living. Free Love Generation. LSD. Grass. The Hog Farmers. Woodstock.

Disjointed thoughts, memories, swam through Suzanne's head as the time machine piroutted down the years to 1969. There had been quite a lot on the three-day event that had taken place in August of that year. Suzanne had been amazed at the bulk of literature and references the name Woodstock had been linked with. She had even watched the Warner Brothers film in an attempt to understand everything that had gone on during the festival.

Newspapers of the time had yielded little real information. Some of them, whose names Suzanne recognized from her own history studies in college, had described the Woodstock happening as an event that went against everything that the United States had stood for. Other periodicals had praised it for being everything the country had been founded on. Free speech, life, liberty, the pursuit of happiness.

One of the main themes, though, that had been written about the festival was the presence of drugs.

And that was what interested Suzanne most.

Somewhere in that maze of barbiturates, uppers, downers, and mind-expanding drugs, there had to be something that would help her mother. Suzanne was determined to find it, then drop back in on Mexico City 2074 to help Jackson. He may have thought he had gotten rid of her, but that only saved an argument at a time when their feelings were already mixed up.

Memories of the way Jackson had held her and kissed her enveloped her, making her wish they had never parted during the night. But they were both too much their own persons. She wouldn't try to delude herself into thinking anything other than that.

Without warning, the time machine became weightless, then the bottom fell away.

Suzanne waited for the usual nausea to burn its way into her throat and was surprised when it didn't.

The crystel window cleared in front of her as gravity snugged her comfortably into the seat again, exposing her to a panorama of color. Trees filled the horizon, vying with the blue of the sky for space. Lower, below the branches of the big tree nearest her, a handful of people sat on blankets staring at her.

Without taking her eyes from the onlookers, Suzanne keyed up the exterior auditory receptors.

A young man with braided long hair hanging down his back and wearing only cut-off jeans took a hand-rolled cigarette from an even younger girl that Suzanne assumed was dressed in the mode of Indians of an earlier day.

"Man, I told you, didn't I, man? Told you people from everywhere was coming to this scene, man." The young man with braided hair took a hit from the cigarette and coughed.

"Far out, man," the other young male on the blanket said. He took the cigarette when it was offered.

The remaining two girls watched Suzanne in blank-faced attention. One wore a fringed bikini and calf-high moccasins that were a pale imitation of the first girl's Amerind dress. The other girl had her red hair tied back and wore only jeans and a psychedelic halter top.

Marshalling her courage, Suzanne hit the toggle that opened the door of the time machine. She closed it behind her and set the security system. Evidently her sudden appearance in the middle of the music festival wasn't startling. Judging from the first man's words, she may have even been expected. Or at least someone was.

The time machine didn't really look out of place in the row of vehicles where it had settled. The cars were of various shapes and sizes, some single-colored and some bearing multiple hues. The thing that seemed to be most noticeable was the old bus only a little further back in the surrounding trees. Psychedelic waves of lemon yellow, pea green, sky blue, cardinal red, and cotton white flowed across the metal skin of the bus, each line of color alternately thinning and fattening as the design flowed from one end to the other.

Suzanne approached the five young people as they continued to share the ill-smelling cigarette. She knelt and gave them a smile designed to show her peaceful intentions.

"Where'd you come from, beautiful?" the man with braided hair asked. He wore a small smirk beneath the dulled blue eyes.

Beside him, the girl in the Indian clothing shifted subtly, drawing away from the man's side. Her dark eyes flashed angrily at Suzanne.

"Springfield," Suzanne answered.

"All the girls in Springfield as pretty as you?" the man asked.

Suzanne flushed. This wasn't what she had expected. According to the resources she had read, the event at Woodstock had been filled with parties, orgies, and drugs. Somehow she hadn't pictured people like the five before her as being connected. They were young, still impressionable, still searching for themselves. She felt disappointed because she didn't see how they could help her.

"Jake," the girl beside the man said warningly. She placed a hand on the man's shoulder and Suzanne could see the girl's nails bite into the bronzed flesh.

Jake ignored her, shrugged away as he leaned forward to extend the cigarette to Suzanne. "Take a hit, beautiful girl, and become one of the ranks of beautiful dreamers around you. The next show won't begin till later today. We're just mellowing out till the music starts. Dig?"

"What day is this?" Suzanne asked as she accepted the cigarette. She puffed on it, feeling the harsh smoke scratch at her throat, coughing uncontrollably for a moment when it constricted her lungs.

Jake laughed and all but the one girl joined in.

"Take it easy, baby," Jake said. "There's plenty more where that came from. They're giving it away around here. Got more grass here at this scene than they do food." He laughed again. "I'd rather be stoned than starving."

"She wants to know what day this is," the other male reminded Jake.

"August 16," Jake answered.

"1969?" Suzanne asked.

The group laughed again. "You must have been doing some serious partying, baby. What's your name?" Jake asked.

"Suzanne."

"Well, Suzanne, I'm Jake. This here's Bobby. The redhead is Michelle. This is Angie. And the Indian princess is LaDawna."

Suzanne tried to hand the cigarette back but Jake waved it away.

"Try it again," Jake insisted.

Suzanne put the cigarette to her lips and inhaled slowly.

"Now," Jake said, "hold it inside and close your eyes. That's right. Hold it as long as you can. Now, let it out through your nose. Slower. Slower. Let it last as long as it can. Yeah. How are you feeling now?''

"Fine," Suzanne said, surprised to hear the strain in her voice. It felt like someone had loosened the hinges holding the top of her head on. Was this something her mother could use, one part of her mind wondered, while at the same time she asked herself how dangerous the narcotic was.

"What are you doing here?" LaDawna asked.

Suzanne could tell the girl's voice was carefully modulated to produce a sultry rasp. She decided to be honest. She had nothing to fear from these people. They hadn't been surprised to see her materialize from nowhere, nor had they appeared to be hiding the drug they were smoking. "I'm looking for drugs."

"Baby." Jake's voice had softened, and a hard gleam filled his eyes, the effects of the drug making them look like the crystal eyes of the Time Police. "You just said the wrong thing."

Suzanne tried to get to her feet, but Jake's hand flashed out and captured her wrist. She twisted and tried to get free, but Michele and Angie grabbed her legs. She was thrown violently backwards, and Bobby darted around her to hold her by her shoulders.

Jake pressed his face into hers. "What kind of narc are you, bitch?" the man screamed. "Didn't they even teach you in narc school that you don't say drugs? It's mary jane, weed, marijuana, yellowjackets, acid, H. Not *drugs*." He reached behind his back.

Freeing a leg, Suzanne lashed out, smashing her knee into the side of Jake's face. Before she could move again, LaDawna had seized the free leg and anchored it to the ground. Her heart hammered inside her chest as she arched her back to find some leverage she could use.

Jake wiped at the trickle of blood leaking from his nose. He reached behind his back again brought his hand back around.

Suzanne saw the small iron bar in his hand, heard a metallic snik, and tried to get away from the double-edged blade that licked into view.

"I knew she was trouble the minute I seen her, Jake," LaDawna said.

"Yeah, well, I was stoned, what can I say." Jake leaned forward, touching the knife to Suzanne's throat. "I'll make up for it now."

Suzanne could feel the throb of her pulse beat against the sharp edge of the knife.

Chapter Twenty-Two

Long minutes passed while Jackson waited under the tarp in the pickup. Voices passed around him, sometimes loud and raucous, sometimes low and passionate. Had someone found the time machine? Where was he? He stretched under the tarp, trying in vain to loosen kinked back muscles.

Lifting a corner of the canvas material, he eased out of the pickup, wondering how he was going to find his way back to the junkyard.

The truck was parked in the graveled lot of a small tavern. The winking neon lights advertising BUDW IS R flickered in uncertain pink in the corner of a window where handmade curtains hung. A highway ran in front of the bar, leading to a residential area a little further inland. A dim shape Jackson identified as a suspension bridge connected with the highway back the way the pickup had come from.

How was he going to get back?

And back to where?

Before he did anything he was going to have to figure out where the junkyard was. He had tried counting the turns and remembering to reverse their direction on the way back but had quickly become confused. The area was hilly and filled with twisting roads that may or may not have had as many turns in them as he had figured.

A vid, he told himself as he turned toward the bar. He had to find a vid. Public Information would give him the junkyard's address.

Loud music met him at the door with an almost physical presence. Smoke stung his eyes as he walked in and he could see it hanging in layers under the low-hung, low-wattage bulbs that illuminated the small room. The bar occupied one corner. A fat bartender with a big cigar stood behind the chipped plywood counter cleaning shot glasses. The cigar bisected the man's round face for a moment as he took another drag from it.

Jackson lowered his gaze and headed for the vid in the back, passing the dozen or so patrons scattered among the tables set closely together. To his left the jukebox glowed in the semi- gloom of the bar as it beat out a crescendo of ancient rock-n- roll. There was no mistaking the singer's voice, though, nor the timelessness of Elvis Presley's "Heartbreak Hotel."

For a moment he was puzzled by the vid. It had a hand-held receiver that he was not accustomed to, and seemed to demand money rather than a Fedcredit ident. He squinted against the dimness of the room and made out the instructions. It took a dime to operate the vid. He didn't know what a dime was. Damnit, he could conjugate verbs in several different languages, living and dead. Ancient monies were not a forte of a linguist. Spying the slot at the top of the vid, he rummaged in his pocket till he found one of the small coins he had gotten in change when he paid for the motel room in 2074. He dropped it into the vid and a connection hummed to life in his ear.

Turning around, Jackson put his back to the wall so he could watch the other people in the bar. No one seemed to be paying him any undue interest. Two of the men at the tables had to be the ones who owned the pickup but he was at a loss as to who it might be.

"Wheeling operator. May I help you," a woman's nasal voice said into his ear.

"Yes. I need some information."

"Yes, sir."

"I need to know where the junkyard is."

"What junkyard, sir?"

"Fratcher's junkyard."

"Hold on just one moment, sir."

Jackson could hear pages being flipped. It was so strange communicating on this vid. He was so accustomed to being able to see the person he was speaking to. Even if you caught someone in the shower, the vid had built-in circuitry to generate a computer-image of the person so it seemed like you were facing them. He watched the pool table on the other side of the jukebox. A lone figure played the game, dressed in black leather with silver studs. No one else in the bar seemed to acknowledge the man.

"Here we are, sir, Fratcher's Salvage." She gave him the number.

"No, wait," Jackson started to say, but the connection was broken before the woman heard him. He checked through his coins again but found nothing small enough to fit the vid. Feeling eyes on him as he recrossed the floor, conscious of the dirt-stained white suit Paress Linnet had chosen for him to wear in Mexico City over a hundred years in the future. He paused at the counter until the fat bartender decided to notice him.

"Something to drink?" the bartender asked in a gruff voice.

Jackson shook his head. "Some information, please. I need to know how to get from here to Fratcher's Salvage."

"What you want there?" the bartender asked.

"My vehicle broke down. I'm hoping to find a replacement part."

"This time of night?"

Jackson nodded.

"You go out there this time of night and old man Fratcher would sooner shoot you than look at you."

"I'll take my chances."

"You damn sure will if you go out there," the bartender agreed. He finished polishing the last glass he was working on and leaned across the counter. "Take the old bridge across to Market, then go north till you cross the railroad tracks. Fratcher's old place sits on the east side."

"Thanks." Returning to the back of the bar, Jackson let himself into the bathroom, intending to relieve himself and get a drink of water. The small coin might have worked in the vid, but there was no way he could convince anyone in this sleepy little town to take any of the paper money he carried.

A trough lined the floor on one side but Jackson disregarded it, choosing a stall instead for the protection it offered. He was just zipping his pants when he heard the door open. A giant, distorted shadow fell across the stall as someone stepped in front of the small bulb hanging on the wall.

There was quietness in the room when the door

closed. He knew someone was in the bathroom with him. He could feel it. Just as he could sense that whoever it was didn't want him to know he wasn't alone.

Slipping the latch on the stall, Jackson opened the door and peered out, seeing the leather-clad man who had been at the pool table.

"Come out of the stall, Jackson," the man ordered. He lifted his right arm to show the pistol he was holding. With his other hand, he swept the dark sunglasses from his face, revealing the crystal eyes of a Time Policeman.

"Let her go, Jake."

Suzanne kept her eyes on Jake's face, waiting to feel the bite of the knife.

"Stay out of this, Rodor. This bitch is a narc."

"She is with me, Jake," the calm male voice assured.

"She can't be with you, Rodor, she don't know a damn thing about any of us. Don't know nothing."

"Jake, if you don't get away from her this instant, I'm going to kill you."

Jake looked up, his face knotted with rage.

Suzanne felt some of the others moving away, freeing her arms. Still, she remained stationary, not wanting to startle Jake into killing her. She wanted to see who Rodor was but didn't dare take her eyes off the man holding her.

"Come on, Jake," Bobby said from somewhere to Suzanne's left. "Come on, man. Rodor means it, man. Jake, you know what Rodor can do. Man, don't be fucking around with this guy. You're going to get us all killed, man."

Slowly, Jake lifted the knife from her throat. Suzanne's lungs burned for oxygen but she breathed slowly, fighting his crushing weight across her chest. She closed her eyes when Jake moved away from her, taking deep, full breaths in order to ease the trembling that raced through her body.

A man knelt beside her, a reassuring smile on the handsome face. Suzanne let him help her to her feet, leaned on him for the support he offered. The man was dressed in blue jeans and a sleeveless sweat shirt daubed in psychedelic colors. His long golden hair framed his face, only a couple of shades darker than the mustache and full beard.

"I didn't know, Rodor," Jake said apologetically.

"Know now, Jake," Rodor said. "This woman is with me."

Jake nodded.

Rodor took a clear bag of powder from under the sweat shirt and threw it to Jake. "Party's on me, man. Peace."

Jake smiled like a kid with a new toy. "Alright, brothers and sisters, gather round." He looked at Rodor. "You and your lady want to join us, man?"

Rodor shook his head. "Later, man." He guided Suzanne away from the group, angling down the small hill. "How are you doing?"

"A lot better now."

"Your first time to the concert?" Rodor asked.

Suzanne nodded. "I wasn't expecting something like this, though." Something was wrong with what the man had said, but she couldn't put her finger on it.

He smiled at her and she decided she liked the expression. He seemed like he smiled easily and often. The hazel eyes blazed brightly under the shaggy eyebrows.

She let him lead her to a small silver camper a little over a hundred yards from her original jump spot.

"The fesitival isn't really like what you just saw," Rodor said as he unfolded an aluminum chair for her to sit in. He opened another for himself. "There are a lot of paranoid people here, though, and it doesn't take much to set them off. But overall, the feeling here is an expression of love and oneness." He spread his arms to encompass everything. "You'll never find another time like this one no matter how hard you search."

"Your name is Rodor?" Suzanne asked.

The man grinned. "Today it is. Maybe tomorrow it will be something else. Would you like something to drink? I've got several different beers on board as well as a number of liquors."

"And drugs?"

"And drugs. Bennies, black mollies, dream dust, coke, hash, white horse, and some things that haven't even been invented yet. These people around us have never even heard of crack."

Pieces started falling into place in Suzanne's mind. Things that haven't been invented yet. You'll never find another time like this. Your first time at the concert. But there was no first time, Suzanne told herself, because there was no second time. She watched Rodor thumbprint his way into the silver camper. On board? That was a nautical term. Why use it concerning the camper? And thumbprint locks, like the security system used to protect the time machines from unauthorized personnel, had not been invented in this decade. It had happened much later.

"What is your name?" Rodor asked as he returned with two glasses and a bottle of wine.

Suzanne turned the cold bottle over in her hands when he gave it to her to hold while he searched for a corkscrew. The information on the label told her it was a 1975 Gold Medal winner in its division. "Suzanne," she said dully.

"Well, Suzanne," he said when he turned back around. He popped the cork and poured. He gave her that dazzling smile again as he handed her a glass. "To us then, Suzanne, and to the moment. Griphra knows there are a lot of them. Especially for people like us who can search out and seize each moment over and over again." His hazel eyes twinkled. "So tell me, Suzanne, when are you from?"

Jackson looked down the barrel of the mini-Matthews, knowing he had crossed the path of one of the contingent of Time Police nestled in Wheeling, West Virginia. And the man had known him. Obviously Brelmer had already alerted the men about him. But was it from the latest foray into the business of Temporal Projects or from the first time?

The knife was a solid weight against his chest, but he knew he could never reach it before the Time Policeman ripped him in two with a burst of automatic fire. The thought of stabbing the man without warning almost made him sick. His mind already had far too many images to play with.

"Get out of the stall, Jackson," the Time Policeman ordered.

Taking a step forward, Jackson noticed that the man stepped back quickly. As if he was afraid of him. Why? Had he seen the knife? No. If he had, the man would have made him get rid of it. It wasn't that. Something else then. But what?

"We're going outside," the Time Policeman said, "and we're going to wait for my commanding officer to arrive."

"Why wait?" Jackson asked. "Why not kill me here?"

For a moment he thought the man might do it, as anger fired through the crystal eyes in a ruby flare of emotion. Then just as suddenly the man lowered the Matthews again, centering the pistol on Jackson's abdomen again.

The loop. The Wheeling Loop. Jackson turned it over and over in his mind. The Wheeling Loop.

"Move, Jackson."

Ignoring the command, Jackson stood his ground, waiting to see what the man would do. The Wheeling Loop. The time machines dumped a lot of people here without a warning of any sort. Why would the Time Policeman hesitate over killing him here?

The Time Policeman took a step forward, a tall and broad menace armored in black leather.

Why hadn't the man simply shot him? Jackson knew what Brelmer's orders concerning him had been.

"Move or I'll carry you out of here," the man said. The dim light gleamed from the dark barrel of the Matthews, cascaded hotly from the crystal eyes.

The Wheeling Loop. It had to be the reason. Why? Because the Time Police stationed there acted under relayed orders, not because they were pursuing an on-going mission. They were stranded in Wheeling, in the years 1968 and 1969. To direct traffic. Traffic being the people that were periodically dumped there. What happened to those people that were caught? Someone had to assess their present status, Jackson reasoned. What if the person was someone who needed to get on to the next jump site in one piece?

Jackson dropped his hands to his sides and laughed

at the irony of it all. Of all places the time machine would take him, he was probably most safe in Wheeling, West Virginia. Under the confusing spell of the Wheeling Loop.

"Get your damned hands back up, you little sonofabitch," the Time Policeman growled as he wrapped both hands around the butt of his weapon.

"You can't shoot me," Jackson said as the full realization of the time trap hit him. "You don't know when I'm from. If you kill me too early, your present will change if I have done something to affect it. And there is no telling when anyone is from in Wheeling."

There was the slightest hesitation in the Time Policeman's movements, a fractional dropping of the pistol muzzle.

Then Jackson turned and fled, conscious that he might be proven wrong at any moment if the bullets ripped into his back and burst through his chest. He hit the door with outstretched palms and almost ripped it from its hinges. He heard a cry of pain from the Time Policeman, then a crash as the man's heavy body hit the wooden floor.

Jackson ran.

Past the bar and the fat bartender. Past the group of men clustered around the tables. His breath screamed into his lungs till they seemed to reach the exploding point. Then he was in the graveled parking area with the clumping of the Time Policeman's heavy boots thundering in his ears.

His feet slipped out from under him as he tried to cut back around the building too quick. He bruised his elbows and palms on the sharp rocks. Rolling to his feet, he ran for the cloistered darkness waiting behind the tavern.

He paused at the corner of the building when he realized the Time Policeman was no longer pursuing him. It couldn't be that easy to escape.

The sound of an engine ripped through the still night. It rumbled low, then gained in intensity. A bright light circled around the tavern from the opposite side and Jackson saw the Time Policeman swing his motorcycle toward him, pinning him against the wall with the beam.

Jackson dove away at the last moment as the heavy machine sliced through the spot where he had just been standing. He got to his feet before the man could bring the motorcycle around, hearing gravel pop and spit from the spinning tire. He dodged between the parked cars, trying to keep as many obstacles between himself and his pursuer as he could, searching hopefully in each vehicle for some method of escape.

As the motorcycle roared at him again, Jackson dodged between the pickup he had arrived in and a small car that bore the name Mustang. Bullets from the Matthews nipped at his legs for a flesh wound, every fourth round a green tracer. The back glass of the small car shattered and spilled out. Ducking down behind the Mustang, Jackson glanced inside, saw the keys hanging from the ignition.

Without hesitation, he dove inside the car, swiveling around painfully to fit himself behind the steering column. The controls weren't much different from the Volkswagen he had learned to drive . . . earlier whenever. Beneath the hood, the small car's engine shivered to life.

Shifting it into gear, Jackson pressed the accelerator to the floor and released the clutch. The rear tires spun crazily in a desperate grab for traction. He saw the motorcycle approach again, coming head-on this time, made unreal by the swinging fuzzy dice that hung from the rearview mirror.

Then the Mustang shot forward, plunging toward the motorcycle.

For a moment Jackson was sure his borrowed car and the motorcycle were going to collide. Then he was by, watching the Time Policeman spill from the machine.

He shifted again and felt the Mustang respond with renewed vigor. Once on the highway, he slid in front of oncoming traffic, wanting to put as much distance between himself and the Time Policeman as he could. He glanced in the rearview mirror as he sped toward the suspension bridge. Market. The bartender said turn north on Market. What the hell was north?

He clutched the steering wheel tightly, watching the overhead structure of the bridge loom into sight. Had the Time Policeman called for back-up? Were more men already heading toward him?

A single light glared into his rearview mirror, and Jackson knew immediately who it was, amazed at the way the motorcycle seemed to eat up the distance separating them. Seeing no one in the oncoming lane, he manuvered the Mustang into the center of the road, grimly aware that the motorcycle could still edge through on either side.

Even over the whining shrill of the car's engine he could hear the approach of the motorcycle. The Time Policeman's face was stained red by his taillights. Then the man was no longer behind, was coming alongside instead.

Dark waters slipped under the bridge as Jackson roared onto it. He glanced over his left shoulder and saw the Time Policeman raise the Matthews in one gloved hand, saw the muzzle flare fan out from it. Then the side mirror disappeared.

Memory of the crystaled picture he still carried came into Jackson's mind. The scarred features, the amputated arm, the burned knot of an ear. Knowing there was nothing else he could do, that the man hunting him had already reached his decision, he turned the wheel hard left as he slowed slightly.

The nose of the Mustang swung outward into the motorcycle. There was no noise of breaking bones over the banshee keening of the engines, but Jackson was sure it existed. For a brief moment the man and motorcycle flamed against the low rail guarding the sides of the bridge, then they were tumbling over the edge into the placid blackness below.

Shaken but afraid to stop, Jackson regained control over the vehicle and drove on. He stopped at a gas station long enough to get directions.

He didn't pause when he reached the entranceway to the junkyard, driving haphazardly through the rows of wrecked cars till he found the row with the small shack. He powered the car into a tight turn, colliding with one stack and seeing it come tumbling to the red mud only feet behind him a second after the Mustang ripped free again.

The car was still rocking when he cleared the seat and ran down the narrow clearing leading to the time machine. Gratefully, he sank into the plushness of the contoured seat, even more satisfied when he saw the power level reading full. He strapped in, pulled the helmet on, reset the coordinates that had previously been there, then triggered the jump. Someone smothered him in a cloth stained with oranges and ammonia, taking his breath away as Time screamed through him, ahead of him, always dogging his heels.

Chapter Twenty-Three

To Suzanne, lost in the sea of people and sitting half-way up the huge bowl depression from where the concert stage was lighted by high-intensity lamps, the music seemed too loud. She was more used to purchasing holo-auds and listening to them in the quietness of her apartment. But this was something entirely different. Even with the binoculars Rodor had given her from his camper it was hard to see the performers. Every time she found a clear view, someone or several someones would shift and get in her way again. In some ways the holo-auds were preferable, because she at least had the opportunity to watch the singers. But here everything seemed so much more alive. So much more joyous.

And maybe that was the effect of the hallucinogens Rodor gave her to sample.

Suzanne had taken what he had offered at first simply to see for herself what kind of product she could acquire for her mother. But as the night wore on, she looked forward to each new dose he administered. The marijuana that continually cycled through the crowd kept the glow slowly building inside her. She wondered what kind of plateau she would eventually reach.

"Who is singing now?" she asked Rodor. She had to lean across to him to make herself heard.

"Creedence Clearwater Revival," he yelled into her ear. "Do you like them?"

"Yes." Someone tapped Suzanne's shoulder and handed her another cigarette. By now she was smoking as expertly as the people around her, drawing the smoke in deep and holding it as long as she could before releasing it through her nose. She watched Rodor take a hit when she passed it to him, watching as the man seemed to thoroughly enjoy the experience.

So far Rodor had managed to remain an enigma. That he was from the future there was no doubt. But which future? And what was he doing here?

He had been full of questions back at the camper as they waited for the evening's shows to begin, evasive when she asked her own. But for some reason unknown to herself, Suzanne liked him. He had to be nearly ten years older than her, never mind how many centuries far removed, yet seemed as irresponsible as the young men and women surrounding them.

The band finished their number and immediately began another. Evidently the crowd recognized it because they started clapping at the beginning.

"Is this really your third time here?" Suzanne asked.

Rodor nodded, sliding the yellow-tinted, round-lensed glasses he wore back up his thin nose. He pointed in one direction, then another. "I'm currently over there, and over there." He gave her another of his disarming smiles. "And no telling how many other places around here."

"What do you mean?"

"I mean Woodstock is a favorite time of mine. I intend to return here again and again. If that will be possible, then I am already here in other places that I know nothing of so far."

"Aren't you afraid of being noticed?"

"There are half a million people here, Suzanne. I could easily lose a hundred other selves here and never bump into myself unless I actively went out of my way to do it."

"When are you from?" Suzanne asked.

Rodor laughed and glanced at her. Even though she sensed derision in his tone, she still couldn't get mad at him. He was too damned likeable. Innocent in a way, almost. "You must be a scientist, Suzanne," he said. "You'd have to be a scientist to come up with these questions all the time."

"Actually, I'm a record-keeper. Or was until I was demoted."

"Another job requiring a neat and tidy mind." Rodor shivered, as if the thought of such a mind was uncomfortable to him.

Another cigarette came by, and Suzanne snatched it, halting its flight for a moment before passing it to Rodor. "Do you have a job?" she asked.

"Ah, circumlocution. How devious a woman's bag of tricks becomes when the anticipation grows too great."

Suzanne laughed at herself with him, knowing part of it was due to the narcotics she had taken in.

"Actually," he said in a poor imitation of her voice, which brought gales of laughter to both of them.

Suzanne wiped tears out of her eyes.

"Actually," he said again, "in my time I happen to be one of the indolent rich."

"Really?"

"Really."

"How did you get the time machine?"

"I found it in my grandfather's attic."

Suzanne laughed again, amazed at her lack of control.

Rodor laughed with her, then said, "No, really. I promise you, I found the time machine in my grandfather's attic when I inherited the house. Of course, at the time it wasn't constructed around a camper shell. I had a company do that after I figured out what the damn thing did."

"What was he doing with it?"

"I haven't the foggiest notion. It was just sitting up there collecting dust."

"Your government doesn't control and monitor time travel?" Suzanne asked incredulously. "Don't the senators know how dangerous that is?"

"Suzanne, in my time we have a game show that gives away time trips as prizes. Usually they are limited to a couple hundred years back, to a period before the Time Wars."

"The Time Wars?"

"Centering around 2249 and 2250, Suzanne. Your present."

A cold chill pushed away some of the lambent glow inside Suzanne. "What happened?" she asked, wanting instead to ask who won.

Rodor lifted his shoulders and dropped them. "Nobody knows, Suzanne. No one cares. Anything past the two-hundred year point is a confused jumble of history. And anyway, the time machines are set so they won't jump back any further than that."

"So time travel is governed."

"No, it's just that the ones most people have access

to are somehow governed not to go back past that time. Nobody knows how. And, like I said, nobody cares. Every now and then you read about one of the time machines malfunctioning and stranding someone back in an impossible era, but that's what makes the winning so thrilling. The chance that you might be sent off and never return. Of course, the game show makes you sign a paper waiving your family's rights to hold the network responsible.''

"Isn't anyone curious about what happened?"

"No. We have our own lives to lead, Suzanne. Whatever happened happened. Nothing can change it."

"But you can change it."

He smiled at her. "If it's been changed, Suzanne, then in my time it has already been changed."

"And if you're the one who is supposed to change it?"

"Why me?"

"You have a time machine that travels past the point where most of your time machines won't go. Why not you?"

"Because, Suzanne, I don't care to change things. I am used to a calm and carefree life, no responsibilities. I refuse to change."

Suzanne looked away from him, trying not to let the hurt show on her face. She damned her emotions for being so close to the surface, knowing it was the chemicals inside her that were eating away at her control.

"Don't be angry with me, Suzanne. You have no right to be. Look around you at all these people. Do you have any idea of what they are committed to at this very moment?"

Suzanne didn't say anything.

"Most of these people, despite their anti-social behavior by the present-day society's standards, are protesting a very unpopular war that is claiming the lives of 18- and 19-year old boys every day. Did you think of that when you time-traveled back here? Or were you just thinking of picking up something from history's largest drug culture to take home to momma? Don't give me the selflessness hype if you're standing on a glass soapbox."

Stung, Suzanne looked back at him, seeing a surprisingly serious gleam behind the yellow-tinted glasses. "You're right. I'm sorry. I had no reason . . ."

He placed his hand on her mouth, the familiar smile back in place. "You have every reason to say what you did, Suzanne. But they're not my reasons. I'm here to party. That's the way I want to spend my life: partying. Maybe someday I'll grow up, but the time will creep up on me when I'm not looking, I promise you."

"Peter Pan," Suzanne whispered against his fingers.

Rodor removed his hand, grinning. "Maybe something like that."

"Then why did you stop Jake this afternoon if you don't want to get involved? You knew I was a time traveler. You told me yourself that you saw my time machine arrive."

"Because," Rodor said as he leaned into her, "you're a very beautiful girl." He kissed her tenderly, just as she knew he would. She felt herself responding and clutched the back of his neck tightly, closing her eyes as she gave herself over to the feeling. Abruptly, she pushed him away as thoughts of Jackson intruded.

The half-smile Rodor wore looked out of place. "Did I do something wrong?"

"No," she said honestly, "you did everything right.

It's me who is in the wrong. I've got my feelings confused. It's partly whatever you've been giving me and partly the whole thing around us."

"It's Woodstock," Rodor said sagely.

"Maybe," she admitted. "But it's not me."

"It could be if you would give yourself over to your feelings."

"I'm not even sure if they are my feelings."

"Is there someone else?"

Suzanne was silent, not knowing how to answer, not know precisely how to explain the confusion that lay between her and Jackson Dubchek.

"Do you love him?" Rodor asked.

"I feel responsible for him."

"Responsibility is an anchor, Suzanne, that too often charts your course through life."

"I didn't choose the full extent of this responsibility," Suzanne said, "but I can't turn my back on it either."

"Where is he?"

"Somewhere in the future, in our past, taking responsibility for something that is not his doing either."

"Birds of a feather," Rodor intoned neutrally.

Sensing she had hurt him, Suzanne leaned forward and held his hands. "Rodor, it's nothing to reflect on you or what we shared today. It's just that he may need me, and I have to be there."

He traced her chin with a forefinger in a way that made her tingle all over. "Do you love him?" he asked again.

"I can't," she replied simply. "But I have to go. I have to try to help him." She tried to get to her feet and felt the inside of her head twist and slip in a manner much worse than in the time machine.

"Wait until later," Rodor said.

Stubbornly, Suzanne shook her head and immediately regretted it. She tried to stand again and only succeeded because Rodor helped her.

"You don't love him," Rodor said as he led her back to the silver camper, "but you owe him this much loyalty. He's a very lucky guy."

"He wouldn't think so," Suzanne replied, wishing she weren't so sure of the validity of her answer.

When he looked in the mirror on the morning of the day of the assassination, Jackson almost didn't recognize himself. His beard had grown considerably, and he couldn't remember when he had last used a dilapitory. His eyes were red-rimmed from reading and rereading the newspaper clippings he had taken from the last time he had been to 2074. For two days he had studied the details provided in the news stories, spent time walking around the plaza till he identified every building mentioned. He slept fitfully only after passing out from sheer exhaustion.

He stood under the cold shower in the hotel room and let it chill him into wakefulness, then toweled off and moved back to the chair he had positioned to look out over the fountain in the center of the plaza, dropping the towel across his lap to cover himself.

He still had trouble believing he was doing this. That he was actually planning on taking the lives of other people. It wasn't something a linguist would do. It wasn't something any sane and civilized person would do. But he was here, in this chair where he had spent so much time doing the planning, with the knife never far from his reach and a Taurus 9mm. automatic, which he had gotten from a greedy pawnbroker lacking a certain knowledge of ethics, tucked neatly between the mattress and box spring of the bed. Extra clips of mercury-tipped bullets filled a spare pouch built into the shoulder holster the pawnbroker had given him as well. The mercury tips, the old pawnbroker had assured him, would make certain that whatever Jackson shot would stay down.

But who would he encounter on the thirteenth floor of the Chavez building?

Jackson wished there was someone else he could take the plot to. Wished there was some way he could make the local law enforcement authorities believe him. He had made anonymous vid calls two days ago when he first arrived, trying to persuade some of the signers not to go to the meeting. Miguel Franco's reply had been a quiet but firm no, stating that he would not be put into fear for his life, that he considered the signing of the Second Plan worth the risk. Then the man had hung up.

Glancing at his chronometer, Jackson found less than three hours remaining before the assassination was slated to occur. He stood and dressed, feeling shabby in the days-old beard and wishing he had thought to buy a razor. There wasn't much remaining of the money that Paress Linnet had originally sent. The pistol and ammunition had cost more than the car he had bought to leave Mexico City the first time.

The car he would buy, Jackson corrected himself.

He scabbarded the knife at his back, under the loose folds of his white silk shirt, and pulled a lightweight jacket on over the shoulder holster.

The platform where the signing would take place had been carefully erected. Baloons and streamers decorated the plaza area, and already a huge crowd had gathered.

Excited children scampered from weary adults, and the buzz of conversations reached Jackson's ears even on the fourth floor.

How many would die? he wondered as he looked down. Even if he succeeded in saving Ana's ancestor, some of those people gathered below would be dead in three hours. It all felt so hopeless. He let the curtain drop and moved away.

With a final look around the room that had been home to him for the last two days, Jackson locked the door behind him as he stepped out into the hall. The hotel bill had been settled in advance, since he knew he wouldn't be staying any longer than today. One way or another.

He walked down the corridor to the elevator, nodding to the two small children of a vacationing couple he had almost become acquaintances with during his stay. When the elevator doors erased them, he could still see the faces the children made at him.

The heat in the plaza hit him with oppressive force, taking his breath away.

For two hours he wandered, drinking in the sights of the festivities, trying not to see skulls with empty sockets behind every smile. He felt the tension build inside him as he glanced at the clock tower in back of the plaza, like the slow wind of a mainspring. In less than an hour, he and Suzanne would be arriving, running through the crowded street. The thought of being able to meet himself made him uncomfortable. But he yearned to see Suzanne again.

Without knowing it, his wanderings had taken him back to the hotel where he and Suzanne would stay later and make love. A wistfulness ignited inside him as he looked up the side of the building. Which room would they stay in? He wasn't sure from the outside. Somewhere on the fourth floor. He counted stories, then scanned the windows. They had stayed on the side facing the plaza, so one of them was the one to their room. Would be the one to their room. Buddha, but this was so confusing anyway without this additional circle-through-itself in time.

Just as he started to look away at the men and women starting to gather on the raised platform, he heard his name called from above.

"Jackson!"

He looked up to see Suzanne hanging out of a third-story window waving happily at him. He felt a smile spread across his face, unsure of where it had come from. What the hell was Suzanne doing here? This was the last place she should be.

"Jackson!" She waved at him to come up.

Taking a last glance at the clock tower, knowing he didn't really have the time to spare, Jackson turned and jogged into the hotel, shouting, "I'll be right there."

Chapter Twenty-Four

Jackson trotted down the corridor of the hotel's third floor, some of the loneliness that had settled onto him over the past few days dissapating as he moved. He didn't know why Suzanne Brelmer was here now, and part of him wished she wasn't so close to the violence that was about to happen. Visions of the scarred buildings that had surrounded the plaza area scattered through his mind. There had been broken windows, too. He was sure of that. What if Suzanne was shot and killed by a stray bullet?

He would warn her. Tell her to stay out of the way. Tell her to stay in the hotel room till he could get back to her.

If he was able.

A door creaked open beside him and he halted in mid-stride.

"Jackson," Suzanne said as she swung the door inward and stepped back.

He was in her arms before he knew it. For the past two days he had sat in the hotel room on the other side of the plaza and thought of nothing but death and dying.

Hoped for nothing more than being able to create enough of a diversion for the signers of the Second Plan to escape.

Now, wrapped in her arms and listening to her laugh gaily in his ear, he could feel alive again.

"Jackson," she said as she squeezed him tightly, "I was so afraid something had happened to you."

He pushed her back, surprised to find the tears in her eyes. Her face was smudged with dirt and she looked more tired than he could ever remember seeing her. She wore a sleeveless T-shirt and lacy pink panties, as if she had just gotten out of bed. "Look," he said, holding her by the shoulders, not wanting to break the physical contact between them, "ever since you left I've been sorry about the way we treated each other. I didn't want to leave it the way it was between us, but I didn't know what else to do."

"It's okay, Jackson," she said as she touched his face gently. "Really. We've been waiting for you since this morning. I can't remember how many times I've hung out that window searching the crowd for you."

"We?" The pronoun confused Jackson, making him think she meant herself and her father. He glanced around the empty bedroom. He would not let anyone stop him from attempting to upset the assassination. Not after all the hell he had put himself through while sitting in that hotel room. Not until he was sure he couldn't return Ana to Martin.

His hand moved to the butt of the Taurus 9mm. when the bathroom door opened. He was expecting a member of Brelmer's Time Police and was surprised to see the long-haired blonde man step into the room.

The long-haired man was wearing a stereo headset, obviously more into the music that played for his ears alone than he was aware of his surroundings. A twisted cigarette danced between his lips as his head moved to the silent tempo. He was having trouble knotting the green towel around his waist.

Before Jackson knew it, the pistol was in his hand, aimed at the other man's chest.

The man noticed him for the first time as he approached Suzanne. When he saw the gun Jackson held, his hands came to an automatic rest on his head. The unlit cigarette and the towel hit the floor at the same time. A facetious grin spread across the man's face. "Hey, man, be cool. Ain't nothing going down here. Don't get your imagination in an uproar. Be chill with the gun, okay? You don't want to hurt anyone." The hazel eyes focused on Suzanne. "Tell him to put the gun away before it goes off."

Jackson kept the 9mm. centered on the man's chest, trying to make sense of it all. Why was Suzanne here now? Who was the man? How did he know Suzanne? The dialect seemed to be archaic, like something from the 1960s, when slang was so popular. The linguist part of his mind kept itself preoccupied with dating the man's speech patterns. Jackson the man just wanted away from the situation. He was already in over his head in the technical and ethical aspects of what he wanted to do without being confused emotionally as well.

Suzanne reached for him and he brushed her hands away.

He looked at her as he backed toward the door, saw the tears streaming down her face. Had she made love to the man?

"Jackson . . ."

"I don't have time for this, Suzanne." His voice

sounded bitter even to his ears but he didn't blame himself. Sure, there had been no soft words between them after they had made love, but he hadn't deserved this. How could Suzanne be so cruel? Unless she thought he didn't care for her. Could that be it? Either way, there was no time to sort it all out now, and he doubted there would be time later. For a man who dealt in Time, he seemed to be amazingly in short supply. His chronometer showed him that less than forty minutes remained before the first bullet was fired into the plaza.

"Listen to me," Suzanne pleaded. "Jackson, I can explain."

"Nothing to explain, Suzanne. I guess we both made some mistakes."

"Damnit, I want to help you."

He gave her a false smile and tried to sound flip. "You're not really dressed for it, Suzanne."

Suzanne's tears dried up instantly and she turned away from him. The blonde stranger shrugged in perplexity and smiled as if at a private joke.

Jackson pulled the door shut as he slid the pistol back into the shoulder holster. He damned himself as he ran to the elevator, slammed the palms of his hands into it as it refused to open when he pressed the button. He opened the fire escape door and started running down the steps, surprised to find a number of people already making their way down them too. Shouldn't ever have gotten involved, he chided himself as he dodged between the people. Should have kept her at arm's length the way you started to. Shouldn't have let her have the chance to get to you the way she did.

A feeling of *déja vu* came over him as he bounced between the men and women in the fire escape stairway.

He had fought the crowd like this the first time and had arrived too late then. Was history doomed to repeat itself? At least this time?

He gripped the bar and swung himself over to drop onto the next set of stairs leading down, almost falling over a man helping an old woman. Then he was on the bottom floor, racing toward the Chavez building, wondering what he would find there, and wondering, too, if Death would find him.

Praetor Centurion Lieutenant Colonel Brelmer phased into 2074 ten minutes ahead of the time he had assigned his men to arrive. Ten minutes to check the security of the site they had chosen and to shake the time-traveling nausea before they got there. He didn't like any of the men seeing him when he was not completely in control of himself and his faculties.

He forced himself out of the time machine ahead of Sgt. Jameson, his only passenger on the jump, and ripped the nausea bag free once he was sure he had his stomach securely back in place.

The site he had chosen was behind a row of deserted warehouses, on the north side of Mexico City, that had been shut down years before when the factories moved to the other side of the country. No one was around.

A handful of minutes later the open space behind the warehouses was flooded with nine time machines holding the thirty-six men Brelmer had chosen for the strike team.

The Time Policemen fell into formation before him without being ordered to, knowing his procedure.

"As you know," Brelmer addressed them, "there is going to be veritable chaos in that city within a few minutes after we get there. We cannot go in as a team because we would draw immediate attention from any security people posted in the plaza. We all know those men failed in their jobs the first time. But I don't want you to think that they will fail again. Your very presence here, now, makes everything you have seen questionable. Maybe it happened and maybe it didn't. For us, this is not a past. It is our present. You can die here just as surely as you can in 2250. If we were to travel back to the ceremony from this point on, there is every chance that we would find some of your corpses lying there." He paused to let that sink in, steeling his face to reflect none of the emotions that typhooned inside him.

"As you also know, my daughter exists in this time frame. And so does Jackson Dubchek, the man who kidnapped her. If one of you men so much as injures her, give yourself to whatever gods you believe in because your ass is mine. I'll personally escort you back to the time you were born and let you watch me blow your infant self's head off. Do you understand me?"

The unit answered as a single man. "Alabama, Colonel."

Brelmer put his hands on his hips. "According to our records at TP, the assassination actually took place, and we don't want to foul that up. If it looks like one of those people on the platform is going to get away, don't hesitate to put that person down. Understood?"

"Alabama, Colonel."

"There will be a bonus for the man who brings me Jackson Dubchek's corpse."

"Alabama, Colonel."

Brelmer checked his chronometer, adjusted to fit the new time frame they were in. 14:40. He waved an arm. "Move out."

Suzanne tucked her shirt into her jeans and brushed by Rodor angrily.

The man grabbed her arm. "Why are you mad at me, Suzanne?"

"I don't have time to talk to you." She yanked her arm back as she picked up her tennis shoes and sat on the bed to slip them on.

Rodor still hadn't made a move to get dressed and seemed entirely comfortable in the nude. "I thought you said you didn't love him."

"I don't." When she bent down to tie the first shoe, Suzanne got a headrush that almost made her pass out. She forced herself to keep moving, the thought of Jackson facing an unidentified assassination team by himself foremost in her mind.

"You don't act like it," Rodor said petulantly.

"He's doing something brave, damnit, and he needs help."

"And you intend to help him?"

Suzanne glared at him. "If I can. At least one of us needs to act like we belong to the human race."

Rodor spread his hands before him and grinned. "You forget, Suzanne, this is all ancient history to me. Forgotten history. I have no place here."

"There are a hell of a lot of people out there who are going to die if something isn't done."

"They've already died somewhere. Somewhen. You saw it yourself."

Suzanne felt her anger build to the boiling point. Rodor was right to an extent. It wasn't his fault that she had still been spaced out enough from the drugs to forget she was in a state of undress when she had asked Jackson to come up. She was lucky that he had even involved himself enough to bring her here to this time. Rodor had only agreed to try to help her mother find a solution for her pain. And she couldn't blame Jackson for thinking what had obviously passed through his mind. Hell, she really couldn't blame herself for what had happened between them. Any of them.

"Fine," she said as she got to her feet. "Stay here, then, and I'll come back to you when the shooting's over."

"I may be gone when you get back," he warned.

She paused with her hand on the doorknob, reminded of the way a young child taunted when it didn't get its way. "Then don't be here, Rodor. I know where to find you when I need you."

She could hear his heavy sigh across the room. "Wait, Suzanne, and I'll go with you."

She watched him pull a pair of jeans and a concert T-shirt with Journey 1983 stenciled across it from the duffle bag he'd carried in from the silver camper time machine. "Hurry," she said as she flung the door open and went out.

The Chavez building was deserted. A sign in Spanish and English declared that all businesses inside had closed for the national holiday.

Aware that the time for preventing the assassination had all but exhausted itself, Jackson stepped back from the glass door and cocked the 9mm. He triggered three shots in rapid succession, surprised at the recoil the weapon had, then waded through the broken glass into the building. With any luck, the alarm system would alert the security team gathered around the platform if the sound of the shots didn't.

The elevator didn't respond to his touch, and the lights above it remained blank. He felt defeated as he raced for the fire escape, knowing he would have no strength left at all by the time he reached the thirteenth floor. Where was the assassination team?

Brelmer took up a post behind one of the sturdy columns behind the fountain. He glanced at the clock tower. In a moment or two all hell would break loose. Where was Suzanne? What if she had been killed in the initial assassination? He had not thought to check the bodies. Maybe that was why he had found no trace of her or Dubchek.

The earphone whistled for his attention.

"Report," Brelmer ordered, feeling apprehension knot up in his stomach.

"McKay, here. I've found your daughter, sir."

"Where?"

"She and Dubchek just got out of a green pickup and are heading into the plaza."

"Intercept them."

"Alabama, Colonel."

Brelmer moved from behind the column, unable to stand still any more. He triggered the telescopic lenses in his crystal eyes and peered out over the crowd, searching for McKay and Suzanne and Dubchek. There. He realigned the telescopic lenses, centering on Suzanne's blonde hair. She and Jackson were running into the plaza. Running to their deaths? McKay followed them, a small lumbering man almost lost in the crowd Dubchek and Suzanne ran through easily.

"Knickmeyer, here, Colonel. Don't know what the hell McKay is talking about. I've got your daughter spotted coming out of a hotel at four o'clock from your position. A blonde man I can't identify is with her."

Swiveling his head, Brelmer checked the validity of the new report. What the hell was going on? There was no doubt in his mind that Suzanne was running toward the plaza at this very moment. He tracked the woman racing from the hotel across the street, magnifying her features into identifiable size.

His breath constricted in his throat.

Suzanne.

He looked back at the first two figures.

Suzanne.

In both places.

A sinking feeling spead through Brelmer when he realized his daughter had effectively doubled her chances of getting killed during the assassination by time-looping back on herself. But why had she done it? Where the hell was the second Dubchek?

Autofire sounded from the business building across the street. Only this time it wasn't immediately raking the crowd gathered around the signers of the Second *Plan de Iguala*. Using the telescopic capabilities of his implanted eyes, Brelmer watched the other Suzanne run through the shattered frame of a door at the bottom of the Chavez building. The same building the assassination team was using as a base of operations.

Brelmer broke the Matthews free of its holster under the poncho, tossing his hood back to clear his peripheral vision. He lifted the collar with the hidden microphone.

Jackson reached the thirteenth floor in agony. His lungs burned for oxygen and his knees felt like the ligaments were pulled taffy. His hands shook as he wrapped his fingers around the butt of the pistol, crouching down painfully to make a smaller target.

For two days he had played this scene over and over in his mind. More times than not it had ended with his death. Now the moment of decision was at hand.

He held the 9mm. up, beside his head, ready to drop it into target acquisition at a second's notice. Had the intervening floors muffled the sounds of his shots as he broke in? Or were the assassins waiting for him?

He breathed rapidly through his mouth in an effort to get enough oxygen into his system. He wanted to run down the corridor until he found the office the assassins had picked, wanted to get the anxious minutes over.

How long before they fired into the signers? Somewhere along the way he had lost all sense of time.

He was halfway down the corridor when a man dressed in a maroon one-piece uniform stepped out of an office near the elevator at the other end. The man wore a helmet of the same dull maroon and carried a short rifle with three barrels. Dark bubble goggles masked the upper third of his face.

Jackson tried to sink back into the recess of the closest door, knowing it would be too late.

"Security breach!" the helmeted man sceamed as he swept the tri-barreled weapon around to cover Jackson. "Damnit, Reese, I thought you said this building would be empty!"

Pressing into the doorjamb for the protection it offered, Jackson lowered the pistol and squeezed the trigger, feeling the recoil kick repeatedly into his palm. A string of bullets from the rifle tore patches from the carpeted hallway, quick-stepping toward Jackson's position.

He expected to feel the impact of the bullets as they chewed their way up his legs. Instead the firing died away as his shots scored on the assassin, knocking the man backward. Blood covered the white wall behind the man as the mercury-tipped bullets ripped his chest apart. The assassin hung there for a moment, crucified against the wall, then slid slowly downwards in a crumpled heap.

It took Jackson a moment to realize the pistol had

stopped firing because the clip had emptied and the slide
had locked back, as the pawnbroker had told him it would.
Staying behind the scant protection offered by the office
doorway, he took an extra clip from the small pocket on
the shoulder holster and slammed it into the butt of his
weapon, flicking the slide release that fed the first bullet
into the chamber.

A helmeted head peeked through the doorway the
other assassin had come from.

Jackson sent it into quick retreat with a handful of
shots. He pushed away from the doorway, realizing that
if he hoped to stop the assassination he had to take more
active measures. He could feel perspiration dripping into
his eyes and rubbed a sleeved arm across his forehead.

Hadn't someone noticed the firing?

Buddha, let someone have heard the shots.

He crept closer, intending to take the tri-barreled rifle
from the dead assassin.

When were they from? He could identify nothing
about their uniforms.

Just as he was about to curl his fingers around the
barrel of the rifle, a voice said, "I don't know who the
hell you are, asshole, but you just bought yourself a whole
lot of trouble."

Jackson jerked back away from the weapon, seeking
running room as he tried to bring his pistol up. He saw
the lined face of the assassin as the man stepped unhur-
riedly from the doorway, noted the crimson sergeant's
stripes painted on the helmet. He saw the pistol in the
assassin's hand jerk back and felt a burning right cross
blaze into his shoulder, knocking the 9mm. from his
numbed fingers. He kicked out, trying to avoid the next
shot.

The assassin leveled his pistol to a line directed at Jackson's face, stepping forward with a cold grin.

Jackson froze, tensing for a last minute move if the opportunity presented itself, wondering if he would feel the bullet explode his head. His right shoulder felt like it had been anesthetisizied.

Something exploded nearby, robbing Jackson of his hearing. Then the whole building seemed to come apart as the ceiling came tumbling down on him and the assassin.

Chapter Twenty-Five

A man stood in front of Brelmer, obviously intending to try and stop him.

Brelmer pointed the Matthews at him, aiming at a thick leg. When he pulled the trigger the man crumpled to one side.

"McKay, break off the pursuit. Acknowledge."

"Alabama, Colonel," McKay's breathless voice whispered through the earphone.

Brelmer vaulted over the fallen man and activated the hidden microphone again. "Leave Dubchek and my daughter alone as they approach the fountain. They've looped back on themselves here. Suzanne has just entered the Chavez building. Make sure her past self is not injured."

"What about Dubchek?" Jameson asked.

Brelmer stumbled over a woman lying face-first on the ground, hugging it for protection, crying and pleading in Spanish. Damnit! It would have been so much easier to deal with only one Dubchek and Suzanne. "Protect them both, Sergeant."

"Alabama, Colonel, I'm taking out a man in pursuit of them now."

"Don't miss," Brelmer warned. More shots ripped from overhead, a solid statacco burst. The assassins?

"Colonel?"

"Identify," Brelmer ordered as he slid to a halt beside the broken door of the building. He peered inside through the darkness for Suzanne.

"Coleman, sir."

"Report."

Gunfire opened up from overhead and Brelmer watched the bullets take their toll in the frightened crowd. He closed the wailing from his hearing. Uniformed law-enforcement people were yanking the signers of the Second Plan roughly from the platform. What had happened? Brelmer wondered. The last time the assassination had been flawless. What had changed? What was the extent of Jackson Dubchek's involvement?

"I've located the assassination team, Colonel."

"Where?"

"Thirteenth floor of the Chavez building."

Cold talons knifed through Brelmer's midsection, slicing deeply into his emotional control. "Corporal Sapir."

"Yes, sir."

"Are you near the Chavez building?"

"Yes, sir."

"Two rockets, corporal, in quick succession on my mark."

"Yes, sir."

Brelmer gripped the Matthews tightly.

"Ready, Colonel."

"Thirteenth floor. I want the assassins taken out."

"I see them, sir."

"Fire," Brelmer ordered as he dove inside the door.

He felt the impact of the rockets before he heard the explosion. The building shimmied and shook under his feet, making it hard to keep his balance. A closing door to his left drew his attention. He halted beside it, fisting the Matthews in both hands.

A bare-footed blonde man ran into the building.

Brelmer pointed the Matthews at him.

The man's face paled.

"Get out of here," Brelmer ordered.

The man nodded. "Color me gone, daddy-o." Then he left the building as quickly as he arrived.

Brelmer yanked the fire escape door open and swept the open area, scanning up the metal stairs. Two floors up, using her hands to pull herself along, he saw Suzanne. He called her name.

She looked at him and a mixture of emotions showed on her smudged face. "Father, you've got to help him."

"Who?"

"Jackson. He came back here to prevent the assassination."

"The assassination is supposed to take place, Suzanne." Brelmer walked up the steps slowly, not wanting to startle her into renewed flight.

She shook her head. "No, it's not. Someone changed it. Jackson's sister-in-law disappeared because her great-grandfather was killed out in the plaza today. We've already tried to stop it once. We were too late."

"It's too late, now, Suzanne. If he's up there we can't help him. I had the men rocket the thirteenth floor. If he was up there, he's surely dead now."

"No, damnit, no." She propelled herself up the stairway again.

Brelmer sprinted after her, the heavy weight of the

Matthews dragging at him. He watched her, closing the distance, wondering if he would be in time. The assassination team wouldn't stay in one spot now that they knew someone else was onto them.

"Colonel?"

"Yes, Sapir."

"There's still movement on the thirteenth floor, sir. Some of the assassins are still firing into the crowd."

"Two more rockets, corporal. Mark."

The building shivered again as Brelmer clung to the metal framework of the stairs. Two flights above Suzanne's head, the door to the thirteenth floor exploded outward and flames leapt out to bathe the fire escape walls.

"No!" Suzanne's scream of denial was pained and piercing. She slipped on the staircase, allowing Brelmer to catch up. "Jackson!"

Holstering the Matthews, Brelmer threw his arms around her waist and tried to pull her back from the flames.

"No!" Her scream ululated in the hollow space. She turned to Brelmer and pummeled his face and chest with her fists.

Another explosion rocked the building, this one coming from an inside source.

Realizing the whole building might come down, Brelmer rocked his daughter's head back with a solid right, catching her limp body before she hit the stairs. There would be time for regrets later, and maybe forgiveness as well, if he could get them safely out of the building. He shouldered Suzanne and started down the stairs, hoping there was time.

A bullet ricocheted from the railing near his hand.

He looked up to see a maroon-clad soldier pointing a rifle at him, knowing he could never get clear before the bullets ripped through him and Suzanne.

Smoke and dust filled the corridor. Jackson spat them both out as he stood. He blinked against the stinging in his eyes as he searched for the 9mm. Broken boards and plaster shifted only meters from him and he saw the assassin who had been about to murder him come into view. The man seemed disoriented at first, then started bringing his weapon up.

Stepping forward, Jackson kicked the man in the face, hearing a sharp snap, and watched the assassin fall back unconscious.

Vicious explosions of autofire still sounded from the office the assassins had chosen as a base of operations.

Was Miguel Franco still alive? Buddha, could he have gone through all of this only to fail again?

He found his pistol under a broken two-by-four and picked it up, handling it with his left hand because he wasn't sure of the strength in his right. He rested briefly against the cracked wall as his head spun. The amount of blood staining his sleeve amazed him. But there were holes on both sides of his arm, which meant the bullet had gone through. That was good news. At least it always was on the holos he had watched as a boy. Did this classify as a flesh wound? He measured the blood flow again, realizing it had to be something more serious. If he didn't have medical help soon, there was a good chance he would bleed to death.

He staggered away from the wall, holding the pistol up.

Another explosion pounded against the side of the building.

It seemed as though Jackson's head separated from his body, then pulled back abruptly like there was an elastic band connecting them. He toppled forward, landing on his knees.

Get up, he ordered himself, willing his legs to work.

He forced himself up and walked over to the body of the man he had kicked unconscious. He laid the 9mm. on his thigh while he searched the man's clothing. There was no mistaking the oblong egg-shape he found in one of the assassin's pockets. Nor the purpose of the toggle insect on it at one end.

Something in the wall exploded, showering Jackson with plaster and slamming him into the opposite side of the corridor. A vague impression of a fireball billowing into, then through, the fire escape door passed by him. His senses reeled as he watched a maroon-clad assassin kick the unhinged door further open.

The autofire coming from the office had almost dwindled to nothing as Jackson got up again. He tasted blood and realized the inside of his mouth was split. He carried the pistol under his right arm as he walked toward the office. He heard the scream and recognized it as Suzanne's voice only heartbeats later.

Pitching the grenade inside the office after flipping the toggle, Jackson managed a stumbling run for the fire escape door as he wrapped his fingers around the butt of the pistol. He stood in the warped doorframe, searching through the dark smoke that roiled out of the corridor, saw the assassin aiming his rifle at someone below. Unable to help himself, he looked down and saw Brelmer carrying Suzanne.

Was he already too late?

He triggered the pistol, feeling it chug into his hand,

feeling no sympathy now. That was Suzanne below. He owed no loyalty to Brelmer. Temporal Projects had only succeeded in making his life a hell of uncertainties and maybes. But he and Suzanne had shared something. And it meant something to him even if it had meant very little to her.

Behind him, the grenade went off, throwing him painfully into the railing. In front of him, pushed by the bullets that ripped through the maroon uniform, the assassin spilled over the side of the railing without a sound.

Jackson peered down the stairway, waiting to see what Brelmer would do. He watched the Praetor lift his pistol and center it on his forehead.

Jackson was barely able to throw himself back onto the thirteenth floor before the bullets spun and spit from the concrete wall he had been standing against.

Brelmer watched the smoke from the Chavez building being carried away by the breeze that wound through Mexico City. Suzanne slept in the back of his time machine, evidently exhausted from her ordeal. So far no one had appeared to track him or the remnants of his team from the plaza area. According to the reports Jameson had logged, most of the Second Plan's signers had lived through the assault. He would check on the validity of the claim Jackson Dubchek had made concerning his sister-in-law. That would be easy to confirm. But he was sure he would find that the story checked out. The weapons his team had recovered had been of some future design they had yet to encounter. But what had been so important about the signing of the Second *Plan de Iguala?*

He sighed heavily, feeling the pull of sore muscles.

Maybe it was something he would never know. But some things were better off left unknown. Just like the uncertainty over whether Jackson Dubchek had died when the top of the Chavez building imploded and dropped the top five stories into the streets. The man had saved their lives, his and Suzanne's, but he had also been the one who had gotten Suzanne involved.

He climbed into the time machine when Sgt. Jameson waved him over.

"Sapir found Dubchek's time machine, sir," Jameson said.

"Is he sure it belongs to Dubchek?"

"Yes, sir. It was set for a time two days ago and showed he came from Wheeling 1969."

"He got caught in the Wheeling Loop before he arrived here?"

"It looks that way, sir."

Brelmer nodded. He buckled himself into the seat and fit his nausea bag into place. Then he gently fitted one unto Suzanne's face, trailing his fingers through her blonde hair, permitting himself to be a father for just a moment before stepping back into his role of Praetor.

"What do you want us to do with the machine, Colonel?" Jameson asked.

Brelmer released his daughter's hair and looked at Jameson coldly. "Destroy it." One way or another, he was going to make sure Dubchek stayed away from Suzanne and Temporal Projects. He would tell Suzanne that Dubchek had died while bravely stopping the assassination team.

He listened to Jameson relay his orders, satisfied he had tied up all the loose ends.

"*Señor,* are you well?"

Jackson looked up at the hotel clerk, taking his eyes

from the task of directing his every step. "I was in the plaza," he said weakly. "I got shot."

A concerned look filled the clerk's round face. "Let me help you, sir." He came from around the counter and draped Jackson's uninjured arm over his broad shoulders. "I will get you a doctor as soon as I can, *señor*. But I fear it will be a while. There were many people wounded."

"I know." Jackson leaned against the wall of the elevator once they were inside, grateful for the coolness. "I can wait. I've got most of the bleeding stopped. All I need is a place to lie down."

"I don't have many rooms, *señor*. This was a holiday, and many people came to see the Second Plan signed. But there are a pair of rooms open because the Aguila families, father and son and their wives, were not able to come."

Jackson looked at the clerk through his blurred vision, knowing he had seen the man before, then realized it was the same man who had checked him and Suzanne into the hotel. Or would be checking them in, he corrected himself. It was only a matter of minutes one way or another. He grinned to himself over the twists of Fate. Or maybe Fate had nothing to do with it. Maybe at the animal level he was operating on now, he had subconsciously chosen the hotel out of all the others.

"What of the signers?" Jackson asked as the clerk helped him down the corridor.

"I am afraid some of them are dead."

"What of Miguel Franco?"

"He lives."

"Good."

"*Señor?*"

"He is connected to my family. That is why I was so concerned."

The clerk nodded. "It is a good thing to be concerned over one's family, and Miguel Franco is a good man."

"At least he's going to live long enough to be a good great- grandfather," Jackson said as the clerk opened the door.

Images of the frantic and stumbling run through the Chavez building flashed inside Jackson's mind as the clerk helped him remove his shirt and wrap a towel around his shoulder. He ignored the worried look on the clerk's face, hoping it wasn't because the man was afraid he would die in the room.

He closed his eyes when he lay down, feeling the throb of pain begin in the shoulder. Rat's teeth seemed to be tearing their way through the arm from the inside out.

The clerk patted his good arm. "I will be back with the doctor as soon as I can, *señor*."

"Thank you."

Even then, when he was surrounded by death, Jackson had not been as dismayed as he was when he found the wreckage of the time machine and realized he was trapped in 2074. He had no doubt that it had been Brelmer's doing. And Suzanne had not stopped her father from doing it.

Voices came to him in the quietness of the room. One of them screaming, the other soft. The soft one was easily recognizable. Suzanne. He started to sit up, then realized her voice was coming from the room on the other side of the wall even as he recognized the other voice as his. Then there was no more speaking as the noises became something else, a celebration of the mysticism of creation.

He felt dead inside, empty, as he tried to close his sense of hearing off, tried to focus on the almost blinding pain in his shoulder. But the noises, the gasps of pleasurepain continued, amplified by the memory in his mind.

Suzanne.

Buddha, how he wished he was not alone.

Warren Norwood spent his childhood summers reading *Tarzan* and *Tom Swift* books one right after another, so it's little wonder he grew up to write science fiction and fantasy adventures. His first novel, *The Windover Tapes: An Image of Voices* was published in 1982, and was followed by three more books in that series. He has since published *The Seren Cenacles,* on which he collaborated with Ralph Mylius, *The Double Spiral War* series, *Shudderchild,* and *True Jaguar.*

Norwood and Gigi—his wife, fellow writer, and collaborator—live outside of Weatherford, Texas. In addition to his writing, Warren teaches at Tarrant County Junior College, and is learning to play a growing collection of musical instruments, including a mountain dulcimer.